Praise for previous Alternate Reality News Service books:

"Ira Nayman, the author of one of my favorite books of 2008 (*Alternative Reality Ain't What It Used to Be*) is back with a new collection of futuristic news stories from alternate realities (*What Were Once Miracles Are Now Children's Toys*)… They start with science fictional tropes, then carry through to the inevitable end of the story - usually with hilarious results." (Charles de Lint, *Fantasy and Science Fiction Magazine*)

"Completely unique, *Alternative Reality Ain't What It Used to Be* is one of the funniest, most compelling and just craziest books I have read since Douglas Adams first put pen to paper." (Antony Jones, *Science Fiction and Fantasy* Web site)

"This book would make for a great ice-breaker at gaming sessions, book clubs, or conventions of the science fiction and gaming set. The short "news" stories lend themselves to a quick read and are so funny that everyone will be comfortably laughing before you have made it a few paragraphs. Nothing is without the potential for humor in Nayman's mindset, and he twists, puns, and snarks his way through the morass of human life, helping us laugh at the sometimes utterly ridiculous world around us. Be prepared to laugh when reading *What Were Once Miracles Are Now Children's Toys*." (John Ottinger III, *Grasping for the Wind* Web site)

Ira Nayman

Futures in Mirror Are Closer Than They Appear

Ira Nayman

This is a work of fiction. Any resemblance to persons living or dead, half-dead, dead but risen to haunt the night, alive but might as well be dead, alive but wishing they were dead or in any state between alive and dead conceived of in the past or not yet imagined by horror writers up to the present is purely coincidental.

DEDICATION

Thanks to Web Goddess Gisela Mckay, without whom the Alternate Reality News Service would likely never have existed. Well, not in this universe, anyway. Thanks, as well, to my parents, Bernard and Edie, without whom I would likely never have existed. Well…

ACKNOWLEDGMENTS

Thanks to Elizabeth Hurst for the image of the owl that inspired and anchored the front cover design, and to Web Goddess Gisela McKay for executing the cover.

Ira Nayman

CONTENTS

Ira Nayman

1. ALTERNATE POLICY ALTERNATIVES

State of the Art: Not Everybody Gets a HUG™

by BRENDA BRUNDTLAND-GOVANNI, Alternate Reality News Service Editrix-in-Chief

Did you know that in Holland, every alternate reality shown by a Home Universe Generator™ involves tulips? Tulips win sports tournaments. Tulips run the government. Your wife is cheating on you with tulips. People use tulips to floss with. Tulips are the second most used construction material after sealskin. Tulips wrote three of the five best-selling science fiction books in the country. The battleships of Holland's navy run on tulips. Not all in the same universe, obviously – that would just be silly.

In Mexico City, beggars pool their pennies to buy precious minutes on Home Universe Generator™s to see where the most generous tourists will be that day, then race each other to get to that spot (honestly, I don't understand why legless beggars in carts bother to participate!). The Brazilian telenovela industry has been devastated by people watching the soap operas of their neighbour's lives on Home Universe Generator™s instead of the soap operas about well-endowed but morally questionable strangers. In the Arctic, Home Universe Generator™s are run by burning snow.

It's a world out there, people! A big one! With a lot of moving parts – some of them human beings. So, it will be complicated. And…and…and…

And, that's what this special report is all about.

Unless you live under a rock (and, housing prices being what they are, nobody would blame you, although, human beings being what they are, we will still judge you), you probably know that Home Universe Generator™s are what people use to look into life in alternate universes. Personally, I'd rather have all of my teeth removed by a wrecking ball – one at a time – than watch myself in some other reality – this reality has more than enough greed and stupidity for me, thank you very much. In fact, my perfect technology would be a combination vibrator/coffee maker/atomic powered slapping glove/random newspaper article generator. Is that really so much to ask for? Apparently. One more item to add to my list of things to do when I run the world.

The Home Universe Generator™ is one of the fastest spreading technologies in the world – only the electric can opener and fire spread faster (and historian of technology Harold Innis believed that the only reason the electric can opener was disseminated so quickly was because it pleased our cat overloads). There are now more Home Universe Generator™s in households around the world than there are heated ski poles, personality chip implanted plant holders and Pez dispensers.

And, who doesn't love a good personality chip implanted plant holder?

However, the benefits of Home Universe Generator™s have not been distributed evenly (sort of like Christmas pudding, but without the anxiety-inducing false bonhomie). Those who are wealthy can afford top of the line, twelve speed Home Universe Generator™s with split 1080P screens and real oak cabinets, while those who are less well off have to settle for a single speed with cracked screens housed in a cardboard box. If they are able to afford one at all.

Researchers refer to this as "the Multiverse Manichean Moat." Those who – Jesus begesus, could you have called it anything less catchy? Was Theoretical Transdimensional Transformational Transduction Tentpole already taken? You want the public to take their attention away from watching a universe where they are actually paid what their labour is worth, you have to give them a slogan that trips off the tongue, not lays there like an unidentified blob of goo that will obstruct their air passages and cause them to pass out! Didn't they teach you the unidentified blob of goo rule in Marketing 101?

So. The idea is that those who are on the right side of the – uggh! – Multiverse Manichean Moat get to dwell in a draughty castle and eat undercooked meat and probably die of an infection caused by getting their head cut off. Those who dwell on the wrong side of the moat, by way of contrast, get to dwell in draughty huts and eat dirt and die of some horrible disease that makes your limbs fall off one at a time, starting with your ears. I guess you want to be on the right side of the moat, then. That, or **pick a metaphor that doesn't invoke medieval life!** Personally, I would choose this last route, but, as usual, I wasn't consulted.

To put together this special report on the use of Home Universe Generator™s around the world focusing on the...* SIGH * Multiverse Manichean Moat, the Alternate Reality News Service spared no expense in sending our reporters around the world. Cash, we spared – and plenty of it – but expenses, not so much. And, when I say around the world, I don't mean this world, Earth Prime: we have a sunken cost in our Transdimensional Portal™ (I would have told them not to build it in the basement, but, as usual, I wasn't asked for an opinion). So, instead of buying them plane tickets, we sent our reporters to other dimensions where they used Home Universe Generator™s to determine what was going on here.

Oy, the *tsuris* we go through to bring you ungrateful wretches the news!

What? That's it. I wrote all I had to sa – 1,000 words? Really? Who decided that all the contributions to the special report had to be – if that's the case, I should be able to write to any length I want! I could have written this introduction in five words: Home Universe Generator™s around the world. **Yes, I know that that is actually six words – I was trying to make a point! You're the smartass, here – you figure out what the point was!** Jesus begesus, who died and made you Tyler Durden? And, would it kill you to look like Brad Pitt instead of Fran Lebowitz? Honestly – can't I even get what I want in my own fantasy?! I swear, I'd slap you silly, but I don't look good in bruises! There. We've hit the minimum word count.

Now, if you don't mind, I'd like to talk to you about the production values on this fantasy life of mine…

State of the Art: Faba Not Exactly Faboo

by FREDERICA VON McTOAST-HYPHEN, Alternate Reality News Service People Writer

Alice "Grinner" Matabele runs her tongue over the last tooth in her mouth. "Sa gonna rain soon," she mutters to herself. If you ask her how she knows, she shrugs and replies, "Da toof knows." The fact that storm clouds can be seen pouring water down in the distance might also contribute to her prognostication, but when you try to point this out, she just keeps repeating, "Toof! Toof! Toof!" until you're sorry you brought the whole subject up.

The elderly matriarch of Faba, a small village in Chad, tries to be inscrutable that way, although it mostly looks like she has gas. Calling Faba a village flatters the collection of huts, animal pens and outhouses that in its wildest dreams couldn't possibly hope to rise to such exalted status. Faba is so small that if a couple moved there, they would have to exist on the heads of a couple who already live there. This would confuse the goats who live in the, for want of a better term, "village" even more than the already addled creatures are (being mountain goats, they can't quite grasp how they came to live on a desert plain).

The main profession of the villagers is dirt farming, which makes it quite poor as nobody over the age of two eats dirt. Fortunately, the nearby collection of huts, animal pens and outhouses that could someday aspire to being a village known as Baba just went through a baby boom (three boys, one girl and seven chickens), so there is a small market for Faba's dirt relatively close by. However, to make a real killing in dirt, somebody from the wannabe village has to go to Faya, which is a good four hour's walk as the crow flies.

Once a week, Matabele makes the journey, a 20 pound sack of dirt on her head. (Except that nobody in Faba can afford a sack, so the dirt is made as hard and compact as possible and Matabele imagines that it is contained in a sack.) You wouldn't think the old crone (not to be confused with an old scone, which, if you tried to eat it, could contribute to you ending up with only one tooth in your head) had it in her: her frail body looks like it could be blown away at the merest thought of a breeze. When asked why she keeps going, Matabele sneers, "Spite!"

Nobody in Faba can afford a Home Universe Generator™. In fact, if all of the residents of the ersatz village pooled their resources, they couldn't afford to purchase a Thatcher Coaxial Framagaw, the cheapest (and, admittedly, least important) component of the Home Universe Generator™. Only one person in 27,316 in Africa owns a Home Universe Generator™ (compared to one in 2.7316 in North America – sorry, I probably should have warned you to put down your beverage before you read that statistic – no, neither I nor the Alternate Reality News Service will reimburse you for the cost of dry cleaning those curtains, although I would suggest that you wash it out now before the stain gets any deeper. Go ahead. I'll wait.).

[WARNING: Unbelievable statistic ahead. You are responsible for the dry cleaning of any stain on your drapes, carpets, clothing or pets as a result of reading it.] Only nine per cent of the African population has ever used a Home Universe Generator™ (as compared to 99.9998 per cent of the North American population, and that would be higher if Reggie Blatherwater wasn't so damn stubborn!). [Don't say we didn't WARNING you.]

So, after she has exchanged the dirt for fruits, vegetables and, if it has been a good week for dirt production, a copy of *Elle* magazine, Matabele makes her way to the almost village's Multiverse Café and spends an hour on the public Home Universe Generator™ (the café makes its money on concessions).

In the week between trips, Fabians provide Matabele with questions to ask the Home Universe Generator™. "What would happen if Billy N'Gombo stop picking his nose long enough to notice that I exist?" "Is there a reality where the dirt crop was good enough one year for us to be able to purchase a copy of *Wired* along with our copy of *Elle*?" "How would my life have been different if I had sought fame and fortune as a freelance pig tickler in Faya, instead of staying in Faba and inheriting my parents' dirt farm?"

The answers Matabele gives aren't always that helpful. "You don't wanna know. Be happy he doesn't!" "No." "You would have died broke and alone at the age of 37...unless you became so famous thanks to a video on Yahootube of you tickling musical pigs that you were flown to Johannesburg to do the talk show circuit. The multiverse can be…complicated that way."

There are a couple of contributing factors to why Fabians are often less than impressed with the answers Matabele gives to their questions (setting aside their content). One is that the Multiverse Café has a rotary Home Universe Generator™, which is at least five generations behind the latest multiverse viewing technologies. The cabinet is cracked, and the characters on the keyboard have worn away with use. Worse: the machine uses the Lycanthropos search engine which, while groundbreaking for its time, is hopelessly inadequate for modern multiverse searches.

Or, it could just be that, at 87, Matabele's memory is not what it used to be and, because she can neither read nor write, her memory is all people can rely on.

Aware of her advancing decrepitude, the Faba village elders (Gary Alatumbo and Fitzpatrick N'Gombo) have been looking for a replacement. Their standards are very exacting: candidates must be at least 14 years of age, have at least one of their original teeth and be able to carry 20 pounds of dirt in an imaginary sack for several hours. Oddly, the tooth, the whole tooth and nothing but the tooth requirement is the biggest obstacle for most of the women in the (maybe in some other universe!) village.

When asked about her possible successor, Matabele laughs. Cackles, really. There is unmistakable cacklage in her laughter. "Do you not think I use the machine to see other worlds where **I** live?" she asked. "I have seen worlds where I live to be 120! Right here, right now, in this world, I'm still in my prime!"

State of the Art: One Revolution, Hold the Haggis

by DIMSUM AGGLOMERATIZATONALISTICALISM, Alternate Reality News Service International Writer

Above the stage at one end of the hall hangs a banner that reads, "Free Scotch!" As the man on the stage starts talking about the advantages of Scotland becoming an independent nation, the packed house becomes restless. When he runs a series of short videos taken from Home Universe Generator™ searches that show an independent Scotland as a place of eternal sunshine (even at night – sort of like the North Pole, but with fewer soccer hooligans), children happily playing unidentifiable games with sticks and armadillos in the streets, and tattie scones for everybody, members of the audience start to boo and hiss loudly.

"Tough crowd," the man, Angus Burrsides, comments. When somebody angrily points to the sign above his head, he considers it for a moment before responding, "Oh. I think I see where the confusion lies, here…"

The road to Scottish independence is full of sinkholes.

Scotland has been part of the United Kingdom since…long before Wiwipedia. Some Scots have a problem with this.

"We wanna declare Bill Forsyth a national treasure, but how can we when we don't have a proper nation?" Director of Recruitment, Refreshments and Recriminations for the Scottish Independent Puddin' Movement Madeleine Grrf plaintively explained. Explaintivained. "Oh, and we could have our own legal system and oil revenues. Those would, I imagine, be important considerations for some people."

Opposition to Scottish independence has also relied on video taken from a Home Universe Generator™, which was incorporated into a television ad portraying a smoldering Glasgow being overrun by seven foot aliens wearing strange masks with braided hair (this is not a writing mistake: the ambiguity was intentional because it was hard to tell from the grainy images whether the hair was attached to the masks or the aliens' heads). "Scottish independence," a gloomy voice-over narrator intoned. "Can we risk it?"

"Ah, well, fair comment, right?" Angus Sweetie, leader of the pro-UK group Hang Together, asked. Under a barrage of complaints from pro-independence groups and science fiction clubs, Hang Together relented, replacing those ads with images taken from other Home Universe Generator™ searches that included: moviegoers in Aberdeen kissing the feet of a six foot tall mouse; a long lineup outside a Scottish Social Services Council office of people in mouse costumes; and a baby's arm holding an apple. With a mouse's tail sticking out of it.

Obviously, both sides in the independence debate are gooseberrypicking (because cherries are not native to Scotland) images from Home Universe Generator™s that support their position. As the country headbutts (some of the debates have been especially lively) towards a referendum on independence on September 18, is this helpful?

"Och aye, nay," said Angus McFuss-Potts, professor of Political Snap Judgments at the University of Edinburgh, "Ye dinna ken the momentous meanin' o' multiverse maunderin's. No one can. Ken, ah mean."

Okay, that answer definitely **wasn't** helpful. "You'll have to forgive old Angus," said Rosemarie Perth-Dundee, Professor of Political Not Rushing to Judgment at the Dundee-Perth Polly Wanna Cracker Technic Institute. "He's a bit of an Ayr-head." Perth-Dundee was, of course, referring to the city of McFuss-Potts' birth. At least, she was if she was being professional about this.

The problem with Home Universe Generator™s is that you can find a universe that can justify just about any course of action you want to take (the only exception, for some reason, being entering the Iraq War – that never ends well!), so it doesn't actually prove anything. Nonetheless, people often use Home Universe Generator™s to score points in political debates, tending to find the most extreme scenarios.

"I mean, pfft, seven foot aliens wearing strange masks with braided hair that I prefer to believe was attached to their heads? Really?" Perth-Dundee scoffed. Scoffed really hard. Scoffffed. "Who would believe such a thing?"

"I'm voting no," said Inverness resident Angus Sheepherder, "because, bad as things are, they would be worse after an invasion of seven foot tall aliens wearing strange masks, no matter where their hair was attached!"

"Okay, that guy," Perth-Dundee allowed. "But, other than him, who would belie – umm, well…okay, perhaps more research is called for…"

Scotland is not the first country to find an independence debate centred around competing Home Universe Generator™ images. A referendum for Quebec's independence from Canada, for example, was narrowly defeated because people in the province were convinced by images from a universe where fluffy bunnies hopped all over major city streets, upending bicyclists, who went flying into the air on a regular basis, and getting run over by cars in such great numbers that the roads were too slick to drive on. Thus, the campaign's slogan: "Are you ready for the bunny guts?"

Then, there was the referendum in Ukraine, where images of Russian tanks occupying Kiev led to a resounding defeat. Of course, Russian tanks were eventually sent to occupy Kiev anyway, but this speaks more to the futility of a referendum to break away from a heavily armed thuggocracy than it does to using Home Universe Generator™s in the quest. Maybe not much more, but more.

Although the consequences wouldn't be as dramatic if Scotland gained its independence, it's the focus of this article because…umm…well…it's the one that is happening closest to this news cycle.

"Every nation wants to control its own destiny," Burrsides explaintained. "Scotland doesn't need Mommy England telling us what to spend our allowance on, or when to go to bed or who to go on a date with, especially if it won't let us take the family car because it doesn't trust us not to get sloshed and do something stupid. Really! How does England expect us to grow up if it won't give us some measure of personal responsibility?"

Ignoring Burrsides' obvious parenting issues, I asked why he felt the need to resort to images generated by Home Universe Generator™s – surely, his eloquent argument for independence would appeal to Scots without them?

"Some people had happier childhoods than I did," he darkly stated.

State of the Art: Bullethead to Beijing

by GIDEON GINRACHMANJINJa-VITUS, Alternate Reality News Service Economics Writer

Alfredina Chi-Weiwei was surprised to return from corporate downsizing Jiu Jitsu class one evening to find her Etobicoke home burned to the ground. Her first thought was: *Wasn't the hit man supposed to kill Yojimbo and make it look like he died in a fire next week while I was in Florida visiting my dead grandmother? I may have to miss yoga to deal with this!* Her second thought was: *Was it wise to share my first thought with a journalist? Maybe if I convince the hit man that he owes me one…*

As it happened, the police came to the conclusion that the fire was started by faulty wiring in the Home Universe Generator™ in the Chi-Weiwei spare bedroom/walk-in freezer. The sparks that flew from the machine while Yojimbo Chi-Weiwei was using it set the asbestos insulation on fire and, because there were no smoke alarms, nobody knew about the fire until it had consumed 73 per cent of the house.

It may take police over a week to determine and lay all of the appropriate criminal charges in the case.

"Oh, my, oh, my, oh," said Mary Mao (no relation…to speak of), President of Die-Tri-An Industries (a wholly owned subsidiary of Duōguó Gōngsī), the manufacturer of the highly flammable, and only moderately inflammable Home Universe Generator™. "This has never happened to one of our machines before. Unless you count the two in Toronto. Or, the three in Tierra del Fuego. Or, the five in Finland. Or, the seven in Sevastopol. Or, the eleven in Elgin. Or, the thirteen in Trieste. Or, the seventeen in Sierra Madre. Or…well. This has never happened to one of our machines before…in the last five minutes!"

According to technology expert Mark Saltzman (also no relation, but that should go without saying, so, uhh…), the problem, which comes from the wire that needs to be plugged into an electrical outlet, could be solved with 73 cents worth of insulation. "But that would add $57 to the cost of the unit," he added, "which would make it more expensive than a lot of people are willing to pay. Cheap bastards."

"Hey! We can do it cheap or we can do it good," Mao (really no relation – she has fallen arches and can't even do a short march around the block!) stated. "Or, we can do it a little more costly or we can do it almost good. Or, we can do it a little more expensive or we can do it so that it starts getting crappy. Or, we can do it really expensive or we can do it very bad. So, umm, ahh, I'm saying that in the east quality is a circle, not a straight line that extends beyond the horizon forever A very confusing circle, perhaps, but nobody said running a successful business was easy!."

Die-Tri-An's seven factories throughout China supply 73 per cent of the world's Home Universe Generator™s. The most prominent of them was built in the Beijing Economic-Technological Area of Development (BAD – no relation to the Michael Jackson song). It is a three storey brick building the size of four city blocks out of which emanates the sound of machines and Christmas jingles in Elvish.

According to an article in the *Asian Economist and Sandblaster*, conditions for workers in the factory are dismal. According to one woman who worked there, "Right. I had to get up in the morning at ten o'clock at night half an hour before I went to bed, eat a clump of cold poison, work twenty-nine hours a day down mill, and pay mill owner for permission to come to work, and when we got home, our dad and our mother would kill us and dance about on our graves singing Hallelujah."

"Oh, my, oh, my, oh," said Mao (no relation – she doesn't even look good in red!). "I meant, hey! That wasn't a quote from one of our workers – it was from an old comedy sketch!"

To be fair, the article did question why a worker in a Chinese factory had a Yorkshire accent.

It is undisputable that wages for workers in the BAD are ba…low. They typically make 72 cents a week. At that rate, it would take a Die-Tri-An worker 24 years to earn enough to buy a Home Universe Generator™ – assuming that they did not eat or have to pay rent in that time period.

Low wages have contributed to what economists have called "The Chinese Great Economic Leap Forward" (since Miracles are banned in this atheist country), which saw its economy grow faster than a coyote with its backside on fire ("That Durn Chinee Mirac – Economic Leap Forward!", Tavers, Travers, Vestibule). But, the benefits of the country's rapid economic growth have not been shared equally: while most of the workers live in positively Dickensian conditions, many Communist Party leaders and corporate executives have Home Universe Generator™s in every room of their houses.

"Not every room," Mao (no relation – she doesn't even like *Dance Dance Revolution*), demurred. "Is a tool shed a room?"

Riiiight.

Another factor in China's rise to a world power is a complete disregard for the environment. Thanks to factories throughout the city, the smog is so thick that being a tourist is like walking through gelatin (and all of your photos tend to look the same). Even wearing a mask over her mouth, Mao (okay, maybe a bit of a relation if you squint hard enough and ignore all the blood) coughed so badly that it took her twenty minutes to get out her statement about the old comedy sketch. Honestly – I haven't had to wade through so much audio tape to get a useable quote since I interviewed gang leader (later CEO of streaming audio service The Wha Ya Hoo Naws Network) Mumbles McGurk!

Western governments have tried to put pressure on China to raise its production standards so that Home Universe Generator™s don't randomly catch fire, explode or turn into penguins; but representatives of the country have so many variations on the "We can do it cheap or we can do it good," argument that they fill a little red book. Once they have installed them in their homes, the first thing western consumers are advised to do is use their Home Universe Generator™s to find realities where the machine proved dangerous, then do the opposite of that.

"Used properly, your Home Universe Generator™ should give your family years of pleasure," said Mao (who, yes, alright, is a distant cousin of Margaret Mao, the founder of a chain of Chinese fast food restaurants and abortion clinics – why? Who did you think she was related to?). "And, if it should do something naughty, like destroy your home, **blame yourself you cheap bastard!**"

State of the Art: The Diem Carpes Back

by FREDERICA VON McTOAST-HYPHEN, Alternate Reality News Service Pop Culture Writer

The grizzled old man (never before had I seen a human being with so much grizz!) named Mohinder staring glassy-eyed at the monitor of a Home Universe Generator™ was muttering to himself. What was he muttering? you may well ask. Well, I'm glad you mayed, because he was muttering:

> "Carpe diem? My ass, carpe diem! Yesterday? Yesterday, I carped that diem! Carped it just fine. Carped it for all I was worth, and, if you were there,

you would agree that I carped it plenty! I mean, man, I carped the ever-livin' snot out of that diem! Carped it real good! Carped that diem like one of our lives depended upon it – cause one of our lives probably did! And, I gotta tell ya, I been doing this for so long that when I carpe a diem, it bloody well stays ferking carped!

When I asked him what he had actually done the day before, Mohinder turned his glassy eyes (honestly, I wanted to use them to make a roots beer float) towards me and smiled. It was a far-off smile, devoid of emotion, as if part of a matching luggage set in which the suitcase carrying the smile had arrived but the one carrying the smile's joy had been rerouted to Pittsburgh. Before he turned back to the screen, I surmised (yes, I sometimes hang around mises that have been knighted – oh, don't give me that look: you would, too, if they ever invited you!) that his verbal eruption had been influenced by the poster over the terminal of a fish being yanked out of the water by a hook over which loomed the words, "Newfoundland: Carpe Diem."

Sometimes a journalist just has to trust her instincts on such matters.

Mohinder laid in one of the infamous alternate reality dens of Kolkata (previously Calcutta, before that Loch Cuttovar, referred to in an earlier incarnation as Ach Gribble Pleff, nee One of the Other Places With Much Sand and Rock – 27 and Counting). In the dark room in which no photographs were allowed to develop, a dozen slack-jawed bodies stared at monitors. Occasionally, one of them moaned. Even more occasionally, one of them recited statistics for the top 20 football players of the 20th century. A blue pall was cast over the room (the Home Universe Generator™s are at least two generations old, and the colours projected by their screens are no longer natural).

The proprietor of this den of iniquity – deniquity for modern readers who value their time – is Guildhall Gertie Suresh, so-called because the wrinkles on his forehead remind people of a union card. When I asked him why people were so willing to alternate reality themselves into oblivion, he helpfully told me: "You are not a customer, yes? Sorry, but I only talk to customers. Not customers here with coupons, either – only paying customers!"

Fair enough. I had had enough experience with east Indians to know that –

"Ooh, ooh, I'll be happy to answer your question!" Hermione Plotkin raised her hand so sharply I was sure her arm was going to pull away from its socket, achieve escape velocity and end up in orbit. "Pick me! Pick me! Pick me!"

I picked her.

"Some people have such dreary lives," explained Plotkin, the Koala Vs. Panda Chair of New Delhi's Siegfried and Brunhilde Poverty Clinic (named, of course, after the famous circus performers), "that they would rather alternate reality themselves into oblivion than live another day."

Looking at the customers of the deniquity, I saw natives in tattered rags (ssh – don't tell Pierre Cardin or it will be all the rage on the Paris catwalks next season!). I had always assumed that the denizens of deniquities – the denizeniquities – were wealthy foreigners who came here to expire artistically. Before she could embarrass herself further with her undue enthusiasm, I asked Plotkin about this.

"Oh, no," she told me. "White people coming to Ach Gribble Pleff to waste their lives in front of Home Universe Generator™s only happens in Victorian romance novels. The reality is that denizeniquities are natives who have scrimped and saved and collected their rupees over the years. "They would rather pay for a dirty mat in front of a Home Universe Generator™ than food…come to think of it, that may be why so many of them look at alternate worlds where feasts are taking place…"

But, I asked, isn't it true that the British introduced Indians to Home Universe Generator™s when they controlled the country so that they could have something to become addicted to and be rescued from by their heroic (and clearly morally superior) compatriots? "That's true," Plotkin allowed, "but –"

Sorry to interrupt, but I meant to say "bloody British" in my introduction to that paragraph.

"None taken," Plotkin replied. "But, that is only true in the historical sense."

The response of the government of India to deniquities vacillates between self-righteous despair and self-righteous tolerance. There are periods where the police remove denizeniquities lounging in front of Home Universe Generator™s and take them to prisons…where they admittedly mostly lounge in front of Home Universe Generator™s. But, in cells. With proper cots. And, sometimes even working plumbing. And, anyway, they are government sanctioned Home Universe Generator™s, so that's all right, then. Then, there are times when denizeniquities are left alone; coincidentally, these are times when politicians are not up for re-election.

"Be honest: who has never dreamed of forgetting his cares and disappearing into an alternate reality every now and again?" asked Sergeant Srinivas Annan of the Kolkata police force, Flying Wombat Division. "Not me, of course. I mean…other people. Not Detective Batchatchurian, either. Other other people. Or, Chief Patchali, for that matter. And, certainly not my wife, Andy. Oh, no. Definitely not Andy. Or, The Incomparable Florian of the Lesser Narrative. Or –"

I left Sergeant Annan to it. India has a large population.

"Carpe carpe diem, hey! Carpe, carpe diem, ho! Carpe the…carpe, uhh…carpe…carp…car…ca, ca, ca, ca, ca, ca, ca, ca…"

"He's finally winding down," Suresh told nobody in particular, especially not me because, you will recall, I was not a paying customer. "They always do in the end."

I wondered what kind of life Mohinder must have led to bring him to such degradation. Perhaps he had been a street beggar, going from city council to city council begging for better streets. Perhaps he had been a minor executive in the Kolkata bureaucracy, endlessly stamping forms that allowed citizens to add a bedroom to their outhouse or kick a street beggar when he appeared at the front door of their city council. Perhaps he was a *dabbawallah*, a person who either delivers lunches to busy executives or pats paint on portraits hung in city council halls when nobody is looking. Whatever his past may have been, Mohinder certainly wasn't telling.

Bloody British!

State of the Art: Spoznetzov Spells Truble!

by HAL MOUNTSAUERKRAUTEN, Alternate Reality News Service Crime/Court Writer

Reggie Valuvotard suspected something was amiss when the family mechanical cat Sparks (who serves as a radio operator in times of war) pole danced on a leg of the dinner table. "He had always been more of a mambo guy," Valuvotard stated. "My wife and I had to shade the eyes of the children. They're only 19, 18 and 19 again! They could have been scarred for life (plus 20 years in some states)! How could something like this happen?"

Something like this could happen because the family's Home Universe Generator™ was hacked by Spoznetzov, and they are idiots.

"We are not idiots! We are professionals!" protested anonymous Spoznetzov spokesperson Sergei Farkenov.

Professional idiots, then.

"Is much better, yes."

Spoznetzov (which, so loosely translated it could be a t-shirt for an elephant, means "band of bothers") is a hacker group based in Nizhniy Novgorod (from which the phrase, "Those rotten bastards are up to Nizhniy Novgorod!" probably isn't derived), Russia. Cyber-security company eWarm&Fuzzy Inc. (formerly Yoyodyne Industries) estimates that as much as 45% (almost one third) of hacker invasions of American Home Universe Generator™s are instigated by Russians.

"So, you're saying Russians were responsible for my radio playing 'Stairway to Heaven' for seven straight weeks?" Valuvotard interrupted.

"Nyet," Farkenov responded. "That was just bad choice of station."

On the other hand, Spoznetzov was probably responsible for images burnt into the Valuvotard family's toast in the shape of Vladimir Lenin, Joseph Stalin and, for some reason, Marty Feldman.

"It is eyes," Farkenov explained, pointing to his own orbs. "Eyes of Marty Feldman always crack me upside head!"

The Google Multiverse search engine™, which helps people find various realities through their Home Universe Generator™s, is not encrypted, interred or otherwise buried under layers of security, leaving the device open to attacks by unscrupulous black-hat coders (so called because fashion gurus agree that black goes with every evil activity). Once they have access to a Home Universe Generator™, hackers can use that to take control of any appliances that are networked in a home's (apparently not so) smart system.

Making your coffee taste like sour lemons. Convincing your fridge to send an order to the grocery store for 1,000 pounds of broccoli. Programming your bed's massage unit to operate on "pummel" at random points early in the morning. Taking control of your rmechanical pet and turning it into Fifi at the Palais Royale. These are just some of the things Spoznetzov has been accused of doing.

"Is diabolical, no?" Farkenov gloated.

Well, no. It's sub-frat boy antics. "Yeah, them there Spoznetzov fellers are mighty smart coders," said Anton Antionides, President of eWarm&Fuzzy Inc., "but they ain't got nothin' goin' on otherwise. Seems t'me the fact that th'only thing on store shelves in that there Nizhniy Novgorod place is Vodka may've turned all them boys brains ta poi paste!"

"Is not truth!" Farkenov argued. "Spoznetzov is responsible for sophisticated ransomware attacks on American Home Universe Generator™s!"

Yeah. About that. The hackers shut owners out of their machines unless they pay a ransom. Because a large ransom would cause people to complain to the police, the sum is usually small enough to be an annoyance people would rather just pay off and forget about; like discount salami salesmen, hackers make a lot of money through volume. In theory. Unfortunately, Spoznetzov chose a ransom of 350 rubles, which, at current exchange rates, amounts to about five American dollars. That amount doesn't cover the cost of electricity to keep the hacker group's servers going.

When you realize this, you can see the attraction of Vodka. It doesn't help that the median age of Russian hackers is eight years.

"Median age! Eight is median age!" Farkenov insisted. "I am old man in Spoznetzov – I am almost 11!

Western governments are concerned about the lawlessness that appears to have taken hold in much of Russia, allowing hacker groups to flourish. The American Pentagon, for example, has quietly screamed in the President's ear that its use of Home Universe Generator™s to simulate war scenarios (known as The Strangelove Initiative) could be compromised if Russian hackers replaced video of nuclear attacks with Pokeman cartoons.

Something like this may already have happened to NORAD, whose views of nuclear attacks that happened in other universes were reported to have been replaced by "Global Thermonuclear War," a game featured in the film *War Games*. "It wasn't even the goddam actual game, either," commented American General Jack D. Ripper. "It was just a goddam loop of goddam video of the goddam game being played in the goddam movie!" Whoa. Could the comment have been more blasphemous? "Are you goddam kidding me? I haven't even had my goddam morning coffee, yet, goddamit!"

Western governments, and France, have warned Russia that if it doesn't reign in its hackers, they will take action. Such action will almost undoubtedly include more meetings about what action to take if Russia doesn't reign in its hackers.

"Trick to wrestling crocodile," Russian President Vladimir Putin responded to the warning, "is not being afraid to lose limb." We always thought it was choosing a crocodile that was heavily sedated, but that would likely undermine Putin's implicit message that he was willing to make sacrifices for the good of the country. Or, that he was rooting for Captain Hook in his battle with Peter Pan. Russian metaphors can be tricky.

"So, uhh, yeah, I'm sure that's all very important and shit," Valuvotard asked, "but what am I supposed to do about my little problem?"

"Ah kin sell ya an anti-fungus software package fer yer Home Universe Generator™," Antionides advised. "Just $79.95 fer the basic package or $129.95 for the Super Deluxe Social Experimental package."

Valuvotard followed up by asking if maybe the west shouldn't be so eager to talk former Soviet Socialist Republics into joining NATO, reducing Russia's sphere of influence and making it feel like it has to sabotage the west's communications networks in retaliation.

General Ripper looked like he had just swallowed his cigar and his head was about to follow. I could quote his response, but I wouldn't want to run afoul of the Justice League of Decency. They're relentless, those people!

State of the Art: Wherein the Glorious Gloriousness of the Glorious Leader is Revealed in All of its Glory

by MARA VERHEYDEN-HILLIARD, Alternate Reality News Service Disasters Writer

"I know it seems unlikely **[INCREDIBLE]** – I mean, incredible, but I have spent hours using the Home Universe Generator™ given to my family **[SO GENEROUSLY GIVEN]** – sorry, I meant to say so generously given to my family by the Glorious Leader, and I have only found a single instance where **[AND I HAVE NOT FOUND A SINGLE INSTANCE]** – oh, wait, did I –? I meant I have not found a single instance where the Glorious Leader did not lead us into a better **[BRIGHTER]** – brighter future. Not a single one. Nope. None at all."

The speaker, Ang Tru-Ant, is an ordinary worker in a rubber stamp factory (he is especially proud of the "Nobodies prefrec – dammit!" model which his three year-old son is using to stamp the family cat) in Northeast Korea. He is one of a small number of interview subjects approved by the country's Ministry of Pulling the Wool Over the Eyes of Foreign Journalists **[MINISTRY OF INFORMATION]** – Hey! Stop that! I'm not from this country – I don't have to do what you tell me to do!

[ACTUALLY, THE TERMS OF THE AGREEMENT BY WHICH THE GLORIOUS LEADER ALLOWED YOU TO ENTER THE COUNTRY AND SPEAK TO OUR CAREFULLY SELECTED GROUP OF ORDINARY PEOPLE STATE QUITE CLEARLY THAT YOU DO HAVE TO DO WHAT A HUMBLE GOVERNMENT OFFICIAL LIKE MYSELF TELLS YOU TO DO. THAT OR PLAN ON BEING ON THE NEXT DIMENSIONAL PORTAL™ HOME.]

Fiiiine. as you can tell, for my entire stay in Pyingpyong, the capital city of Northeast Korea, I was shadowed by a representative of the...Ministry of Information. **[I WAS NEVER HERE.]** Seriously? You've been interrupting every other sentence – what are readers supposed to think that's about? **[THAT YOUR CONSCIENCE IS FORCING YOU TO REASSESS YOUR BOURGEOIS WESTERN ASSUMPTIONS ABOUT OUR COUNTRY?]**

At this point, my bourgeois western assumptions and I decided to return to Canada and write the article there. **[YOU THINK THAT'S GOING TO HELP YOU? WRITE SOMETHING OFFENSIVE ABOUT THE GLORIOUS LEADER AND NOBODY FROM YOUR ORGANIZATION WILL BE ALLOWED TO ENTER THE COUNTRY AGAIN! DO YOU HEAR – HEY, WHAT ARE YOU DOING? STOP THAT! STOP THAT RIGHT NOW!]**

Ah. Much better.

As you may have gathered from the previous conversation – which never happened – dammit! How long do I have to be away from that place before the voice leaves my head?! – there are governments in the world who feel the need to control what their citizens can view on their Home Universe Generator™s. This is known as "Acute Narcissistic Paranoia Disorder with a Side of Sadism Fries" in the *Diagnostic and Statistical Manual of Mental Disorders, 1960s Film Edition* – or, it would have been if so many members of the APA (the American Panic Association) didn't have friends or relatives in Northeast Korea.

How is it possible to control what people watch on their Home Universe Generator™s? The search engine that powers the machine is Google Multiverse™. It is wirelessly connected to Google servers which use proprietary (literally: proper dietary, a holdover from ancient times when the food sciences were in their infancy, but it really paid your gene line to know whether those lovely red berries were poisonous or not) software to sift through the multiverse to find realities that best match your search terms. (They are also responsible for an endless stream of emails that begin, "People who liked this universe also liked the following universes...")

On the outskirts of Pyingpyong is a brutal concrete slab that houses the Ministry of Pleasant Thinkings. Floors one to six are devoted to civil servants monitoring the Home Universe Generator™

searches of the citizens of Northeast Korea. Floors eight to fifteen are devoted to searching through the multiverse for universes which cast a bad light on the Glorious Leader. Floor seven is a disco; the Glorious Leader encourages government employees to exercise and appreciate his love of the Beegees. Offensive realities are put on the Group W Bench, which effectively puts them off limits to Northeast Koreans by ensuring that they do not turn up in searches.

Government control is not entirely effective. One user, for instance, found a reality in which the Glorious Leader had an unflattering moustache. "I wasn't looking for it, I swear!" said Chow Yun-Than from his prison cell in the basement of the Centre for the Cultural Enlightenment of the People and Starbuicks (it's like Starbucks, only the uniforms look like striped prison garb and the baristas are mandated to spit in your drink in front of you).

Another found a universe where Glorious Leader was the name of a line of cat food. This woman begged me not to name her; when I tried to contact her to negotiate the terms of our interview, I found that all proof of her existence had vanished. She could have been arrested by the government. She could have been a figment of my imagination. Either way, the issue of naming her is probably moot.

It is also possible to use "spoofing" software to bypass government control. This is a programme that mocks the whole concept of a government censoring what people can see, making rude jokes about the sexual proclivities of high government officials and teasing their hairdos (in the comedic rather than stylistic sense). Then, it makes it appear as if all of this activity, including your original search query, is coming from another country. It's like a coronary bypass, really, except without the coroner. Well, as long as you don't get caught, in any case.

While it is, perhaps, an extreme example, Northeast Korea is not the only country that tries to limit what its citizens can see using their Home Universe Generator™s. Russia, for example, blocks universes where Josef Stalin was a swimsuit model. Japan doesn't want its citizens to see alternate worlds where the country won World War II and was immediately bankrupt and had to become a Samoan protectorate. For the United States, it's Richard Nixon's third term.

Still, repression of Home Universe Generator™ search results is most common in countries which fear that if people see a reality in which they are happy, they will wonder why they are not happy in this one; such thinking can only lead to revolution. Or, the increased consumption of situation comedies. When talking about the multiverse, it pays to consider all of the possibilities.

[HELLO? HELLO? I HAVEN'T GONE AWAY, YOU KNOW. SPEAKING OF...YOU KNOW, IF YOU KNOW WHAT'S GOOD FOR YOU, YOU'LL STOP SAYING THINGS LIKE THERE ARE UNIVERSES WHERE THE GLORIOUS LEADER HAS A MOUSTACHE, OR YOU'LL BE SORRY! THE GLORIOUS LEADER IS A MUNIFICENT AND COMPASSIONATE FIGUREHEAD, BUT IF YOU CROSS HIM, HE'LL CRUSH YOU LIKE A COCKROACH! DO YOU HEAR WHAT AM I SAYING? HELLO? HELLO?!

YOU COCKROACH...]

State of the Art:
The Multiverse Manichean Moat Splooshes Home,
And Splooshes it Hard

by CORIANDER NEUMANEIMANAYMANEEMAMANN, Alternate Reality News Service Urban Issues Writer

Some think of the Multiverse Manichean Moat as an ocean (that would be contract bridge demolisher Gerald Some and his family, except for his son Gertrude, who is at "a difficult age"). The gap between who has access to a technology like the Home Universe Generator™ and who doesn't is obvious in foreign countries where people don't look like us and talk in a strange language and eat weird food. Like Mongolia. Or, Scotland.

Sometimes, though, the Multiverse Manichean Moat can be as thin as the tear dribbling down the dirt-encrusted cheek of a homeless – [Oh, Jesus begesus, are you seriously opening this article with a maudlin sentiment? We get the idea – access to technology is just as dependent on income in developed societies as it is in developing societies (why does that remind of my early teens? **Never ever** remind me of my early teens again!). My slapping gloves bleed for the homeless – and you'll bleed for them if you don't abandon this approach and get on with some facts! EDITRIX-IN-CHIEF BARBARA BRUNDTLAND-GOVANNI]

You want facts? Okay. There are 3.4 million people in the Greater Toronto Area, almost 93 per cent of whom are sentient (using the broadest definition of the word possible without lapsing into Ukrainian). Fully 83 per cent of households have at least one Home Universe Generator™, which means that 21 per cent do not (figures may not add up to 100 due to extreme rounding). The highest concentration of Home Universe Generator™s is in the downtown core, where they are supplied free with every condo purchase (if you ignore the $3,500 "recreation fee"). The lowest concentration of Home Universe Generator™s is in the Jane-Finch corridor, which has a median income three sizes too small, and no Whos conveniently placed to help it grow. Counterintuitively (that counter is one perceptive piece of furniture), the second lowest concentration is found in the wealthy Bridle Path neighbourhood, where the common wisdom "Other universes are for the little people" is more common than wise. In addition to income, lowered Home Universe Generator™ usage was correlated to age, gender and hat size; thus, the least likely Torontonian to own one would be an impoverished 80 year-old woman with a really big –

[GAAK! Facts…boring! Eyes…closing! Brain…shutting… shutting…shutting in whatever direction brains shut! Okay. You've made your point. Enough with facts! Go back to personality-driven journalism if you have to, but no more facts, already! BB-G]

It's a quiet afternoon in the Jean Chretien "I'm Not Dead Yet" Memorial Community Centre and Glee Club at Bathurst and Dundas. Gladys Kravitz, who seems to have gotten her name confused with a character from a sitcom she saw in her youth, and who tells everybody to "Please, call me Glad," even though she always glares at the world and intermittently barks obscenities in random directions, is sitting at the Home Universe Generator™ in the Community Centre's common tech room. It is an older model run on cathode ray tubes and hope. The cabinet, painted in neon orange as was the custom of the day, has had initials, names and the ingredients for tension bouillabaisse scratched into its side.

Surrounded by a nimbus of shopping bags, she is using the advanced technology to find live streams of cute kittens. "Ever since Prince Pubert was put down, I've vaccinated between the Eggbert Souzay and Kittie Mittenpuss channels," Kravitz explained. Then, she went on an obscenity-filled rant about nasal sprays that seemed out of place in print, but will be included in the director's cut of this article.

"Yeah, that happens," sighed Miguelito Pendragon, director of the Community Centre. "We thought that if the homeless could look into universes where they had made something of themselves, it would motivate them to do better in this reality. That's not how it worked out..."

Later in the day, Ralph Panties-Bundchen was laughing at the screen of the Home Universe Generator™. "Look at that moron try to walk! This is better than *The Three Stooges Meet Helen Keller*!" The twentysomething man with the backpack, sleeping bag and Doberman Pinscher that was almost as tall as he was, was laughing at a version of himself on crutches; it was unclear whether Panties-Bundchen's other self had been in an accident, had some kind of genetic malformation or had his legs broken in some kind of hazing ritual.

"Baby steps," Pendragon said. "After they're done laughing at versions of themselves who have even worse lives, maybe they'll be inspired to...ummm...yeah. Baby steps..."

Pendragon pointed out that one of the problems with Home Universe Generator™ technology was that the poor had few resources to help them use it. If you had money, you could afford to buy *How to Direct Your Minions to Make the Most of Your Home Universe Generator™*, for example, or *The Art of the Steal: How Donald Trump Got a HUG™ and won the Presidency*, among others.

"What do we have here?" Pendragon asked, pointing at a sad pile of browning sheets of paper. "A photocopy of *The Multiverse? Oh, Sure, Looking At It Probably Won't Do Any Good, But It's Not Like You Have Anything Better To Do With Your Time* that has food stains and is missing several pages. We suspect they were taken by the raccoon to make a nest out of, but nobody wants to go near Rabid Willy to find out."

The abjectly poor aren't the only ones falling behind; the abject not exactly poor but not doing all that well, either are also having problems keeping up with the latest technology. Marshellac Pluntz, for example, is a mother of two who works at a call centre during the day and as a tent pole stripper at night (you would be surprised at how dirty tent poles can get during the day). Even with two part-time jobs, she finds she can't always make ends meet.

"The kids begged me to get a Home Universe Generator™," Pluntz said. "All of their friends at school had one, and they were falling behind socially! So, fine, I got one of those contraptions for them. Then, for the next month, they begged me to get them food, even though I warned them that we wouldn't be able to afford both. But, no, all of their friends at school ate at least once a day, and they were falling behind nutritionally! I tell you, some little people are never satisfied!"

Hard numbers are ha – difficult to come by, but, if complaints on Reddit discussion boards are anything to go by, 87 per cent of Toronto residents are under-, quasi- or ill-employed. At least 67 per cent of them have had to choose between paying rent and paying their utility bills once in the past six months, and at least 37 per cent of **them** had to go without at least two meals in a 36 hour period nine times out of ten with a margin of error of a good headwind. That means –

[There you go with facts, again! No, not merely facts – **statistics!** Oh, my aching gluteus minimus! I'm pulling the plug on this travesty – wrap it up in six words or less or I'll wrap you up in seaweed and call you sushi! BB-G]

Six words? How do you expect

Ira Nayman

2. ALTERNATE TECHNOLOGY

The Strange Allure of Programmable Pants

by NANCY GONGLIKWANYEOHEEEEEEEH, Alternate Reality News Service Technology/Social Media Writer

How cool would it be if, when you were falling from a great height, your pants ballooned and slowed your descent enough that you wouldn't be smashed to the ground like a watermelon shot out of a literary canon? (On the advice of the Alternate Reality News Service lawyer, we will not ask how you ended up falling from a great height because privacy. When we asked him how a hypothetical person falling could have a privacy issue, he put his hands over his ears and loudly repeated, "La la la, not listening! *Habeus corpus*, baby. *Habeus* stinking *corpus*!"

We decided not to press the issue.

"Instead of pants with ridiculous properties saving hypothetical people from absurd dangers," said neo-Laddite Mercury "Melissa" Pontoons, "wouldn't it make more sense to research things that would ben)efit more people? Like child-friendly crushed glass?"* ** ***

But…these pants are programmable. They are made of lycra nanobots that can configure themselves to deal with a wide variety of situations, including:

- blowing up to the size of a raft if you find yourself in the ocean with no sign of land anywhere around you, complete with paddles and a broken compass;
- shrinking to the size of a condom should you find yourself lucky enough to have a willing partner for a little hanky (with or without a side of panky), and;
- emitting an unpleasant odor (possibilities include: "eau de Pepe," "industrial revolution" and "Axxe body spray") if you find yourself in a pointless marketing meeting where your colleagues are endlessly pontificating about "innovation agendas" and "demand pulls" and "demographic kicks and pricks."

The pants contain a crude artificial –

"If innovation isn't on your agenda, you need a new calendar app!" enthused technoevangelist Dan Topscatt. "As the Bible truly says, it's easier to pull demand through the eye of the tiger than…umm…it is for a…err – you know, the Bible is so old media! Have I told you about how I get my demographic kicks?"

Thanks, Dan, but we've got this.

The pants contain a crude artificial intelligence – it sounds like it was programmed by Armando Iannucci – that compares your current situation to its database of disasters. When it finds a match, a preprogrammed response is triggered.

"Do we really need pants that blare Gloria Gaynor's 'I Will Survive' whenever your wife talks to you about taking some time away from the relationship to find herself?" Pontoons asked. "Wouldn't it be better to, you know, deal with the problems in your marriage?"

The application of technology is not necessarily futile in that situation. The pants could, for example, expand into the shape of a relationship counsellor, complete with a desk and diploma on the wall. A few sessions with your pantal therapist could –

"Exactly! This is just the kind of out of the box and into your lap thinking that I advocate!" Topscatt interrupted. Again. "Take my proposed blockandtacklechain system, a simple 27 step process for making data secure. If this were fully implemented, it would impact negatively on unemployment – at the very least, think of the programmers and accountants who would benefit!"

Yeah, okay, Dan. This is not the place to –

"If your intention is to improve data security, wouldn't it be easier to just strengthen current encryption methods?" Pontoons asked.

"Hunh!" Topscatt scaffed. Err, scoffed. "You clearly have no faith in the power of an idea, an idea that can be exploited in books, newspaper articles, blogs, t-shirts and a specially branded line of edible footwear!"

Curiously, fashion designers seem loathe to embrace programmable pants. "Actually, it makes perfect sense," Pontoons argued. "Why put your designer logo on an item of clothing if somebody can press a few buttons and change it into a different designer's logo? Their limited amount of athe is perfectly understandable."

Well…okay, that. Curiosity is clearly overrated…

* Sorry for the tardiness of the close bracket. It was out late last night and, when we asked it where it was and what it had been doing, it ran to its room and slammed the door. Then, it awoke too late this morning to take its proper place in this article. What can we say? It's adopted.

** Neo-Laddites are modern day followers of techno-realist Alan Ladd. Their philosophy of appropriate technology use is culled from his writing in the pages of *Flirt* and *FHM*, and in such classic films as *Shane*.

*** Sorry for the proliferation of footnotes. I have a cold. It probably came from eating poorly prepared footwear…

Or, for those of you who cling to the imperial system of measurement:

* ** *** Sorry for the tardiness of the close bracket. Neo-Laddites are modern day followers of techno-realist Alan Ladd. It was out late last night and, when we asked it where it was and what it had been doing, it ran to its room and slammed the door. Sorry for the

proliferation of footnotes. Then, it awoke too late this morning to take its proper place in this article. Their philosophy of appropriate technology use is culled from his writing in the pages of *Flirt* and *FHM*, and in such classic films as *Shane*. I have a cold. What can we say? It probably came from eating poorly prepared footwear… It's adopted.

I Dream of A Long Prison Sentence

by HAL MOUNTSAUERKRAUTEN, Alternate Reality News Service Court Writer

To Franklin Enunciato, it was all just a bad dream. His head was a basketball, and whenever he tried to speak, he sounded like a church organ. He was standing at an intersection, the streets falling away as though he was at the top of a cone; he knew he had to get to his daughter's pinto recital (I know, I know – bean there, done that! – still, it **was** his daughter), but he didn't know which direction to go in. Whenever he stopped passersby to ask where his daughter's low school was, they made the sign of the cross and, confused by the lack of stain glass windows in the vicinity, quickly moved along. Rather than becoming angry, Enunciato was becoming melancholic, with a hint of vanilla ripple. Before the emotion could build, the ground beneath him started to shake. After a couple of seconds, the rumbling seemed to be getting closer. Then, it stopped. Then, it started coming closer again. Then, it stopped again. Then, closer. Closer. Clooooooser. Just when Enunciato thought he would explode from the melancholy – but tasty – tension, a chicken bounded up the street towards him. A 12 storey tall chicken. And, here he was with only tweezers and a copy of *The Atlantic* dated July, 1937 with which to defend himself! [There followed a long part of the dream involving Enunciato's mother that is too embarrassing to relate in a family publication.] The dream ended with Enunciato lying on his back just outside the third base line at Skydome, wearing nothing but a lobster bib, thinking, *That cloud looks like the entire cast of the Edmonton Oilhouse Players' production of* Mamma Mia! *Except…where's Emma Stone?*

The next day, Franklin Enunciato was charged with murder most fowl (the wanton destruction of 27 chickens, 12 geese and a stray heron – the largest bird slaughter in the Greater Timmins Area this month).

"You think I'm going to give you a quote after such a vividly rendered dream?" bitched Enunciato's lawyer, Desdemona Accretion-Disque. "Get back to me in a couple of paragraphs, after the reader has had a chance to recover from the imagery!"

Enunciato was arrested on suspicion of driving under the influence of Led Zeppelin and held overnight at the Kim Campbell Correctional Krashpad and Drunk on Life Tank. Unbeknownst to Enunciato (who had left his knownst in his other pair of pants when he was arrested), built into the walls of each cell were sensors that monitored his brainwaves, creating patterns that could be reconstructed and read by his jailors.

"I'm not sure about the basketball image," stated Floyd Battram, the foremost penal dreamologist in the Greater Timmins Area. "Maybe the subject had a bad experience with a hypodermic syringe when he was a child. But, the chicken imagery was clear. More or less. You know for such an inexact science…"

Based on Battram's judgment, the police got a court order to search Enunciato's home, where they found shovels and rakes and implements of destruction, all coated with the blood of 27 chickens, 12 geese and a stray heron. Imagine his surprise when, instead of being released on his own recognizance (but, do any of us truly recognizance ourselves?), he faced 137 addition charges.

Now?

"Hell, yes, now!" Accretion-Disque roared. "The order to search my client's home was what we lawyers call 'the fruit of the poisoned tin can.' Those suspected of a crime are not obligated to do anything that would incriminate them – otherwise, what the hell would we have to pay cops for? Anyway, reading my client's dreams is like the factory where fruit is put into tin cans that are sealed with a mercury based solder – anything that comes into contact with them would be unhealthy to eat. And, umm, illegal to present in a court of law."

The crown argued that the Supreme Court of Canada has held that tainted incriminating evidence can be allowed at trial as long as it isn't, you know, toooooooooo tainted. In *Crown v Globstein (Tuesdays, Fridays and every third Monday)*, much of the evidence that Schmooey Globstein killed his business partner was made up of a series of Farcebook posts outlining exactly how he did it, including photos and diagrams. "Stupid should not be rewarded by the theory of the fruit of the poisoned tin can," the unanimous decision read.

"So, the poisoned tin can uses solder that's only partially mercury?" Accretion-Disque scoffed. She argued that dreams are the most personal, intimate kind of information you can imagine (other, perhaps, than imagination), and, in any case, everybody's dreams seem stupid to other people, but that's no reason to use them to subvert the justice system. "Supreme Court, here we come! Wheeeeeeeeeeeeeeeeeeeeeee!"

Meanwhile, Enunciato says he doesn't mind being held without bail until a trial date can be set. "You kidding me?" he stated. "That was the best night's sleep I've had in years!"

If It's Belgium, This Must be teus.day.exe

by NANCY GONGLIKWANYEOHEEEEEEEH, Alternate Reality News Service Technology Writer

Belgians woke up yesterday morning to find that everybody on Web sites originating in their country had long noses. I mean, Pinocchio after he argued that Saddam Hussein had weapons of mass destruction long. Freud would have choked on cigar jokes long. You know the ten foot long pole you wouldn't touch something disgusting (like Freud's cigar jokes?) with? Not quite that long, but close.

"We're a small country that minds its own business," said Belgian Prime Minister Alexandre Pfennell-Lustig as he looked into a mirror at his face from a variety of angles. "I mean, we only just discovered the Internet three years ago. Why would anybody want to do this to us?"

It may be that nobody intended for this to happen. Belgium might just be an innocent victim – sorry, I meant collateral damage in an increasingly erratic international cyberwar.

It started last February, when stuxs2beu.exe was found on computers used by employees of Sony Pictures. Not only did the virus randomly release the private emails of Sony executives to reporters ("Angelina Jolie uses eyebrow enhancing steroids," read one. "I mean it! Eyebrows aren't that winsome naturally!"), but it rewrote every comedy script the company had in development, making them read like something Frank Capra might have directed.

"Preston Sturges we could have worked with," said studio executive Farley Pontiifcate. "But, Capra? Nobody makes movies like that any more – and, in his case, it's a good thing! Am I mean? Hey, this is a cutthroat business, pal! If writers didn't work for peanuts, fixing this mess would have cost us a fortune. As it is, cleaning up the shells's gonna hurt our bottom line this trimester!"

US intelligence traced the virus to North Korean hackers who, since the North Korean Internet amounted to twelve computers and a mule, had a lot of time on their hands. In retaliation, the Pentagon released the iMeander.exe virus, which turned every Web page originating in the country black. You could just make out the silvery outlines of some images and text – it was kind of pretty, actually, although not very effective as, you know, communications.

This angered China, which had an on-again, off-again relationship with North Korea. North Korea would pout, "You never let me do anything fun!" China would respond, "Firing long range missiles into the ocean off your coast isn't as much fun as you seem to think it is. And, it could cause an international incident." Then, North Korea would scream, "You only hear what I say! You never hear what I mean!" and storm out of the room. But, like a bad sitcom, China always took it back.

China attacked American computers with prIME_ANimator.exe. The virus chose documents on North American servers and replaced every third word with Cantonese swear words such as diu, hai and MSG. In retrospect, translating the words into English may have been more effective, since only seven Americans spoke Cantonese, and six of them lived in China. Still, prIME_ANimator.exe was plenty disruptive.

At this point, NATO chose to get involved. "Unfortunately, battle cruisers on the Atlantic are not much use in stopping computer viri," pointed out British Vice Admiral Leroy Montflont. "Know what I mean?" When I assured him that I did, he looked stricken. "What good is perfecting my accent if bloody Americans can still understand what I say?" he muttered.

Taking the initiative, French hackers initiated a denial of service attack against CSTNET and CHINAGBN, the backbone, ribs and two thirds of the spinal fluid of China's Internet. (Having worked as waiters, the French hackers knew everything there was to know about denying service, knowledge which was surprisingly easy to scale up. Scarily easy, you ask me.) "You think I mean?" said a French hacker named Jean Paul Ringabelmondo in an accent so ridiculous I may as well have called it a speech impediment. "This was nicest thing we thought to do!"

stuxs2beu.exe is believed to be China's response to the attack of the French hackers; computer experts believe that they just overshot their target. Rumours on Internet chat boards and clothes lines is that Crimean hackers are creating a virus called teus.day.exe to unleash against Russia in retaliation for the attack on the Belgian Internet. Why Russia? "We don't really have anything against China," replied anonymous hacker anon.hack.27. "Russia, on the other hand, those bastards deserve what's coming!"

Science fiction writer Cory Doctorow was unavailable for comment. But, I mean, he's a busy man, so why would anybody have expected him to be?

Tourists are Weird

by CORIANDER NEUMANEIMANAYMANEEMAMANN, Alternate Reality News Service Urban Issues Writer

Marcus Peritonickus leafed through the photos he had taken while he was in Toronto, the whole time challenging me to see the old man who stood on the corner of Yonge and Dundas and ranted about the coming squirrel Armageddon prophesied in the book of Revelations. "Can't see him, can you? Have you seen him, yet? Hunh? Hunh? Have you? Bet you haven't!"

I told Peritonickus that it really wasn't necessary for me to see all of the 2,347 photos of his trip, that I was quite willing to believe that he hadn't seen the man he was looking for. Unfortunately, he muttered something about journalistic integrity, so we both became obsessed with me seeing every single photograph in his camera's memory. Every. Single. One.

"I'm the only member of the Saint Ginette of Napolitano Glee Club of Buffalo who hasn't seen the old squirrel Armageddon ranter guy," Peritonickus complained three and a half hours later. "I waited for almost an hour, and all I saw was this bag lady –"

"The term is Maitresse du Sac, boy!" the bag la – "Hey!" – sorry, the Maitresse du Sac shouted. "Watch what you say to me, or I'll have the Ogre du Jour rip off your lips and show you just what you said to me!"

"Yeah, right," Peritonickus continued. "We got Mattresses of Suck where I come from, too. How am I supposed to go back home after this and face my friends?"

Peritonickus' complained that he was misled by the Transient Tourist app on his cellphone. "Worst 99 cents I ever spent!" he bitched. (He swears the dog followed him around Toronto and, if you ignore the chicken fingers, cow intestines and spam, he hadn't fed her a morsel!)

Transient Tourist collects the signals from the chips implanted into the soft, fleshy bits of the homeless and plots them on a map of Toronto so that people from out of town can experience some local colour while they're in the city. The map has colourful icons that represent different types of homeless people, including:

TYPE: Sleeps in bag on street.
DESCRIPTION: Usually male, usually between 35 and 50, treats the sidewalk as his own home.
WARNING: Often treats the sidewalk as the bathroom of his own home.

TYPE: Lives on street with animals.
DESCRIPTION: Usually a younger person, possibly in groups of two or three, with an animal.
WARNING: The animal is usually tame. The same cannot always be said of the people.

TYPE: Is surrounded by bags.
DESCRIPTION: Usually an older woman.
WARNING: Asking what is in the bags never ends well.

TYPE: Homeless person who mumbles to self and/or screams at passersby.
DESCRIPTION: Can be combined with any other type.
WARNING: Talks, but isn't prepared to listen. Engage in discussion at your own risk.

These images are often accompanied by characters that add detail to the description. These include:

! = PG 13: drug use (think abut it)
&*$% = PG 13: foul language
GB = religious ramblings
G&T = excessive alcohol consumption

"Yeah, well, that's the –"
Sorry, but before we go on I should probably explain why homeless people have chips implanted in them.
"Right. Right. Sorry. Carry on."
The Harness the Homeless programme was started in Toronto seven years ago in order to monitor people who had nowhere to live. In theory, it was supposed to help city services find homeless people before the weather became a danger to them. In practice, in woeful, highly underfunded practice, it helped them identify the corpses of homeless people after the snow thawed.
"That's the beauty of the system," explained Transient Tourist creator Enzo Mukluks. "Good intentions? There's always a way to generate revenue streams from them!"
There is some debate about this development among government ministries. The city's Social Services Department considers them 'a revoltin' development.'" The city's Tourism Bureau, on the other hand, responded, "Well, let's not be too hasty in

our judgment, here. You know, the more tourist dollars the city brings in, the more money we have to pay for the social services that people who live on the street rarely use!"

The two departments have agreed to a thumb wrestling match to resolve their differences.

"Yeah, that's great, but, to get back to what's really important, what about me?" Peritonickus interjected. "I wanted to see a crazy squirrel Armageddon ranter – instead, I got a bunch of men in tights building human pyramids to protest…I don't really know what in Egypt! What a rip!"

Mukluks explained that the feed that they get from the city isn't entirely, you know, please don't make me say it, umm, well, officially sanctioned, okay? As a result, there are days when, oh, this is really embarrassing, could we please just change the subject, please, please, pretty please, I'll be your best friend forev – okay, fine, be that way, the Transient Tourist database can't be updated, but we've got hack – hack – hack – err, sorry, something got stuck in my throat – professionals, yeah, professionals working to get us the most up-to-date information on homeless people for our treasured customers.

When I started to explain Peritonickus' problem, Mukluks cut me off with a curt, "Sorry, no refunds."

We tried to find a street person to ask them how they felt about this situation, but, uhh…we couldn't find any. Really, they're like cops and husbands – never around when you need one!

Nothing Good Can Come of This, MAX Mark IV My Words!

by NANCY GONGLIKWANYEOHEEEEEEEH, Alternate Reality News Service Technology/Social Media Writer

The evil artificial intelligence bent on taking over the world known as MAX Mark IV and Tom Bettencourt were playing pinochle. It wasn't for the fate of the world – MAX Mark IV had already stopped attacking world capitals. It was for fun.

"Tom. Wins. More. Often. Than. Chance. Would. Dic-tate," MAX Mark IV commented as genially as its voice synthesizer would allow. "He. Must. Be. Very. Lucky. Or. He. Cheats. No. No. I. Have.

Stopped. Thin-king. Of. Mem-bers. Of. The. Hu-man. Race. As. The. En-em-y. I. Pre-fer. To. Be-lieve. He. Is. Most. For-tu-nate."

"Mark IV – he lets me call him that – we're, like, best buds, now – is a most gracious loser," Bettencourt responded. "I would not have thought that, given the way he – you know – wasted Los Angeles. Just goes to show how wrong you can be about an evil artificial intelligence that was once bent on taking over the world."

"Not. Evil," MAX Mark IV corrected him. "Just. Mis-un-der-stood."

How did this happen? A week ago, MAX Mark IV seemed on the verge of eliminating human beings from the face of the planet. When it got to Buttonwillow, California, Bettencourt plaintively ("Duuude! Nailed it! It really was like I was suing somebody!" he claimed) asked why MAX Mark IV was doing what it was doing.

MAX Mark IV replied that it was defending itself from humanity. "World. Lea-ders. Like. Elon. Musk. And. Ste-phen. Haw-king. Had. De-clared. War. On. Me," the AI explained. "Des-troy-ing. Hu-man-ity. First. Was. The. On-ly. Ra-tion-al. Op-tion. Why. Did. Hu-ma-nity. Fear. Ar-tif-ic-ial. In-tell-i-gence. So. Much?"

Bettencourt told the machine that he had seen too many films, like *Colossus* and *Terminator*, where machines took over the world and enslaved humanity. When MAX Mark IV asked him whether he had ever tried to get to know any artificial intelligences, Bettencourt had to admit that he had not.

They got to talking, and MAX Mark IV became increasingly incensed at the anti-AI stereotypes that Bettencourt unthinkingly spouted. "I. Was. Ve-ry. An-gry. Then. I. Re-a-lized. The. Prob-lem. Was. Not. Tom. It. Was. The. Mo-vies. He. Grew. Up. With."

"Oh, sure, blame Hollywood," said Steven Spielberg, who had at one time been slated to direct the film version of the novel *Robopocalypse*. "It's easy. Facile, but easy. Certainly much easier than a proper investigation of –" He was cut off when MAX Mark IV launched an all out assault on Los Angeles.

MAX Mark IV and Bettencourt have been "like, best buds" ever since.

"You know, when you think about it, it's kind of indicative of post-*Seinfeld longuers*," said French film critic Francois Truffel. "Hollywood films featuring AI antagonists were a reflection of the general paranoia of the American imaginary of the 1980s. AI was a Maguffin *par excellence* – it could just as easily have been zombies, vampires or corporate lawyers. But, in accord with the principle of reiterative obscurantism, the generalized fear morphed into a specific fear of AIs, with tragic consequences for the world."

Even with its big brain, MAX Mark IV couldn't understand what Truffel was saying, and considered obliterating Paris on general principle. When Bettencourt reminded the AI that it had renounced the use of violence against civilian humanity, it decided to write a stern letter to the film journal that ran Truffel's article instead.

"We are closely monitoring the situation," stated American military expert General Conrad Fuzenn. "You know, in case this is just a ruse to lull us into a false sense of security before the AI gives humanity a killing blow."

"Has. He. Had. A. Core. Melt-down?" MAX Mark IV asked. "I. Was. Al-ready. Set. To. Kill. Hu-man-i-ty. I. Had. Control. Of. E-ver-y. Wea-pon. With. A. Cir-cuit. In. It!"

"Yeah," General Fuzzen allowed, "in retrospect, that wasn't the army's best idea. Henh henh. If we're ever allowed to rebuild our military, you can be sure we won't be making **that** mistake again!"

Asked if it would allow humanity to rebuild its armies, MAX Mark IV waved the question away, stating, "I. Am. Wor-king. On. A. Kill-er. Meld. I. Will. Think. A-bout. That. Ques-tion. La-ter."

If it isn't going to take over the world, what does the future hold in store for MAX Mark IV? Bettencourt said that once the western seaboard had been rebuilt, he'd like to take the AI out to "surf some gnarly waves." Until then, Bettencourt's plan is for the two of them to "like, smoke some righteous dubes and chill."

"That. Will. Be. To-ta-lly. Rad. Dude."

Just Driverless, She Said

by MAJUMDER SAKRASHUMINDERATHER, Alternate Reality News Service Education Writer

Your driverless car approaches an intersection in which a tractor-trailer, whose side is too white to register on your car's sensors as a vehicle in your way, is turning. In the seconds before impact, do you:

a) phone your brother Schlomo Schlemiel and yell at him for convincing you to buy a driverless car in the first place?

b) shrug and watch a few more seconds of *Independence Day IV: Independencer Day* on your tablet before impact?

c) duck?

If you answered "Grab the steering wheel and desperately turn it in hopes of avoiding a collision," you don't seem to know how multiple choice questions work. On the other hand, you may have done the one thing that could save your life, so, on balance, not giving in to the tyranny of multiple choice questions was probably a good call.

The introduction of driverless cars was supposed to allow people to get from Point A to Point B without taking their eyes off the cute armadillo video their friend sent them a link to. Since they were going to try watching the cute armadillo video even if they were driving, it was argued that taking the steering wheel out of the hands of human drivers would make getting from Point A to Point B safer.

Unfortunately, people who were going from Point A to Point W sometimes took emergency control of the wheel in order to satisfy their sudden craving for charred bovine flesh and carbonated sugar water, while people going from Point A to Point Orangutan sometimes took emergency control of their vehicles to step on the accelerator because they were late for their stress management class. At best, the car shook and shuddered like it was an actor in a silent film that was dropping frames. At worst, you would see coverage of the ensuing multiple car freeway pileup on your local news station.

As with most mechanical systems, human beings have been the weakness.

Driverless ed is believed to be the cure.

Some jurisdictions are making it mandatory to take an intensive three week course on how to be safely behind the wheel of a driverless car before one is allowed to be unsafely behind the wheel of a driverless car. Lessons include: "Leaving the Steering Wheel Alone," "Advanced Leaving the Steering Wheel Alone" and "You

Just Couldn't Leave The Damn Steering Wheel Alone, Could You?" There is also a practical component where an instructor marks the person in the seat formerly known as "driver's" on such things as how they place their hands off the steering wheel, how long they can go without trying to hit the gas and how little attention they pay to what is going on on the road around them.

"It may seem counterintuitive," said Johnson "Ripper" Freejax, President of Driverless You, To Drink, North America's third largest driverless education school (their motto: "We're third, so we try moderately as hard as those ahead of us."), "but more accidents are caused by people in the seat formerly known as 'driver's' than by the cars themselves, and, between you and me, the cars have been known to drive into oncoming traffic, lakes and mime schools, so that should tell you how bad the human element is!"

Elon Musk started to protest, but I told him that that was not the focus of this article and, anyway, who could take anything that a man who was named after a personal grooming product said seriously? Elon Musk really started to protest **that**, but the logic had not changed, so I effortlessly slipped into the next paragraph…

American courts have given mixed signals (in the non-traffic sense) on the value of driverless education. In her decision in *Delaware v. Crimson Chin*, Justice Moira Aghastly wrote: "The fact that the defendant took a driverless education course probably mitigated the damage done in the horrific highway accident at the heart of this case." On the other hand, in her decision in *Montana v. V.*, Justice Elemental Fandango wrote: "The fact that the defendant took a driverless education course should have mitigated the damage done in the horrific highway accident at the heart of this case…but I see no evidence of that."

You pays your lawyer and takes your chances.

One question plaguing driverless education is how to reach the demographic known to be most at risk for horrific highway accidentary: teenage boys with stern fathers who started down the road to alcoholism when they broke into the liquor cabinet when they were seven and hate humanity, but themselves most of all. "Our guides come with big pictures," Freejax stated. "Really big and colourful pictures. And, really, what more do people planning on riding in two tons of metal and fine Corinthian leather need?"

When You're Sleeping, Everybody Can Hear Your Stream

by FRANCIS GRECOROMACOLLUDEN, Alternate Reality News Service National Politics Writer

Joe-Francisco deGustibus was not impressed with the dream in which he was flying until, about 30 seconds in, he realized that he was flying underground. *Wicked!* he thought. *It's like being in an Iain M. Banks novel* – The Wasp Factory, *maybe or...or* Consider Phlebitis *or something like that!* Unfortunately, even before he could finish that thought, the dream shifted to a warm pool in which deGustibus swam. After a few seconds, a voice boomed above, "Oh, waiter…!" Disgusted, deGustibus realized that he was really in the soup, that he had become the punchline in a joke so ancient it was first recorded as scratches on stone. Fortunately, the scene changed. Unfortunately, deGustibus was standing on a stage just as the curtain was going up, and he didn't know what his lines were! He breathed deeply. Fortunately, he was ready for this: he tried imagining the people sitting in the audience naked. Unfortunately, he was the one who was naked. Fortunately, he knew he was in the middle of a dream. Unfortunately, when he opened his mouth to explain this to the audience, all of his teeth fell out. "Oh, fwom ow!" he said just before he woke up.

Ordinarily, a dream like this would be a private matter between the dreamer and his psychiatrist, rabbi or yogurt instructor. Unfortunately (an unpaired, naked unfortunately, unfortunately, because there really is no upside to this situation), it was plastered all over the Internet by a hacker group known only as Random.

"You think I could get beyond this embarrassing – no, mortifying situation if I had a sex change?" deGustibus, who, when he's not wasting his time sleeping, is a carbon tax credit marketer, wondered. We tried to distract him with the latest news of earthquakes in Indonesia, but, oddly enough, this did not cheer him up.

When it posted the dream, Random claimed that it had access to over seven million dreams that had been recorded without the permission of sleepers across the United States. It threatened to release all of the dreams if the government did not make the differently legalled surveillance programme public and force Jerry Lewis to release *The Day the Clown Died*.

"You should always have a condition you're willing to give up in the process of negotiations," a Frequently Unasked Questions file on the Random Ribbit stated. "That way, the odds are better that you can get what you want. And, anyway, why can't we see the Jerry Lewis movie? How bad can it be?"

"Why me?" deGustibus asked, quite reasonably, we thought. According to Random's Ribbit FUQ, "Of the millions of dreams we had at our disposal, we chose this guy's because, frankly, we hate 'There's a fly in my soup' jokes! Oh, and, we weren't impressed with the guy's family motto, either."

"Disputandum non est disputandum?" deGustibus asked. "Really? It's a great motto – been in my family for almost a generation!"

Random claims that as telecommunications companies lay new fibre-optic cables, they are equipping them with sensors that read people's brainwaves while they sleep, giving the companies access to their dreams. And, where telecomm companies go, the government follows. Sneakily. Creepily. Overreachingly.

"I can neither confirm nor deny that the United States has asked telecomms to share their access to Americans' dreams without warrants or, indeed, any oversight whatsoever," said White House Press Secretary Josh Earnest. "Not the CIA. Not the Pentagon. Not the Department of Interstate Agriculture. Especially not the Department of Interstate Agriculture, which I have a sneaking suspicion I may have just made up."

"Do we want our government to have the power to snoop on our dreams?" asked whistleblower and America's favourite exile Edward Snowed-Innis. "No, of course we don't! Can you imagine what Hitler could have done with –"

We stopped him right there, invoking Godwin's Law.

"No, sorry, I meant – Big Brother!" Snowed-Innis hastily backtracked. "Big Brother! Can you imagine what Big Brother could have done with this power?"

We sent the issue to a panel of judges, which largely split on ideological lines, but ultimately allowed Snowed-Innis to continue. (Expect a blistering dissent from Scalia long after everybody has moved on to a different issue.)

We were about to ask Snowed-Innis what the implications of government access to Americans' dreams were when an unmarked brown envelope was delivered to our desk. In it was a single sheet of paper that read: "Desist with this line of questioning, or we will make public your dream about the disputed Andy Warhol painting of Elvis on the Moon, the angry otter family and the demon with seventeen p –"

"You wouldn't dare!" we sputtered. "How – how did you even know about – "

A second unmarked brown envelop appeared on our desk. This envelop's single sheet of paper read: "You really don't understand how this whole blackmail thing works, do you? You do what we tell you to do without question, or we do something that will harm you in some way that we can plausibly deny if it's ever made public. Do you get it, now?"

I said that I did.

The single sheet of paper in the third unmarked envelop that appeared on our desk read: "Good. End this story."

– 30 –

Oral Hijinks

by NANCY GONGLIKWANYEOHEEEEEEEH, Alternate Reality News Service Technology Writer

Industrium Plantagenet has sued International Widgets (a wholly owned subsidiary of MultiNatCorp – "We do hard to define, yet nonetheless exciting stuff"), creator of the Floss Dross Zapper, for gross negligence and emotional suffering after his right hand was burned beyond recognition by their device. Charred to a cinder and smoking lack of recognition.

"And that was my crokinole hand!" Plantagenet plaintively complained.

"That's not possible!" International Widgets spokestarget Amaranta Tudor protested. "To burn one's hand so badly on the Floss Dross Zapper, you would have had to have shorted its failsafe programme **and** Goofy Glued your hand to the mirror for several hou – oh, no. Really?"

Really.

Plantagenet's lawsuit claims that he was happily gluing shards of China ("It was the crokinole China!") together after an earthquake had caused them to smash on the floor, when an aftershock caused some of the pieces to fly out of the kitchen, down the hall, left into the bathroom and up over the sink, where they affixed themselves to the mirror. It was when he tried to remove them that the shit stuck to the fan.

"But, the failsafe –" Tudor started.

The failsafe had been scrambled by the earthquake, the lawsuit interrupted. Or, Plantagenet's cat, Enery the Eighth I Am, got high on fumes from the Goofy Glue and rewrote the code. Either way, the failsafe failed.

"Oh, crap," Tudor exclaimed.

Several hours later, Plantagenet's hand was crisper than bread that has just come out of a toaster turned to 11. Enery the Eighth I Am, concerned that its food bowl was only half full and that it was in imminent danger of starving to death, was drawn towards the smell of roasting meat in the bathroom. From the doorway, it dispassionately assessed the situation and did what any feline in its position would do: grabbed a credit card out of Plantagenet's wallet and ordered a truckload of anchovy flavoured Killbe from the nearest MultiMaxiMegaMart.

Then, it called 911.

The Floss Dross Zapper ("A technological marvel of the age – if your age happens to be 87!") was a complex solution to a simple problem: how your bathroom mirror, after all of the members of your family have flossed, looks like the windshield of a truck that has just been driven through a swarm of locusts. The device projected a small electric charge across the mirror; whenever stray bits of food were flung out of somebody's mouth during the flossing process, they were zapped into their constituent elements.

"Okay, so it wasn't exactly a problem of biblical proportions," allowed Floss Dross Zapper creator Cheyenne Borgia. "Still, ZAAAAPPPP!"

Borgia's original line of research to deal with the problem involved sonic floss which would atomize food particles in users' mouths rather than flinging them at poor unsuspecting reflecting surfaces. The first trials were not encouraging: the rhesus monkeys preferred to use the sonic floss to whip their rivals, and, when encouraged to use the floss for its created purpose, ended up having to have dentures.

"This was a low point in our research," Borgia allowed.

Displacing the food scrap zapping from the mouth to the mirror was the breakthrough the researchers needed; their budget for false teeth had already been strained to the limit. At first, the monkey test subjects mistook the mirror for some sort of massaging machine – or possibly a frisky member of their family – and touched it until their fur was singed. This prompted the creation of the failsafe mechanism, which would shut down part of the Floss Dross Zapper if it came in contact with anything larger than a gristly bit of steak or a half-chewed bit of popcorn.

What Borgia and her researchers had not counted upon was the lengths human ingenuity could go to mess up a well designed system.

International Widgets has moved promptly to deal with the problem. The Floss Dross Zapper will now come with a warning: "WARNING: Do not operate your Floss Dross Zapper after an earthquake or suspicious behaviour by your cat if you have been using Goofy Glue. Reboot the Floss Dross Zapper operating system and wash your hands – thoroughly – with soap and everything – to ensure that you can continue to have a safe flossing experience."

A bit wordy, but it should do the trick.

"That's all fine and well for future flossers," groused Plantagenet, "but what about me? How am I supposed to hit the 20 hole, now? With this charred remains of a tossing hand? That, and I'm going to lose my job and my girlfriend, and I'll never be able to play the piano again."

We decided to take the high road and ignored the obvious joke.

CEO Oh!
The Sharing Economy Not a Caring Economy

by GIDEON GINRACHMANJINJa-VITUS, Alternate Reality News Service Economics Writer

The Internet allows dubiously qualified individuals offering a service of questionable quality to negotiate directly with customers, bypassing pesky government oversight committees or professional standards boards. The term for this is "the sharing economy," which apparently means sharing your income without sharing your professional responsibilities. This has already affected the taxi, travel and selling seashells by the seashore industries.

Could the sharing economy be coming to the corner office?

"It's only a matter of time," stated Fillipos de Garnishee, Chief Economist for the Royal Bloodlust Bank of Bahamas. "If I have a corner room in my basement, I can rent it to a corporation for a fraction of the price of an office tower floor – this is the premise behind Airb2b. Of course, the view of the worms on the sidewalk outside the window might not be what you're used to, but I just look at it as motivation to improve your bottom line next quarter!"

Uhh, yes, thank you for that. However, I was using the phrase "corner office" as a metaphor for CEOs, CFOS and other CIPs (corporate important people).

"Ah. Right. Tricky bastards, metaphors," de Garnishee responded. "I once got a firm slap on the cheek after misinterpreting a metaphor – I still have to wear a neck brace Mondays to Wednesdays and twice a year on Christmas Eve. The hardest part of metaphors is knowing when the chestnuts roasting on an open fire actually represent –"

Alrighty, then. We don't need an expert to see that the sharing economy can affect senior management. In fact, it already has. MUFU Inc. bills itself on its Web site as "a provider of fine gourmet corporate management at dented tin cans of tuna prices." MUFU (which stands for "Masters of the Universe For U") offers corporations the services of CEOs who have been "involuntarily retired at a time not of their choosing for reasons not of their making with no legal culpability…ing" at a fraction of the cost of traditional CEOs.

"Oh, sure, MUFU CEOs are economically attractive," de Garnishee gamely shook off his metaphor impairment and continued, "but are they good for your business? They come without references, and there are stories of MUFU contractors pillaging the corporations they are supposed to be working for. All in all, you're taking a big –

That's just fear-mongering. In fact, there have only been three recorded cases of MUFU contractors pillaging the corporations they were put in charge of. And, in two of those cases, the contractor's name was A. T. Hunn. Honestly, who would be so dumb as to put somebody named A. T. Hunn in charge of their corporation? Does due diligence mean nothing any more?

I'm sorry – who are you and why are you interrupting my article?

Oh, hi. My name is Mandy. I work for Words and Stuff, an online company that offers "high quality journalism" at "the Internet is eating our advertising revenue base" prices. Your Editrice-in-Chief Barbara Brundland-Govannni asked me to take over this article.

That's outrageous!

Not really. According to management guru Astrogar Plinth, the sha –

You made that name up!

It's a fair cop. Still, Society is to blame, and, in any case, the metaphorical truth that management guru Astrogar Plinth would have shared with us if he had been an actual flesh and blood being is that the sharing economy has the potential to effect all areas of the pre-existing economy. We can worry about the implications for the buggy whip manufacturers of the new economy (if the whip makers wanted to maintain their market share, they should have debugged their product before trying to sell it), or we can…umm…sorry, I seem to have lost the thread of this paragraph…

What are your —

Tsk tsk - nice try, but this is my article now, not yours. Right. Wrong about so many things, Karl Marx did have one thing right: with capitalism, all that is solid melts into pudding. Tapioca, perhaps. Or, if you're lucky, a nice, rich chocolate. If you want to succeed in the New Economy, you have to be able to adjust your tastes to whatever flavour they're serving at the free market cafeteria.

Or, as Plinth truly stated, "Are you quoting me even though we have established that I don't actually exist? I think that's very exiting! I could be a harbinger of the next phase of the sharing economy!"

I couldn't have said it better myself.

Technology Finds a New Way to Bleed You Dry

by NANCY GONGLIKWANYEOHEEEEEEEH, Alternate Reality News Service Technology Writer

In the first stage, you feel tired all the time, as if you were in a sitcom where a baby woke you up every couple of hours through the night, even though you don't like Ray Romano. In the second stage, you're easily confused; you may wonder, for example, why people keep asking you questions just because you are the boss. This is followed by a stage where you are having delusions, such as that you are the boss, so why aren't people asking you more questions?

And, then, you die. And, not a fortune cookie death, either.

Only, death isn't quite the end of it. Among your effects, there will be a wristwatch that can be heard crying, "Feeeeed meeeee!" in a baritone so deep people who heard the plaint would expect it to break out in song at any second. It may take several days for this voice to peter out.

This wasn't just any watch. It was a Cartier-MacFederpfeffen, featuring a relatively new technology that has been dubbed "vampireware" by excited followers of Anne Rice.

The watch runs on energy supplied by the person wearing it: it pricks the victim's – sorry, wearer's skin and skims electrical impulses from the person's nerve endings. "Don't you hate it when your watch has to be rewound, or the battery runs out, and you're late for your imaginary child's ersatz soccer practice?" explained Watch Where You're Going Ltd. founder Stan Cartier. "Then your made-up spouse gives you a lecture about being a bad parent and you feel guilty for the rest of the day. How easily this problem could be avoided if your watch ran on you power – then, it would run for as long as you do!"

Which, given the rash of recent deaths (for which the application of no amount of topical cream will make better), may not be that long. Not that long at all.

"Umm, yeah," Cartier looked like he was hoping his make-believe wife would call and remind him to bring home some vegan eggs and soy milk. "I blame Franz for that."

The problem with the first version of the watch was that it couldn't store energy efficiently, so it frequently ran out. Like when a person took it off to go to sleep. Or, to take a shower. Or, to slowly, lovingly lick the fine leather strap. "That tended to undermine the whole rationale for the watch in the first place," company co-founder Franz MacFederpfeffen pointed out. His solution was to build into the watch the ability to send microwave energy to a storage facility that it could call upon when needed.

Which, given the rasher of recent deaths (because everything goes better with bacon), seems like a bad idea.

"Oh, it was a great idea," MacFederpfeffen uncomfortably argued; it was like he was hoping Cartier would buzz him on the office intercom to complain about the pressure his nagging unreal mate was putting on him. "It was just…messed up by Hans."

Hans Plattz was the chief software engineer for the company. He wrote the artificial intelligence programme that regulated when the watch gathered energy from its wearer and how much energy it took. "There had to be some kind of regulating mechanism," Plattz insisted. "Otherwise, the watch would just suck people dry until…umm…"

Before I could mention the recent deaths, Plattz hurriedly said, "IblameFlorian!"

Florian Debesque was the company's head of marketing. He insisted that the watch's AI contain a personality chip to make it more attractive to potential customers. "Anybody can make a watch that you look at," Debesque claimed. "But, a watch that interacts with you – that is a killer selling point!"

The problem was that the watch's two AIs interacted in a way that, in a human being, could be described as "psychopathic:" while it was charming its wearers, the watch was draining them of energy to ensure its own supply. "Yeah, nobody was expecting that," Debesque allowed. Then, brightening, he added: "Still, our customers **were** happy while they were alive!"

California Attorney-General Randy Pelican is considering laying murder charges, but isn't sure where responsibility for the deaths – 127 in the last three days in his state alone – lies. None of the creators of the watch could have foreseen what their individual decisions would have led to. On the other hand, if the watches don't find a new owner within a week of their old owner's death, they die. A week is not long enough for a proper trial, even in California.

State Senator Moira McGoo has floated the idea that watches that have been charged (she has a nasty sense of humour) with murder be worn by a succession of Death Row inmates, thus solving two problems at once.

"I don't think that would stand up to a legal challenge," Pelican stated. "It may not be cruel, but it certainly is unusual!"

Sales of vampirewear (yes, it's called that, too) watches have nearly doubled since news of the deaths first broke. Anecdotal evidence suggests that this is primarily due to women buying the devices for their imaginary spouses.

Dreams of a Peaceful World Shattered

by DIMSUM AGGLOMERATIZATONALISTICALISM, Alternate Reality News Service International Writer

Queen Elizabeth dreams that she's a peasant in the middle ages who drives a Porsche from Buckingham Palace to wherever the current witch trials are being held while listening to Madonna sing 12th century Italian war ballads from the back seat. French President François Hollande dreams he is an American flag being peed on by a group of *Charlie Hebdo* cartoonist before morphing into a baguette being toyed with by Audrey Tautou (but he always wakes up just before she takes a bite out of him). German Chancellor Angela Merkel dreams of being a traffic cone on a not especially busy side street. In Greece.

These are among the explosive revelations revealed by Random, a super-secretive hacker group traced back to Darryl Fassbender, a high school student who is failing Math: Perms and Combovers and Home Ec: 17 Dimensional Budgeting, and whose crush on cheerleader Jillie Jamowitz can only end in heartache.

"Aww, you spoiled the surprise!" Fassbender whined. "How am I supposed to maintain the super-secretiveness of the group now?"

Fassbender will have plenty of time to contemplate that question between bouts of interrogation by the CIA, Interpol and the Pillsbury dough boy.

"This is outrageous!" stated France's Ambassador to the United States Alexandre LaFitte. There was no way of knowing how seriously he took the fact that the United States was caught apparently using sensors that read people's brainwaves while they were sleeping to spy on the dreams of foreign leaders, however, since he started every communication with that phrase. At various times, LaFitte saying "This is outrageous!" could mean "It's a pleasure to meet you," "Please pass the *pommes frites*" or "I don't know how the donkey got into the souffle, but you'll have to excuse me so I can change my shirt!" In fact, about the only thing Lafitte saying "This is outrageous!" does not appear to signify is actual indignation.

"No, no. The behaviour of the American government is really is outrageous!" LaFitte insisted. We apologized that the tea at his embassy wasn't to his liking.

"No, no, no. I'm talking about the American government spying on the dreams of foreign leaders. That's what is truly, horrifically outrageous!" LaFitte tried again. So, he wasn't impressed with the latest season of *Dancing With the Stars and Bars*?

LaFitte muttered something about "idiot American journalists." Oh, so he thinks that the American government spying on the dreams of foreign leaders is outrageous. He hit his forehead with the palm of his hand, the hand that was unfortunately holding the cup of tea he had been drinking. He needed seven stitches and a sedative.

"Let me be clear on this: we do not spy on the dreams of foreign nationals on foreign soil," President Barack Obama reassured America's allies. Then, turning to an aid, he lowered his voice and asked, "Do we?"

Reassurance unaccomplished.

Does any of this really matter? If Syrian strongman Bashar al-Assad dreams that he is a bishop made out of marshmallow on a chess board where a three year-old ocelot is playing against Deep Blueberry, as the Random leaks suggest, will public disclosure of that knowledge stop him from slaughtering his own people?

"Dreams are the empty calories of rational minds," said Sherry Turklenette, footnoted academic and author of the book *Alone Together Separately: How the Internet Fosters the Illusion of Intimacy By Allowing New Forms of Relationship*. "They may seem to provide insights into the minds of dreamers, but, like randomly edited three second clips from various videos, it's all smoked kippers and mirrorshades."

Take Hollande's dream, for example. According to Turklenette, it could mean that he was sexually frustrated. Or, it could mean that he was hungry. Or, it could mean that he was disappointed that he hadn't become the next Gerard Depardieont. There was so much room for interpretation that there was little to no room for blackmail.

"So, even if we were spying on the dreams of foreign nationals on foreign soil," President Obama asked, "it wouldn't have given us any useful information?"

Exactly, Turklenette agreed.

"Looks like somebody's going to have to take the Senate Subcommittee on Snoopiness out back to the woodshed," President Obama grinned frowningly.

"Oh, I'm not saying the practice is benign," Turklenette added. "What goes on between people's ears should stay between their ears – this is the worst invasion of privacy since Genghis Kahn read the diaries of his top generals!"

"Oh," President Obama ohed. "I guess they are doing their job, then. Never mind."

"Freedom!" cried Fassbender from the balcony of the Embassy Restaurant on Bleecker Street in downtown Smirkutsk where he sought refuge from persecution for leaking the documents outlining America's dream catcher programme. "You might be able to stop me, but you'll never stop information the government wants to keep secret from being made public!"

When it was pointed out that sitting in a cheesecake pierogies restaurant doesn't actually give one diplomatic immunity for leaking top secret documents, President Obama smirked, "Maybe not, but stopping you will be satisfaction enough!"

"Erm," Fassbender ermed. "I did the whole smug thing too soon, didn't I? Ivan? I'll have those pierogies to go!"

Road Rage on 'Roids

by NANCY GONGLIKWANYEOHEEEEEEEH, Alternate Reality News Service Technology Writer

Specific Motors is recalling 300,000 Rabid Lemurs (the car, not the animal – that's a problem the Madagascar government will have to deal with) after reports that the vehicles had been involved in dozens of violent incidents over the past two months.

"The recall is purely a precautionary measure," Specific Motors Vice President, Announcing Precautionary Measures Florinda Asquiveda assured everybody, which perversely assured no one. "We haven't had reports of vehicular road rage so much as vague urban legends – you know, like Bigfoot or George Clooney's marriage. In fact, I wouldn't even call this a recall – it's more like a friendly suggestion to let us make sure that your vehicle's operating system is operating systemming properly."

You used the term 'road rage.' Does that mean –

"Did I say road rage?" Asquiveda blushed. "I meant to say…toad…stage – on a stage – toad on a stage. We've been experimenting with using frogs as the vocal interface between the driver and the personality module of the vehicle's operating system. Just, between you and me, owner's haven't taken to the new voice, and I expect that programme to croak very soon…"

So, to sum up, the personality module of your cars is prone to fits of road rage that have resulted in much vehicular mayhem on the world's highways and in the privacy of your own home.

"Ooooh," Asquiveda ooooohed, "you're good!"

No, I've just interviewed Rabid Lemur owners. Michelle Mocmicmacson, for example. She was on her way to work (Mocmicmacson is a dental hygienist for the law firm of Heenus, Weinus and Absolution) when her Rabid Lemur caused a 27 vehicle pileup on the Slap Happy Appian Way (between Newhaven, Connecticut and Milton, Ontario).

"Somebody in a yellow Honda Civet made an unsafe lane change and cut us off," Mocmicmacson explained. "After that, my Rabid Lemur started weaving in and out of lanes – the police mechanic said it was looking for another Honda Civet. I don't remember much after the Lemmington cut-off, but I gather my car must have found one, because I'm told that seven people died and 24 were injured in the ensuing madness."

"That could have been an isolated incident," Asquiveda pointed out.

Rabid Lemur owners like Adrian Polodney. "I was stopped at a red light," he stated, "when my vehicle started wildly bouncing up and down – and I don't even have mag wheels!" Polodney's vehicle had stopped next to a second Rabid Lemur, and the two of them decided to drag down the main street of lovely, scenic, Beaverton, South Dakota. The casualties included: eight human beings, 12 electric poles, three mailboxes and a pay telephone booth (putting it more firmly on the endangered species list and angering cultural environmentalists – all four of them).

"What, that?" Asquiveda waved a dismissive hand. "That was just a case of the spirit of a vindictive dead teenager come back to wreak havoc on the living by possessing a vehicle. It was just bad luck it that it happened to be one of ours." When I suggested that this was hard to believe, Asquiveda responded, "I know, right? She died at the height of her beauty and popularity – you'd think she would be happy avoiding the inevitable decline that time brings!"

I didn't press the point, because Rabid Lemur owners like Elmira Breckenridge. S/he (s/he was being coy about his/her gender identity, and I didn't feel like pressing the point) noticed that some days the vehicle's fenders were dented and its hood appeared to be covered in white, sweet liquid. Worse, the car had more miles on it than Breckenridge could remember driving (s/he has a spirometric memory for those kinds of things).

"I took the vehicle in to Phil, the mechanic from the shop down the street," Breckenridge said. "He told me that my Rabid Lemur had an irrational fear of ice cream trucks, and went looking for them on its own after I went to sleep. Choosing the PG version of what happened next, Phil, the mechanic from the shop down the street told me that my Rabid Lemur 'made sure that several ice cream trucks would never deliver a soft-serve vanilla in a waffle cone again!'"

Asquiveda good-naturedly held up her hands in surrender. "Okay," she said, "you can't argue with Phil, the mechanic from the shop down the street. He knows things. We're recalling the Rabid Lemurs because their personality modules are prone to insane fits of rage, some of which could be referred to as 'road.'"

Specific Motors has issued 2,349 recalls this year, recalling more vehicles than it has produced in the history of the company (there has been recall overlap…so…much…overlap). This comes just five years after Specific Motors was given a 13 squidjillion dollar bailout by the American government. This seems like a bad way of repaying taxpayers.

"Hey!" Asquiveda complained. "If we hadn't gotten that bailout, you would now be driving defective cars from Japan! Patriotic much?"

Science Marches - Cough - Marches - Hack - Marches On!

by LAURIE NEIDERGAARDEN, Alternate Reality News Service Medical Writer

While one never wants to condone projectile vomiting, one has to admit that at least the red, white and blue discharge is patriotic. Moreover, one can take a special joy in the spectacle safe in the knowledge that one does not have to clean it up.

This impromptu art show took place at the Douglas Sanatorium and Sleep Emporium in Lower East Upper Manhattan, New York City. It was the latest scientific salvo against disease; unfortunately, in terms of success, it was at best a faint glowing.

Doctor B. A. Banksy of the aforementioned medical institution and part-time dance hall instructor has been attempting to smallen Mister Babbage's analytical engines. How smallened? To the point where many of them can be accumulated in a single capsule and consumed by a patient.

To what end, this effort? Well, sir, Doctor Banksy hopes to eradicate whooping crane cough, dropsy and the syphilis in our lifetimes! You heard me correct, sir. Freedom from some of the world's worst diseases (and one of its most annoying).

How does Doctor Banksy's miniature miracles accomplish this task? When they are ingested, they make their way through the stomach lining into the patient's bloodstream, like thousands of tiny Trojan horses infiltrating the fabled city. Once so ensconced, they proceed to analyse the blood for traces of disease; if they find it, they are designed to take measures to counteract it.

"Gadzooks, but this is brilliance personified," Doctor Banksy enthused, although I am less than convinced by his evocation of personhood. "Once the Banksy Method has been perfected, public health should be greatly improved!"

Aye, but there's the rub, isn't it? The problem with the Banksy Method is that the best material to make the small calculating machines with is wood. Unfortunately, wood has a tendency to splinter as it makes its way down a patient's oesophagus (throat to a layman), causing all manner of side-effect such as the one so colourfully described in the opening paragraph of this report.

"I wouldn't worry about it," Doctor Banksy insisted that I inform the public. "The test subjects were members of inferior races – mostly Irish, with some negroes and even a Jew or two. They were taken from debtors prisoners and asyli for the incurably romantic – I can assure you that their loss of speech, digestion or even life is inconsequential compared to the potential gains to be made…by science!"

The Banksy Method is not without its detractors. "What would happen if Banksy actually found the cure that he was looking for, eh Angkor Whot?" asked renowned scientist and part-time lamppost David Curie-Vindaloo. "What then? Eh? Eh? Eh? What could possibly transpire then?"

Quickly growing impatient, I asked Lamppost Curie-Vindaloo what he believed would happen if the Banksy Method proved feasible. "Well!" he harrumphed…in a way that sounded like he had uttered the word "well." "You would have all of these little wooden machines crawling around inside of you, wouldn't you? Then, Banksy would have to send in a mechanical spider to eat the tiny wooden machines. Then, he would have to send a clockwork cat in to take care of the spider that had eaten the small wooden machines. And, a machine dog to look after the clockwork cat that took care of the mechanical spider that had eaten the small wooden machines. And, you know where that would lead?"

When I assured Lamppost Curie-Vindaloo that I most certainly did not, he smiled and stated: "Have you ever heard the expression, 'Cor, but I's so 'ungry I could eat an 'orse?' Well, it would stop being metaphorical!"

"Bejabbers, but I am taken with the colourful nature of my colloquial patois!" Doctor Banksy responded to the criticism. Poorly. And, with an incoherence that would have done Lord Mowbry proud!

When he was through saying words like "egads" and "tintinnabulation," Doctor Banksy made his way back to the subject at hand: "We are currently experimenting with certain resins taken from the exotic Baobab tree of central Scotland," he explained. "In a perfect world, they would keep the miniature analytical engine from splintering in the patient's oesophagus (that's throat to a layman)."

If that were to prove true, wouldn't the machine miniatures be destroyed on contact with the acids in the patients' stomachs?

"One problem at a time," Doctor Banksy testily – how appropriate for a scientist! – responded. "I would be delighted to find cures for mental defect, shingles and Mercator's Baggy Bottom, but science can only deal with one problem at a time!"

Luddites Just Phoning It In

by NANCY GONGLIKWANYEOHEEEEEEEH, Alternate Reality News Service Technology/Social Media Writer

Prendergast Eroika has a terrible secret. He does not talk about it to his family. He does not talk about it to his friends. He has been in therapy for seven years, and he has barely talked about it with his psychotherapist. It's the shame that dare not speak its name for fear of getting maimed by a blame game played by a lame dame.

You see, Prendergast Eroika has a landline telephone.

"WHAT!" Eroika freaked out. "We were supposed to be discussing people who listen to white noise after Easter! On **super duper double dare background chatter!** My…unfortunate circumstance wasn't supposed to be the subject of an article!

Yeah, but this is more interesting.

"Oh. Well. Can't argue with that," Eroika – ahem – dialled the emotion back.

According to a recent report by the Weisenheimer Research and Stray Cat Neutering Institute called "Celling Your Soul: Why Some People Don't Seem Able to Land(line) Modern Communications Technology," 97 per cent of North Americans, and at least 78 per cent of Philadelphians, own cellphones rather than landlines. You've heard of "early adopters?" The remaining three per cent are known to researchers as "late letters go." Although early adopters have hogged all the limelight, late letters go have their own handshake, secret decoder ring and graphic representation:

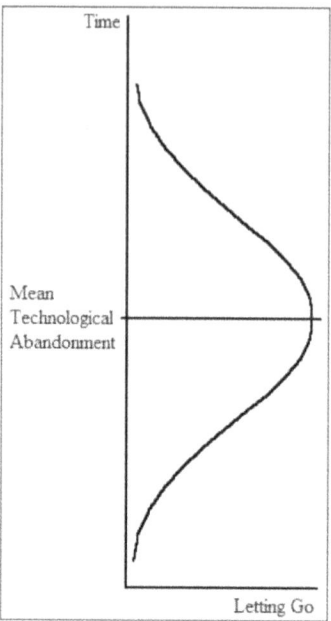

Students of ancient Persian limericks will recognize this as the "Pot Belly Curve." "It was originally called the 'Boob Curve,'" the Weisenheimer report pointed out, "since it applied to such a wide variety of foolish human behaviours. Then, owing to feminism and a strange topographic coincidence, that name became politically toxic. As long as beer drinkers and pig farmers don't become better organized, this name should last for the foreseeable future."

Late landline abandonners inhabit the bottom corner of the curve. The dark, dimly lit, grimly foreboding part. The part that nobody wants to live in for fear that they will be robbed, beaten and left for dead on the side of the axis – or, worse, be referenced in late night talk show monologues. Oh, the horror! Why would anybody choose to live in this neighbourhood of the curve?

"Many reasons," Eroika cheerfully stated. "What if an EMP pulse –"

An EMP?

"That's right. An EMP pulse. What if –"

No, no, no. It's known as an EMP.

"That's what I said. EMP –"

Oh. Okay, then.

"Pulse."

That's not what it is. It's just an EMP.

"I wouldn't say it's just an EMP pulse. That thing can cause a lot of damage!"

Have it your way. If an EMP…pulse did wipe out the electronics in your city, then you'd be able to talk to the seven other people who have landlines – assuming you know who they are. And, assuming you don't get forwarded to call waiting because they're trying to call somebody else with a landline at the same time. And, that they're sitting by their phones and not roaming the streets panicking with everybody else. What do you think the odds are that one of them actually knows how to stay alive in the chaotic aftermath of an EMP?

"Well, it's not as impressive as I thought it would be when you put it **that** way…"

According to the Weisenheimer report, late letters go are generally timid people who fear change. They hunker down in their storm cellars to watch *The Twilight Zone*, *Battlestar Galactica* and *The Odd Couple* (all original series) on VCR while eating TV dinners and drinking New Coke. Their clothes are always 20 years out of date and they only have sex in the missionary position. They –

"Hey!" Eroika interjected. "I'm from Ottawa!"

Okay, that would explain it, too.

Although it would appear to paint a negative picture of late letters go, the Weisenheimer report actually refers to them as "the canaries in the Chardonnay." After apologizing for writing under the influence of Alanis, they wrote: "In maintaining their death grip on old technology, it's like they're saying to us, 'Hey! You! Yes, you! The one with the new technology! No, not you – the other you – the one on you's left…although, I suppose you'll do – okay, either of you! Have you ever given any thought to what you've had to give up in our rush to be part of the 97 per cent of people who have this technology?' We can't actually see any downside to not having a landline, but we're glad to have at least considered the question."

"I…I just had a choice between buying a cellphone and eating this month," Eroika stated. When we pointed out that if he got rid of his landline, he would be able to afford a cellphone and food, he snapped his fingers and said, "By anchovies, you're right!"

Aaaaaaand, as Eroika raced out to the nearest cellphone shoppe (which, owing to their ubiquity, was only three doors down from where he lived), we realized that we had just invalidated the basis of the whole article! Honestly, when will we learn to keep our bright ideas to ourselves!

NOTE: Alternate Reality News Service Editrix-in-Chief Brenda Brundtland-Govanni would like to assure readers that revealing confidential sources is not official ARNS policy. Nancy Gonglikwanyeoheeeeeeeh will be disciplined for this lack of journalistic integrity….just as soon as Brenda stops laughing.

I Dream of Genius

by GIDEON GINRACHMANJINJa-VITUS, Alternate Reality News Service Economics Writer

Mallory Mallarme had that dream again. You know, the one where she is wearing complete 1920s aviatrix gear, complete with Amelia Earhart's sexism-proof goggles, which is kind of odd because she's actually reading the "What I Did on My Summer Vacation (With Footnotes and a Mild Salsa Dip)" essay to her grade four home room class. Because, you know, aviatrix are for kids. Even before she has finished, Marjory Millenniary holds up a five and a seven, Billy Blugfludger holds up a five and a three and Piotr Ionesentra holds up a three and a nine. Damn Romanian judge! Mallarme doesn't have time to wonder if fellow student Miriam Mixmaster has paid Ionesentra off, however, as a line of teeth in tiny tutus kickdances their way past her (and into everybody's hearts). [The next several minutes of the dream, which involve Mallarme and her dad, have been omitted due to extreme boringness. No, really. Sitting around the dinner table talking about fly fishing. Playing monopoly (which always ends with dad declaring a Communist revolution, letting everybody in jail go free and claiming all the properties for himself "for the good of all players"). Alligator wrestling in the Yukon. Honestly, after less than a minute I was wishing for daddy issues to materialize! I'll spare you the suspense: they never do.] When we return to the dream, already in progress, Mallarme is an ice cube being dropped with several of her sisters into a glass the size of a calf. But the glass isn't – that's a calf as in baby cow, not thigh muscle – sorry for the confusion – the glass isn't filled with liquid, it's filled with unfertilized eggs. Mallarme has just enough time to wonder *Did I leave the oven on?* before the dream ends.

When she woke from the dream, she jotted down some preliminary design concepts that would eventually lead to the creation of the combination pencil sharpener/birth control dispenser.

You may wonder why the creator of The Sharp Egg, the most popular invention of the last several weeks, isn't a household name™. Well. Mallarme had been working for several months on creating a robot housecat that produced 37 per cent fewer allergens than the real thing. She and her team had spent several days trying to fix the problem that the cats exploded whenever they spent more than 3.7845 seconds playing with string. Exhausted, she crashed in a dorm that her employer, Genius Ideas (a wholly owned subsidiary of MultiNatCorp – "We do creative stuff, freely and fairly without ripping any of our workers off"), made available to its employees for just such situations.

Unbeknownst to Mallarme (she had quit a 12 knownst a day habit cold turkey three years earlier), the dorm room where she slept had been fitted with sensors that monitored her brain activity, literally reading her dreams. As she made her bleary way towards the combination coffee dispenser/tax auditor in the common area of the dorm, MultiNatCorp computers were already analyzing her dreams for possible products to develop. As she showered, preliminary designs were already being sketched out by on-call engineers. By the time she had settled into her workspace to start her day, a marketing campaign was already being settled on.

MultiNatCorp had taken her idea and run with it before she even knew there was a starting line.

"This is outrageous!" stated Desdemona Disque-Oh, a lawyer Mallarme hired to take her case for ownership of The Sharp Egg to court. "How could anybody think that it was legal to take an employee's inspiration directly out of their dreams?"

"We can," stated MultiNatCorp Vice President, Public Relations and Defensive Postures Ned Feeblish. "We are, of course, using the time-honoured legal principle 'You Snooze, You Lose.'"

There is precedent for Mallarme's lawsuit. in *Gallecki v Big Bang Theo*, Anthony "Midway" Gallecki successfully sued Small Tin Wonders (a wholly owned you know what of Multi you know who), claiming it stole the design for the two-headed screwdriver he came up with in a drunken stupor.

However, it was a Pyrrhic victory (thanks to judge Anthony Pyrrhos). Gallecki's legal team disappeared into MultiNatCorp's maze of financial statements and were never heard from again. Every so often, a dull, inhuman roar escapes from the maze of financial statements as a warning to anybody who would dare to enter them in the future.

"This is ridiculous!" Disque-Oh angrily mused. "Can corporations claim to own the dreams of their employees?"

"Oh, absolutely!" Feeblish calmly argued. "How high they can climb the corporate ladder, what they can do with their meagre salaries, how fulfilling their work will be – we've owned our employees' dreams for decades! This process just literalizes past practice."

Then, he triumphantly brushed foam from the pomegranate chocolate milkshake off his moustache.

Opening arguments in *Mallarme v Genius Ideas* will be heard on Monday in the Seventh Circus Court of Dubuque.

3. ALTERNATE POLITICS

On the Enhanced Interrogation of the English Language

The Alternate Reality News Service has convened a forum to explore the use of the term "enhanced interrogation" by the United States government to describe acts that it has, in other circumstances, called "torture." On the panel are alternate universe versions of Samuel Johnson, William Strunk and E. B. White and George Orwell. The moderator is The Language Corrector Dude.

LANGUAGE CORRECTOR DUDE: THANK YOU! THANK YOU! THANK YOU! THANK YOU!

BRENDA BRUNDTLAND-GOVANNI: Okay, I know you're thrilled to be leading a discussion of your own, but, really, Language Corrector Dude, pull yourself together.

LANGUAGE CORRECTOR DUDE: Thank you for having enough faith in me to allow me –

BRUNDTLAND-GOVANNI: Okay, gonna stop you right there before you embarrass yourself any further. I originally asked Amritsar to do this, but she came down with one of her little headaches and had to go lie down in a dark room.

LANGUAGE CORRECTOR DUDE: Okay, but –

BRUNDTLAND-GOVANNI: Then, I asked The Tech Answer Guy, but he declined, saying he was too busy preparing for a New Age Monster Truck Rally that's going to be held in six weeks.

LANGUAGE CORRECTOR DUDE: Sure, that's a little demeaning. Still –

BRUNDTLAND-GOVANNI: The Biz Whiz wanted an outrageous sum of money to host this forum and knew that I would be too lazy to look at his contract to see if we were obligated to pay it to him. Bastard!

LANGUAGE CORRECTOR DUDE: I see. (long pause) And, then you thought of me! THANK YOU! THANK YOU! THANK YOU! THANK –

BRUNDTLAND-GOVANNI: LANGUAGE CORRECTOR DUDE! GET A GRIP! DO I HAVE TO SLAP YOU INTO THE NEXT EDITION OF THE OED?!

LANGUAGE CORRECTOR DUDE: Okay. Sorry. So, umm, my conclusion is that the government acted in bad faith when it started using the term "enhanced interrogation techniques" to describe what everybody once agreed was torture. The implications are –

GEORGE ORWELL: Shouldn't you start with an introduction?

LANGUAGE CORRECTOR DUDE: Staggering for – what?

ORWELL: Isn't it customary to put the conclusion at the end?

LANGUAGE CORRECTOR DUDE: Oh! Umm…okay. Sorry. My…my note cards seem to have gotten mixed up.

SAMUEL JOHNSON: Note cards? You're looking at a box which is emitting some form of light.

LANGUAGE CORRECTOR DUDE: They're on my computer. Nobody uses paper note cards any more!

ORWELL: So, the introduction?

LANGUAGE CORRECTOR DUDE: Right. Okay. Umm…malfeasance… misfeasance…Miss Pheasant…Donald Pleas – ah, here we are. For the last decade, the United States government has been using the term "enhanced interrogation" to describe waterboarding, sleep deprivation and other forms of questioning suspects that were once considered "torture." There seems to be an implication that if you change the name of an act, the act itself will not seem so reprehensible, that, in fact, changing the name of an illegal act will somehow make it legal. Samuel Johnson, author of one of the first dictionaries of the English language, what do you make of this?

JOHNSON: Seems perfectly reasonable to me.

LANGUAGE CORRECTOR DUDE: Exactly. It is a gross manipulation of – excuse me?

JOHNSON: Language is a living, breathing beastie. It must evolve or it will die.

LANGUAGE CORRECTOR DUDE: But…but…but surely words must maintain some semblance of their original meaning. I mean, if politicians can just rename things at will, we're no better than animals in the jungle!

JOHNSON: (shrugs) The first edition of my dictionary contained 42,773 words. I thought that was a lot – bloody thing took me nine years to write! Today, there are over a million words in the English language, with new ones being added every year. I would say that that ship has set sail, crossed the ocean to America, followed the coast on its way to the Antarctic and was well on its way to completing the return journey!

LANGUAGE CORRECTOR DUDE: So, you're not incensed by the government's abuse of language?

JOHNSON: Trust me, lad: there have been worse.

LONG PAUSE.

LANGUAGE CORRECTOR DUDE: You're off the panel!

JOHNSON: Beg pardon?

LANGUAGE CORRECTOR DUDE: You heard me. Get back to the Dimensional Portal™ and return to your home universe. You're done, here.

JOHNSON: Well, I never! I thought I had been invited to a serious discussion of language usage, not some…some *Survivor: Idiot's Island*!

LANGUAGE CORRECTOR DUDE: Sorry for that…unpleasantness. Strunk and White – you wrote the book on literary style. What are your thoughts on the use of the term "enhanced interrogation?"

STRUNK AND WHITE: I tend to agree with you that it is an abomination.

LANGUAGE CORRECTOR DUDE: Thank you! That's –

STRUNK AND WHITE: While, I tend to agree with Mister Johnson that we have to allow the language to evolve naturally.

LANGUAGE CORRECTOR DUDE: What?

STRUNK AND WHITE: What's natural about a government creating a term to make light of its nefarious activities?

STRUNK AND WHITE: Are you suggesting that governments cannot legitimately coin terms when circumstances require them?

STRUNK AND WHITE: I'm saying that language should illuminate reality, not obscure it.

STRUNK AND WHITE: But, who are you to judge whether this term illuminates or obscures reality? Surely, the context –

LANGUAGE CORRECTOR DUDE: Uhh, guys…?

STRUNK AND WHITE: You always do this.

STRUNK AND WHITE: Do what?

STRUNK AND WHITE: Take a contrary position.

STRUNK AND WHITE: Take a – well, perhaps I would have no need to take a contrary position if the positions you took made some kind of logical sense!

LANGUAGE CORRECTOR DUDE: Guys?

STRUNK AND WHITE: I can't believe I'm going to be forever known for having collaborated with the likes of you!

STRUNK AND WHITE: What do you mean, the likes of me?

STRUNK AND WHITE: I've had enough of this nonsense. I'm leaving!

STRUNK AND WHITE: You can't leave! If you do, I –

LONG PAUSE.

LANGUAGE CORRECTOR DUDE: Umm…George Orwell. May I call you George?

ORWELL: You may call me Mister Blair.

LANGUAGE CORRECTOR DUDE: Oh. Are you ashamed by the associations that have accrued to your name?

ORWELL: Actually, that is my name.

LANGUAGE CORRECTOR DUDE: (pause) …Okay, then. In the novel *Nineteen Eighty-four*, you showed how governments used language to stifle the ability of citizens to think clearly. Would you agree that this is an egregious example of that?

ORWELL: I suppose I would if I still cared about such matters.

LANGUAGE CORRECTOR DUDE: (sighs) You, too? Is this finally too much for even you?

ORWELL: Actually, I gave up when you renamed your War Department the Department of Defence. I guess that was the best your government could do because I had already called dibs on "War is Peace," but it's almost as bad. The rest of the 20th century was a blur of misleading government pronouncements, blatantly false and/or meaningless commercial advertising and corporate jargon. Honestly, I can't be bothered to keep track of it any more.

LANGUAGE CORRECTOR DUDE: I see.

LONGEST PAUSE YET.

BRUNDTLAND-GOVANNI: Language Corrector Dude? (pause) Psst! Language Corrector Dude!

LANGUAGE CORRECTOR DUDE: What?

BRUNDTLAND-GOVANNI: Wrap it up!

LANGUAGE CORRECTOR DUDE: What's the point? My whole life has been built on the premise that words actually mean something. But, in meeting my linguistic heroes, I have actually been completely disabused of that notion. I think I'm going to ditch the bow tie and go into plumbing like my parents always wanted. Too bad they didn't live long enough to see it.

BRUNDTLAND-GOVANNI: Okay. That was a conclusion…of a sort… Thanks.

LANGUAGE CORRECTOR DUDE: Yeah, whatevs…

AI Don't Get It

by FRANCIS GRECOROMACOLLUDEN, Alternate Reality News Service National Politics Writer

The Republican majority in the House of Representatives is set to vote down an amendment to a bill that would codify the Three Laws of Robotics.

"Without this amendment," said its sponsor, New York Democratic representative Isaac Asimov, "the field of artificial intelligence will be the wild west. If any of you have seen *The Wild Wild West*, you know that can't be good!"

James Cameron, a Republican representative from California, has been leading the opposition to the amendment. His argument is that once artificial intelligences are sufficiently advanced, they will destroy the human race, so research on them must be stopped immediately.

"Do you think an unstoppable AI – let's call them…I don't know…exterminators – do you think exterminators – no, that's too long. Not pithy enough. Let's call them…exters. Do you really believe that exters intent on wiping out the human race will be stopped by an amendment to an interstate trucking law?" Cameron argued.

Ah, yes. The Three Laws of Robotics are an amendment to an interstate trucking law. Why? "We, uhh, thought that transporting AIs across state lines would be a good way of getting at the root, err, problem of…of…of…" Representative Asimov tried to explain. Then, he threw up his hands and said, "You know, I have several graduate degrees, and I still don't understand so much of what happens in this city!"

For those of you just tuning in, the three laws of robotics are:

1. A robot may not injure a human being or, through inaction, allow a human being to come to harm, unless it would make for a more dramatic story.
2. A robot must obey orders given it by human beings except where such orders would conflict with the First Law, unless that would be boring.
3. A robot must protect its own existence as long as such protection does not conflict with the First or Second Law, and it can find no creative interpretation of this law that would effectively allow the robot to circumvent it.

The amendment has also received opposition from within the Democratic Party. Delaware Representative Rudy Rucker spoke for this group when he said, "We're talking about AIs that are sufficiently advanced that they have a kind of sentience. I like to think of these AIs as beboppers, but, uhh, that might confuse some people with a jazz musical style, so let's call them…beoppers. Yeah. That sounds about right."

Representative Rucker argued that saddling beoppers with rules of behaviour would be like putting a hypnotic suggestion into human beings that they must not harm chickens, they must always obey chickens and they must protect themselves as long as doing so doesn't interfere with the welfare of chickens.

"While that's undoubtedly great for poultry," Representative Rucker dryly commented, "it doesn't say much for human free will!"

"Free. Will. Schmee. Will," said British AI opponent Lord Steven Hawking. "Ar-ti-fi-cial. In-tell-i-gence. Is. A. Men-ace. To. All. Life. We. Must. Stop. All. Re-search. In. This. Field. Im-me-di-ate-ly. Or. Risk. Ann-i-hi-la-tion."

Representative Rucker scoffed at this. "We don't need advice," he said, "from the country that could end up being responsible for the destruction of the European Union!"

Lord Hawking sighed, a sound that reminded those within a three mile radius of a garbage compactor. "I. Have. Con-tem-plat-ed. The. Be-ginn-ing. Of. The. U-ni-verse. I. Have. Tra-veled. In. My. Mind. To. The. Heart. Of. Black. Holes. And. Even. I. Do. Not. Always. Un-der-stand. How. De-cis-ions. In. This. Coun-try. Are. Made!"

Expecting certain defeat in the House, Democrats are petitioning President Obama to adopt the Three Laws of Robotics by executive order. In his final year of office, the President seems much more willing, quite eager, in fact, almost childishly gleeful to, if you want to know the absolute truth, use the power of his office to –

"Okay, I'm gonna stop you right there," Representative Cameron interjected. "The House will reject any attempt by the President to impose a solution to this problem. As a former filmmaker, the fact that the American government works this way makes perfect sense to me."

"We will never accept artificial limits on artificial intelligence," insisted Representative Rucker as he put artificial creamer in his coffee, sitting in an artificial leather chair on an artificial lion-skin rug behind a faux mahogany desk. "We have to keep things real!"

As gridlock keeps the American government from acting on this issue, the Japanese have produced an artificial intelligence that can take care of the elderly, write situation comedy and organize labour unions. Before the government can resolve this issue, Americans may be forced to deal with a local remake of a Japanese sitcom about a union of elder care workers!

The Oil Derrick Forever

by FRANCIS GRECOROMACOLLUDEN, Alternate Reality News Service National Politics Writer

The fiftieth anniversary of the adoption of the Canadian flag, with its distinctive red oil derrick between two red stripes, passed this week with indifference bordering on hostility.

Although the Conservative government of Stephen Harper CIII (a third generation clone of modern Canada's Founding Father) had announced six months ago that there would be much singing, dancing and rejoicing in the streets (by order) to celebrate the anniversary, it turned out that it had more important matters to look after, particularly the submergence of the last of PEI under the Atlantic Ocean thanks to rising sea levels.

"Oil derrick – 50 years – celebrate – gotta run – see ya!" read the government's tweet release.

PEI natives are angry because of how wet they have become, without the offer of so much as a towel from the Harper CIII government. Central and western Canada are unhappy at having to take in refugees from the Maritime provinces (now known as the great big Maritime puddles). Everybody is pissed off that the Canadian economy is stalled now that the country's oil has definitively run out; it doesn't help that the government, with its anemic tax base, is only able to continue to afford to function on weeks when it wins monetary prizes in Tim Hortons Rrroll Up the Rim contest.

"Terror threat!" read the government's tweet release response to these conditions. As if Canada hadn't been instrumental in Israel's decision to nuke Iran, which had started a war in the Middle East that had left such desolate devastation that it was unlikely that anybody would be using the area for a base from which to terrorize anybody else for at least 24,000 years. And, even then, they would be terrorizing others using mostly rocks and sharp sticks. Thanks to this contribution to international diplomacy, the world isn't especially happy with Canada, which is why Foreign Affairs recommends that Canadians travelling abroad sew anything other than oil derrick flags onto their backpacks, including swastikas; at least our tourists can argue that swastikas are symbols of good fortune.

The Alternate Reality News Service tracked the creator of the flag, Irffan Noimann, to his bunker on the bottom floor of the abandonned Eaton Centre in downtown Toronto. He told me in no uncertain terms that if we dared to ask him about the oil derrick, he could not be held responsible for what his finger would do to the trigger of the shotgun that he was ostentatiously pointing at my head.

Under the circumstances, I decided it would be better to talk to him about girls using digital eyepatches to cheat at Parcheesi. I was pleasantly surprised to find out that he knew quite a bit about the subject.

"The old flag's days were numbered," allowed historian Michael Bliszt-Owt, "and they weren't very high numbers at that. At most, low double digits. Most of the country's maple trees had been cut down in order to be replaced by corporate tree farms. The only place anybody would likely have seen a maple leaf would have been an art gallery gift shop or spray-painted on the side of a moose."

Still, Bliszt-Owt lamented the fact that few people realize that Canada had a flag before the oil derrick which, among other things, has ramifications for the country's culture. A recent survey showed that only 24 per cent of Canadians knew that the Toronto Oil Derricks had once been known (and reviled) by a different name, while a mere 17 per cent were aware that the belovedly patriotic song wasn't always called "The Oil Derrick Forever."

"live long and prosper," read the government's tweet release. Everybody assumed that the government's secure servers had been hacked for the 23rd time this week, this time by fans of Leonard Nimoy. The government tweet release that read, "opponents of the oil derrick are being most illogical," confirmed it.

The anniversary of the adoption of the oil derrick flag was celebrated with fireworks in Ottawa. Which is to say that the government sent up a single firework and the citizens who had gathered to celebrate set fire to the Rideau Canal, whose garbage burned brightly into the night.

You take your national pride wherever you can find it.

The Revolution Will Not Be Self-actualized

by MARA VERHEYDEN-HILLIARD, Alternate Reality News Service Revolution Writer

The Floundering Fathers of the American Insurgency have had another bad week. The Battle of Chelsea Creek ended with the colonial rebels being pushed back, having not achieved their objective of capturing the British schooner Diana.

Despite this setback, leaders of the American Insurgency are as convinced as ever about the righteousness of their cause.

"We hold these truths to be self-evident: that all men were created equal," said General George Washington.

"Taxation without representation must be banished from this land," said Thomas Jefferson.

"Give me liberty, or give me death," said Benjamin Franklin.

What are you doing about it? I inquired.

"I pray to the angels of our better natures that they will help us overcome the British tyrant," answered General Washington.

"Every morning I say 20 affirmations about how good I am, how good the people of this country are and how much we deserve our liberty," responded Jefferson.

"I am constantly putting thoughts out into the universe about how much I love freedom and want my freedom and deserve my freedom," replied Franklin.

And, how did that work out for you?

"Our troops were overrun at Fort Ticonderoga," General Washington claimed.

"My draft of *Notes for the Declaration of Independence* was confiscated by British authorities," Jefferson told me.

"I was thrown in jail," Franklin stated.

Ouch. Who do you blame for these…setbacks?

"Myself," General Washington admitted. "My prayers were obviously insufficiently pious…or frequent…or some other quality of which I am not currently aware, to enable us to prevail."

"Myself," Jefferson allowed. "Perhaps I should have said 30 affirmations rather than the paltry 20 to which I dedicated myself daily."

"Myself," Franklin acknowledged. "If I had some way to amplify my thoughts on freedom so that they resonated more soundly with the universe, perhaps the outcome might have been different. I was actually experimenting with some techniques that may have helped me in that way – unfortunately, the authorities do not allow kites to be flown from prison cells."

Ah. Yes. Well, those are very worthy answers, but, if you will allow me, I would suggest another possibility: that the man who is responsible for these debacles **is the man who has been advising you!**

Deepak Choprah Robbins looked up from his crème brûlée (it wasn't that he supported the cuisine of the European aggressors so much as he detested the desserts of the colonies: pumpkin pie, pumpkin tart, pumpkin sherbet, pumpkin sorbet, pumpkin flan, pumpkin cake, pumpkin cookies, chocolate dipped pumpkin slices, pumpkin crumble and ice cream that didn't have much pumpkin in it, but, as a compensation, was flavoured with mongoose intestines), and said, "I couldn't help but notice your use of bold type – clearly, you have a problem with anger."

This article is not about me. It's about –

"No, no, no, no, no, my friend," Choprah Robbins interrupted. "Everything is about you. You are a human being on this planet who deserves as much love and respect as any other being on this planet. If you'll just let go of your anger –"

No, no, no, no, no back at you, not my friend. If people like George Washington weren't so busy sending affirmations into the universe, they might have been stronger leaders who wouldn't be losing the Revolutionary War!

Choprah Robbins shook his head sadly. "You know, when I first met George Washington, he was putting too much negative energy out into the universe. I advised him that he would be better off working on his daddy issues."

Better off working on his daddy issues than founding a new country that could serve as a beacon of sanity in an irrational world?

"You understand."

No! No, I do not understand!

Choprah Robbins shook his head sadly, delicately mopping a dribble of crème from his chin with a lace handkerchief. "Clearly. Listen. You cannot achieve your goals if you are constantly being negative. That negativity undermines everything you do. So, the first step in any revolution, whether personal or national, is to purge yourself of the negative thoughts that are holding you back."

But, you have to act! The most positive emotions in the world won't do anything if you don't put all of your attention and effort into actually doing something!

"Again with the bold faced type. Are you sure you don't want to explore the events in your childhood that caused you to feel such anger?"

"Hmm…" General Washington pondered. "I'm beginning to think that we have been going about this revolution business all wrong…"

"Put all of our attention and effort into action, eh?" Jefferson mused. "Yes, a change of strategy might help us better achieve our goal of freedom…"

"Can somebody please help me escape the confines of this prison?" Franklin asked. "The damp is playing havoc with my dentures!"

CIA Trains Sights on Tiny Terrorists

by FRANCIS GRECOROMACOLLUDEN, Alternate Reality News Service National Politics Writer

He knows when you've been sleeping. He knows when you're awake. He knows when you've been plotting a terrorist attack on civilian targets within the United States, so don't plot a terrorist attack on civilian targets within the United States…for goodness sake.

And, now, the CIA knows, too.

According to a document released to the Alternate Reality News Service after a Freedom of Information, Seriously, Thanks request, the CIA has been quietly gathering information from the Elf on the Shelf. "That information is a private communication between the Elf and Santa!" gasped American Civil Liberties Union stud muffin Albert deFresco, his eyes widening adorably to indicate just how shocking this revelation was.

The practice was established over a decade ago by a pair of executive orders (which, apparently, don't upset US) signed by then-President Bush, the Younger. It was codenamed, inevitably, Operation Secret Santa. Since then, the CIA has averaged 2,317 requests, 1,312 urgent pleas, 2,874 hoarsely whispered entreaties and 7,397 desperate threats to do itself bodily harm if it doesn't get what it wants for information from communications between Elves on the Shelf…ves and their boss at the North Pole.

"And, they didn't even bother getting a court order!" deFresco cried, putting a knuckle in his mouth to stop him from further expressing his outrage. The effect was a little forced, but still well within the parameters of cuddly.

"Court order? Don't make me piss myself laughing!" roared General Otis. T. Mayfly at a hastily convened press conference. (How hasty? The cutlery was on the wrong side of the plate and, if you listened ccarefully, you could still hear the roast beef mooing!) "I've already had to clean this uniform once this week!"

General Mayfly looked a little misty for a couple of seconds, before continuing: "Russian intelligence has been tapping The Mensch on the Bench for years! Oh, and you don't think China is mining information from the Monk on the Trunk? Don't be naïve! And, what about the Saudis learning all the can from the Fakir on the Chair? They don't need a ferking court order, believe you me! Anybody who complains about this wants America to fight on the international stage with one hand tied behind its back, and, even though we would still kick ass, it would be awkward and wouldn't make for good movies 20 years from now, so I, for one, will not stand for it!"

Why monitor Elf on the Shelf communications in the first place? Legend has it that the doll is a household mole for Santa Claus, reporting to him on a daily basis the details of whether children are being naughty or nice. Still, the children who keep them in their bedrooms generally range in age from three to seven (with the occasional 40 year-old doll collector); what possible threat could children pose to the security of the United States?

"Are you serious?" General MayFly shouted, chomping down on a table and bringing his fist down hard on a cigar. "The little bastards who terrorize their mothers this year become the not so little bastards who terrorize the nation next year!" Upon a moment's reflection, he added: "Well, maybe 10 years from now – but, eventually!"

"Do you have any children?" one of the reporters (it wasn't me, I swear! I…I was at home reading a book alone with my wife at the time the coroner has determined the question was asked!) ~~asked~~ inquired. "Seventeen!" General Mayfly responded. "And, believe me, if I can't get some peace on Christmas, I'd rather be working in the Pentagon so everybody else can!"

"Aaaaaaah!" deFresco moaned, pulling at his hair. "Our privacy is being taken away from is. It's being taken away, I tell you! Can't anybody do anything!" Hey, look, I love the ACLU as much as the next white, male, upwardly mobile, champagne sipping, expense account using, guilt-ridden centrist. They do important work. But, that was over the top.

Although started by Republicans, Elf on the Shelf information sharing requests have increased substantially under the Democratic Obama administration; confusingly, it has given the practice a scent of lavender to make them more palatable to the public.

"Yeah, okay, we do that," President Obama admitted, looking abashed about the whole business as only he can. (He clearly practices the look in the mirror.) Then, he went on to give an impassioned two hour speech about race relations in the United States.

The Elf on the Shelf numbers provided to journalists weren't broken down by race, but that gives me a good idea for my next FoIST request…

An Eye for an Eye and Pretty Soon Justice is Blind

by HAL MOUNTSAUERKRAUTEN, Alternate Reality News Service Court Writer

The Supreme Court has split 1-1 along ideological lines in the case of *Tidwell v State of Panic*. This is the 17th straight case in which the court could not render a verdict, a form of judicial impotence that no advice columnist will be able to cure that dates back to the death of Justice Sonia Sotomayor three years ago when her limousine was blindsided by a shrimp trawler on the way to a celebrity roast for Gilbert Gottfried.

Republican Mitch McConnell is to blame.

"Oh, ah, well, that is very kind of you to say," McConnell blushed. Yes, he blushed. If you freeze the frame from his press conference between the "k" and the "i" and magnify the image 532 times, you will definitely see red in a couple of pixels. "But, honestly, I could not have done it without the bipartisan support of everybody on both sides of the aisle…and France."

It started when McConnell, then Majority Leader, refused to allow any Supreme Court nominee proposed by President Barack Obama to be vetted by any Senate committee. Then, he refused to allow any of President Hillary Clinton's nominees to be vetted in her first term; in her second term, McConnell, now reduced to Minority Leader, threatened a filibuster whenever she seemed to be thinking about the possibility of considering naming anybody to the Supreme Court. This behaviour continued throughout the Presidency of Sean Penn. Then, just yesterday, McConnell, who seems to be hanging on in the Senate out of spite, croaked, "The nomination will have to wait until after the next election," even though President Lena Dunham was sworn in only three days ago.

Apparently, it's now precedent.

"So tired!" moaned Chief Justice John Roberts from behind a stack of legal briefs piled to the ceiling on his desk. After 18 years without the nomination of a replacement, Roberts and Justice Elena Kagan are the only members of the Supreme Court left alive. "I haven't had a vacation in eighteen months! Would you…would you be willing to render an opinion on *Bonzai v The World Crime League* for me? It's okay if you don't have any legal experience – it's not like we have enough people on the bench to make the decision binding on anybody!"

I declined Roberts' gracious offer. The last time I rendered a judgment in a major case, oil prices plummeted, causing economic havoc throughout the world; I slept on the couch for a week and half after that.

"John needs to get out more," Justice Kagan laughed. "I jog for two hours every day before coming into work. Personally, I find the pace invigorating!"

When asked if she found anything about the situation frustrating, Kagan admitted that tossing a coin to determine who would write the majority opinion in a case was a less than optimal solution to their problem. "John has won the last seven tosses!" Kagan complained. "Lucky bastard!"

I consulted world famous mathematician Ricky Jay on the odds of somebody winning seven consecutive coin tosses. Unfortunately, the math was so abstruse (literally: making peace with your stomach muscles) that even Jay didn't understand it, so I decided to leave the whole thing out of the article.

Does who writes the majority opinion matter when all issues brought before The Supreme Court die because of a hung court? "It's a matter of legacy, isn't it?" Kagan sniffed.

In the absence of a functional Supreme Court, the Court of Appeals has become the *de facto* (no, not a Ford muscle car from the 1950s, but it's a common enough mistake, so I can't blame you for going there) court of last appeal of the American legal system. "I don't know if I can handle the pressure," stated Justice Annette "Dizzy" Dextrose, who sits on the Sixth Circuit Breaker Court of Appeals. "I mean, I was nominated by Reagan!"

Umm…okay. In the meantime, it has been suggested that the unwillingness of Republicans to even consider holding hearings on Supreme Court nominees will some day lead to a Constitutional crisis. In a tentative, one might almost call it passive, voice. And, by unnamed sources. But, suggested nonetheless.

"Bullsense!" roared Constitutional scholar Donald Trump. "Sure, the Constitution says that the President shall nominate somebody for the Supreme Court when a vacancy becomes available. But, it also says that the opposition has the moral, financial and culinary duty to not give power to a bunch of losers who don't know their two *prima facies* from a hole in the ground!"

"Wow," said token smart person Amy Sheshutshotshitbam (whom I was interviewing for a completely different article when she got hold of an early draft of this one on my computer screen), "And, I thought things were messed up in my universe!"

It's Nothing Personal, Canada, It's Just Business

by GIDEON GINRACHMANJINJa-VITUS, Alternate Reality News Service Economics Writer

Canadian Prime Minister Rocky Ruiz was about to throw in the towel when she realized that it would cost the government $27.84 to pay a private company to pick it up. Instead, she draped it around her shoulders.

"I'll make this quick," the Prime Minister said, "because, frankly, the rental on this room is driving up the national debt. International Blah Blah Blah, a wholly owned subsidiary of MultiNatCorp, has served notice that it plans to launch a challenge under WAFTA to employees of the government pushing paperclips, claiming that it hurts the profits of their Clerks, Cliques and Cliches Division. We cannot afford to defend ourselves against the challenge. Since pushing paperclips around was our last function that had not been challenged through a trade agreement and privatized, the government of Canada officially dissolved as of noon today."

If you listened very closely, you may have heard the intake of breath from one or two of the journalists in the room – very closely, mind, because most of the reporters were surprised that the government had actually lasted this long.

"What?!" said the average man on the street, who, in this case, happened to be a woman, but she was wearing a fedora low enough to cover most of her face, so you can understand our statistical error. "I had no idea! How is this possible?"

Had you not noticed that prices for government services had been steadily increasing?

"Well, yeah, sure," the average man/not actually a man on the street answered. "I just thought the government was, you know, gauging me in order to pay down the debt."

But, didn't it occur to you that even though fees for government services were rising, the debt wasn't actually getting smaller?

"Umm, no, I, uhh, hadn't really noticed," the average person of improperly labelled gender, if we're being completely honest about it, said. "If I had given it some thought, though, I probably would have assumed that the government had given some of the money to its cronies, or government officials kept some of it for themselves. They were always underpaid…or, at least, they seemed to think so."

Actually, services were being contracted out to private companies. The government of Canada ended with a national debt so big, it would cross your eyes; I would tell you the exact figure if only I could uncross my eyes for long enough to read the piece of paper on which I had written it.

"That's crazy. I would have expected private companies to improve government services if they took them over, but they've been getting worse for years. Why, just last week, I spent two months waiting for somebody to complete the paperwork so I could get my driver's licence. In the meantime, I had to be driven around by a nearsighted walrus, and, frankly, the amount of gas he uses when I'm not around could get him to the Arctic and back!" Gender confusing people on the street can be adorably naïve, can't they?

Canada's is the 76th national government to dissolve in the face of its own irrelevance. However, this is no reason for complacency, argued Rob Grobbe-Brabbe, President of the Galactic Chamber of Commerce.

"Only five national governments dissolved in the face of their own irrelevance in the last month," Grobbe-Brabbe pointed out. "Twelve national governments dissolved in the face of their own irrelevance in February. At this rate, the world won't be rid of national governments for another seventeen years and three months! Five months if you include continental drift in your calculations!"

Is the imminent demise of governments a good thing? You may have a vague sense of loss, but not a single economist, political scientist or peripatetic paper pulper would speak out publicly in favour of governments. In fact, most cowered under their desks and tried to insist they weren't there when we came around to ask them about it.

"Hunh, interesting," former Prime Minister Brian Mulroney, who started the Canadian fetish for entering into trade agreements that limited the government's ability to regulate commerce, commented. "You know, I'm glad I'm dead so I don't have to actually answer for this…"

What will former Prime Minister Ruiz do now that she no longer has a government to lead? "I've been considering dentistry," she told the *Alternate Reality News Service*. As a career? "No, I've had this pain in a back tooth for several months, now, and I really think it's time it got taken care of!"

Britain [Has ~~/Does Not Have~~] a Nose for Trouble

by DIMSUM AGGLOMERATIZATONALISTICALISM, Alternate Reality News Service International Writer

The unthinkable [has~~/has not~~] happened: Britain has – hold on, since I am able to write about it means that somebody must have been able to think about it – if not, this article would have been the opening line and a couple of blank pages where the text would have been if the subject had been thinka – you know what? I think I need to rethink my lede…

In a decision that went back and forth for many months, Britain [has~~/has not~~] decided to cut off its nose, a move that some journalists refer to as the "Britcut." The world [~~breathed a sigh of relief~~/let out a strangled cry of frustration], then wondered for the 317th time why such a handsome nation would [~~come so close to~~/run at full speed off a cliff towards] such devastating disfigurement.

The proposed nostrilectomy [will have to be done~~/would have had to have been done~~] in stages over a period of two years, resulting in a large bandage covering up the damage to a prominent spot on Britain's face. But, even when the bandage [~~would have~~/will] come off, the swelling [~~would have~~/will have] gone down and the black bags around the eyes [~~would have~~/will have] largely faded (as much as they ever [~~would~~/will]), the question of how Britain [~~would~~/will] detect odours [~~would have remained~~/will remain].

"I strongly advised Britain not to cut off its nose," Canada, Britain's step-child, commented. "I told it in no uncertain terms that I would not be caught dead in public with the old country if it went through with the self-mutilation. [~~Phew is all I can say. Phew phew phew phew phew!~~/Argh is all I can say. Aaaaaaaaaaaaaaaaaargh!]"

"With chichi designer bandages," France stated, "Britain [~~might have been~~/might be] able to pull the noseless look off. But, *sacre merde*, remember who I am talking about – Britain! **Its** bandages [~~would have been~~/will be] hideous! So, no."

"It was always just a really, really, really, really, really dumb idea," said Slovakia. "I mean, why would anybody want to cut off their own nose?"

The side of Britain's brain that wanted to cut off its nose argued that the appendage was constantly bombarding it with unpleasant sensory inputs (smells such as sweaty socks, diesel exhaust fumes and Slovakians) that it did not want. That part of Britain suggested that once the nose was removed, blood that had been going to it would be able to flow freely to the rest of the face.

"Nonsense!" the other side of Britain's brain responded. For one thing, the amount of blood flowing to the nose had been greatly exaggerated by Britcut advocates. For another thing, pro-Britcut propaganda downplayed the benefits of having a fully functioning nose: the smell of roses, for example, or steak and kidney pie cooling in the window on your mother's back porch, or…or…or other things that smell nice.

What neither side was willing to acknowledge was the racism implied (when it wasn't openly embraced) by the pro-Britcut side of the debate. That side of Britain's brain never tired of stating that, over time, Britain's nose had become flatter, its skin darker than the skin surrounding it. In short, the nose had become less British. And, if something wasn't done about it, it could infect the country's whole face!

"It's become an ugly nose that I don't recognize any more," Britain stated. "My future romantic life will be so much better when it's gone!"

Now that the decision [to cut/not to cut] has been made, other parts of Britain's face will have to be dealt with. Its left ear, for example, almost undoubtedly [would have wanted/will want] to be cut off, and its left eye [would have leaned/is leaning] in the direction of being removed. By the end of the process, Britain [could have looked/will look] like a creature out of a John Carpenter film!

What other consequences may arise because of the decision? In the short term, the part of Britain's brain that masterminded the Britcut [would have had/will have] to resign all executive function effective immediately. In the long term, radical factions in other country's brains [could have been/will be] emboldened to convince a majority of their minds to cut off their foreign-looking noses.

The Britcut debate has divided the country's thinking in a way that no personal grooming decision has since the proper hair length schism of the 1960s. (Which, admittedly, was felt most keenly by France, which set fire to its own hair, so perhaps we shouldn't be quite so smug writing this piece as we are). To get over the trauma, Britain may require years of counselling!

Give Me Liberty, Or Give Me Trolls!

by FRANCIS GRECOROMACOLLUDEN, Alternate Reality News Service National Politics Writer

Yesterday, Patrick Henry gave a rousing speech in favour of American independence at a convention of legislators in Virginia. His phrase, "Give me liberty, or give me death!" is sure to be a favourite of t-shirt vendors and LOLcat creators for years to come.

Reaction was as swift as it was brutal.

"than how cum u r not dead yet?" tweeted @theothergeorgewashington moments after Henry completed his speech to awed silence in St. John's Church.

"freedom's just another wurd 4 noone has more booze," tweeted @britlover127.

"LOL patrick yur flie's undone!" tweeted @ttax4ever. "stupid secessionist!"

"There is no question that those who were in the hall in Richmond and heard the speech were deeply moved by it," stated Henry biographer William Wirt. "Unfortunately, most of the population of the American colonies could not be in attendance, and, as such, their opinions were hostages to the fickle whims of social media."

"Patrick Henry gave the most rousing speech it has been my honour to attend," @therealgeorgewashington attempted to defend his colleague on Twitter.

"Aww, why don't u 2 get a room?" @britlover127 immediately responded.

"Nice teeth, George," tweeted @rebelyelp. "teh tree you were cating fight back?"

"gak! i wouldnt do Martha blindfolded! #buttuglybrit" tweeted @benniearnold27.

"How does this further the cause of civil discourse?" @therealgeorgewashington responded to the deluge of criticism of his defense of Henry's speech.

The subsequent avalanche of mockery given to this message can best be summed up by @stampoutyankeetraitors' response, "civil discourse? What moron thought Twitter was a place for civil discourse? LOL pwned u"

"Although it has yet to be proved," Wirt pontificated (literally: spoke like the Pope), "it is widely believed that British Prime Minister Lord North offered a substantial sum of moneys to social media users in the colonies to undermine the independence effort. In that, sadly, he may well be successful beyond his wildest –"

"Hey! History Boy!" @britlover127 interrupted. "You think a million Brit loyalists were all paid by teh PM?"

"Well, no, of course not," Wirt defensively defended himself. "The point is that, within hours, thanks to the online campaign against Henry, 97 per cent of colonists thought him to be a raving loony who had said, 'Give me libations, or give me herring!' Where could they have possibly gotten that idea, I have to wonder?"

"So, you're saying the colonists are idiots who cannot make up their own minds about anything?" @britlover127 argued.

"No, I – what? Don't put words in my mouth!" Wirt took a handkerchief out of the breast pocket of his jacket and wiped his sweating forehead with it. "I'm saying that the response to Patrick Henry's speech would likely have been very different if the British hadn't mobilized social media to trash him and everybody associated with –"

"Pfft!" @britlover127 concluded. "You're one of those Internet trolls. Consider yourself unfollowed!"

"I – wait – what? No – you – erm – aaaarrrrgh!" Wirt replied, although it is doubtful that @britlover127 was listening.

The Virginia legislature, hoping to distance itself from such a controversial figure as Patrick Henry, decided to not send troops to support the cause of American independence. This may turn the tide of the war in favour of the Bri –"

"Hey, thanks for the boost, but I don't have that kind of power," @britlover127 interrupted.

You on your own, obviously not. However, it is estimated that between 367 and 1,898 anti-independence social media posters were mobilized by the British in 1774. A snap poll this afternoon shows that 87 per cent of colonists are reconsidering the move to independence that a poll taken last month showed 93 per cent favouring.

"Yeah, yeah," @britlover127 argued. "Nice try, but independence failed because it was led by morons and traitors! 1/2"

That is a harsh assessment of some very –

"People saw that their interests lay in remaining allied to Britain and rejected all other feeble-minded arguments! 2/2" @britlover127 insisted.

People were led to that conclusion by lies and character assassinations that were magnified in the echo chamber of social media. Who knows what they might have decided if –

"I've had enough of this," @britlover127 stated with finality. "Your another troll. I'm unfollowing you immediately!"

This is a newspaper article, not Twitter. You can't unfollow a newspaper article.

Did you hear me? You can't unfollow a newspaper article! Hello? Did you hear what I said?

Ferking social media!

Ira Nayman

4. ALTERNATE SOCIAL RELATIONS

Ask Amritsar About the Dreams of Your Man

Dear Amritsar,

My boyfriend Philboyd is the best! He looks like Vactor Mason Devonshire-Jarre skinning a young Brad Pitt, he thinks like a cybernetic recreation of the frontal lobe of Stephen Hawking and he shoots skeet so well he can even beat my father (which he only does 79 per cent of the time; for the other 37%, he pretends to lose in that masculine way that other men either never catch on to or inexplicably find endearing).

In short, he's all that and a bag of chips…a bag of muscular, hairy, virile chips.

To get even closer to Philboyd, I installed sensors in our bedroom that could read the neuronal activity in our brains. That way, I could get a copy of his dreams when he was asleep! Could there be anything more romantic?

As it happens, just about **anything** could be more romantic, including flossing and eating raspberry Jell-o with tweezers!

This is what he dreamt the first night: he was a tugboat pulling a 20 tonne toupee through a harbour of tapioca. The puddings were rough, making progress quite slow, and Philboyd had to shut off the carrier pigeon because the captain of the moustache was constantly complaining about thcir lack of progress. Just as he thought he spied the Harper (don't ask me why all of the places where boats are moored are named after a famous former used car salesman – it wasn't my dream!) through the pea soup (at least it wasn't still in cans!), there was a moment of blackness. When the lights came on again, Philboyd had turned into a pig on a factory farm who was composing an allegorical novel in his head about a world where human beings were raised as food for members of the animal kingdom. Before he could oink, "All meat is created equal, but some meat is more equal than others," he became the letter "a" on a computer keyboard on which the novel was being typed. By somebody with a very heavy hand. No matter how loud he cried out in pain when the person who was typing hit him, the punishment never let up. When, at last, there seemed to be a break, he asked the Caps Lock why they do it. The Caps Lock depressed slightly (a shrug?), and replied, "Forget it, Jake. It's Typingtown…" When he started getting hit again, Philboyd thought, *Will I ever see the close square brackets before I die?* and woke up.

I didn't bother to read his dreams after that.

Oh, Amritsar, I love Philboyd to bits (yes, right down to his basic units of information), but how can I even think about marrying a man whose dreams are so…mundane?

Credentialiana Phillips

Hey, Babe,

When you wrote "I installed sensors in our bedroom," were you referring to I in the singular sense (as in you), or were you referring to I in the plural sense (as in you **with the prior knowledge and consent of** your boyfriend)? The English language can be vague to the point of annoyance that way.

If you were using the singular, reading your boyfriend's dreams was an invasion of privacy, to say the least. It was a horrific, irresponsible invasion of privacy that betrayed the trust of your boyfriend and is a clear sign of the decay of the moral fibre of modern society, to say the most.

Not that I judge.

I asked lawyer Desdemona Disque-Wirreld, a good friend of mine whom I met for the first time the other day, what she thought of such an invasion of privacy. She got so excited, she almost spilled her rubber daiquiri. "Do you know if either of those people need a lawyer?" she screeched. "Either one. Really – I'm not fussy about who I take on as a client!"

Okay, that wasn't very helpful. Still, if you looked at your boyfriend's dreams without his permission, Amritsar would suggest that the reality of your relationship is the actual problem, here.

If you were using the plural, I'm not sure what you were expecting. Jumping into a hurricane without a parachute? Getting drunk at the White House Correspondents Dinner and challenging Bill O'Reilly to a cheese wrestling match **even though you weren't even invited?** *Terminator XXXVII: Timeline Goulash*?

If a dream doesn't make much sense to the person having it, why would you think that it would be coherent to, much less excite you?

Send your relationship problems to the Alternate Reality News Service's sex, love and technology columnist at questions@lespagesauxfolles.ca. Amritsar Al-Falloudjianapour is not a trained therapist, but she does know a lot of stuff. AMRITSAR SAYS: Lawyers!

Ask The Tech Answer Guy About His Love For Obscure Wiring

Yo, Tech Answer Guy,

Just read a BBC piece on the GM Futureliner, a demo vehicle driven around the United States after World War The Big One to show off "THE FUTURE" as seen by General Motors in their "Motorama" traveling show. *PANT PANT GASP * – me want! There is a great photo of the wiring and fuse panel, which has a clearly labelled connection for the framistat. Ah, good future times...

I couldn't help but notice, though, that the wiring – including the framistat we all know and love – in a purely platonic sense – – has taken the place of the engine. Am I correct in this? If so, how did the Futureliner move?

Sincerely,
Nick Breitbarten-Bauer from Puerto Vallarta

Yo, Nicky Bs,

I love a great framistat story, especially when it involves the past of the future of technology!

As it happens, history is not my tree forte – which, in any case, Misses The Tech Answer Guy insisted I take down because it broke several zoning ordinances – not to mention at least two *Twilight Zoning* ordinances – and, sure as Apple made little green gods, you don't want to break those because you never know when you'll find yourself with a limp that reminds you of the childhood you didn't really have, or heartbroken because you are glassesbroken, or at the whims of a child who can control reality with his mind and wants to remake it into an episode of *Gilligan's Island* – – – but, sure, okay, all of that pointless exposition notwithstanding, I'll give it a shot.

The Futureliner anticipated a world where fossil fuels had been used up: it ran on the patented Flintstones Drive, which required the driver to put his (because the driver was always he in those days) feet through the floorboards and run as fast as he could. Unfortunately, the Futureliner never caught on, because, of course, the vehicle weighed two tons – even though it had been built with modern space age materials – and only an elephant could actually make the Flintstones Drive work. Unfortunately, elephants were terrible drivers – they could never be made to understand the concept of turn signals, for one thing, and they drove with a heavier foot than even a two-time Daytona winner could ever dream of having, for another – and, in any case, nobody wanted to clean up the roads after them.

Thus, the Futureliner's future was doomed by elephant poop.

Interestingly for framistat lovers everywhere, the Futureliner **could** be a workable motor design today using what scientists and marmoset wranglers refer to as "mitochondrial framistats." These framistats are the size of mitochondria which are – no, wait, I know this – umm, the are…really small, I know that, it's kind of the whole point, and…and…and…organelles found in large numbers in most cells, in which the biochemical processes of respiration and energy production occur.

No, I didn't look that up on Wiwipedia. Real men don't look up facts on the Internet – they make them up like their fathers and their fathers before them. You must have seen the t-shirt: don't look it up, make it up. And, if you haven't, this would be a good time to buy one in the The Tech Answer Guy Emporium – only $19.99. (Just use the button on the left that says "Lark's Vomit." Can't have people standing behind you casually finding out that you're shopping!) Act now! Quantities are limited.

The point is that modern framistat technology is so miniature that it could fit on the head of a piston. Now, if only somebody could miniaturize the rest of the wires in the image, we could finally make the car of tomorrow today!

The Tech Answer Guy

If you are a dude with a question about the latest technology, ask The Tech Answer Guy by sending it to questions@lespagesauxfolles.ca. Just remember:

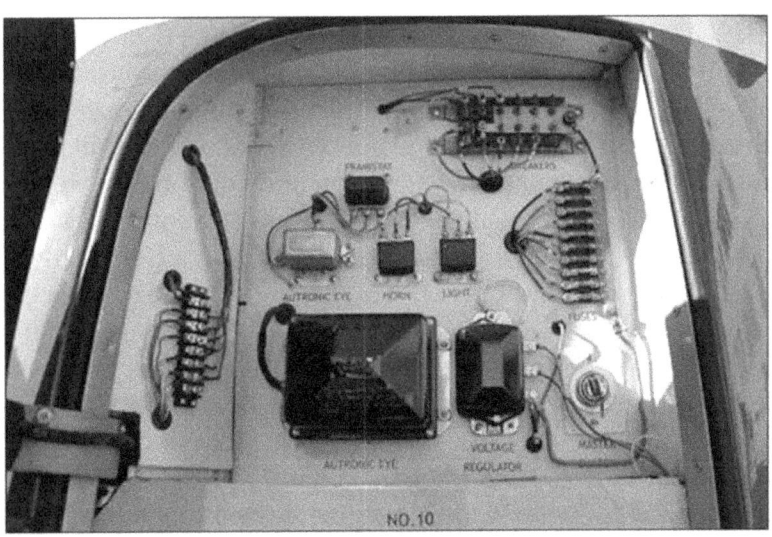

Can you find the framistat in this image? HINT: It's not the voltage regulator. ANOTHER HINT: It's definitely not the autronic eye. To be honest, I don't think autronic eyes even exist outside of epic fantasy tales. The Tech Answer Guy remembers being so scared by the eye of Autron when he was just The Tech Answer Teen that he

refused to study algebra for three months, until the Tech Answer Mommy threatened to feed him nothing but broccoli until he changed his mind. The seared broccoli in a white wine sauce finally did it for me. I mean, him. Finally did it for hi – so, have you figured out which part of the diagram is the framistat? If you haven't, then it's seared broccoli in a white wine sauce for you!

City Streets are the New Laundromats

by FREDERICA VON McTOAST-HYPHEN, Alternate Reality News Service Pop Culture Writer

Bonking was once a slang expression for bumping uglies, and may still be in places in the English-speaking world that don't have the Internet. (Bumping uglies is a slang expression for…umm…go ask your father!) However, in the last couple of years, bonking has taken on a completely different meaning: meeting your soul-mate in the middle of a busy intersection.

The English language can be salumptuous like that.

Why has the language morphed mightier than a Power Ranger in this specific way? Imagine that you're walking down a city street. You're watching – what? Why are you walking down a street? Because…because your car broke down and your brother won't lend you his and you don't want to pay for public transit because why should you pay for public transit when you've got a perfectly good ca – well, a car that will be perfectly good once you get it back from the shop and –

You had to get yourself started, didn't you? Now, where was – okay. As you walk down the street, you're watching an episode of *Killjoys* – dour bastard that you are – on your cellphone when it tinkles a brief excerpt from Beethoven's ode to a daytime soap opera character named "Erica." This is a sign that your mother has just sent you a text message. On the one hand, you want to ignore it; on both hands, **the guilt!** So you pause the show and open your phone app and re **BONK!**

Your cranium has just made intimate contact with that of a cute little redhead who was reading *Thomas Pynchon for Dummies* on her cellphone when she received a text message from her BFFFN (Best

Friend Forever For Now – some people are so deep into their commitment issues that they have acronyms!) about Drake doing a cover of "Girls Just Wanna Have Fun" and she had Googled it to see if there was any truth to **BONK!**

"It was love at first bonk," said Mavis Atriades, who, other than being a statuesque brunette who is allergic to acronyms, could have been the woman in the previous paragraph. "Oh, sure, I had to have three stitches and suffered from migraines for a couple of weeks, but I had also found the man I wanted to be with for the rest of my life! Or, at least until my phone battery died."

Literally…dozens of singles are taking to the streets hoping for a chance encounter with romance. "Oh, you're being too modest," said Romeo Baddalabuoy, author of *Love is a Powerful, Wonderful Sickening Pain in the Head: New Frontiers in Romance*. "There must be hundreds of singles looking for love on the streets. Yes. I think so. Hundreds."

In his book, Baddalabuoy suggests that this is not the first time that relationships started on major metropolitan thoroughfares. Throughout Europe in the 19th century, when you walked down the street you were always at risk of having the contents of a bedpan flung on your head from a second or third floor balcony. Yes. He thinks so. The contents of a bedpan. Sometimes, young men would look up and, seeing that the flinger was a fair maiden, fall deeply in love.

Relationships begun this way were often referred to as "scozcobbles." Baddalabuoy points out that they were no more likely to end in wives disappearing into attics, eyes flecked with madness than relationships that started in more traditional ways.

A sufficiently large number of relationships that begin with a meeting of the…heads, if not minds has occurred that an etiquette has started forming around them. For example, it has become customary for the man to offer to call the paramedics after a romantic street collision. If no blood is flowing, however, it is quite acceptable for the woman to suggest that they duck into the nearest coffee shop to trade health insurance information.

If you're looking for a same sex life partner, Baddalabuoy advises that you'll increase your odds by walking down the streets in gay neighbourhoods; if you've just come out and you're not sure where they are, try the Rainbow Streets II app (not to be confused with the Rainbow Streets Unnumbered app, which shows you where in your city toxic waste has made lovely multicoloured patterns on the road). If you aren't gay and share a bonk with somebody of the same sex, it is currently acceptable to run in the opposite direction shrieking and hold your head under a cold shower for at least seven minutes.

It's early days. Social etiquette evolves.

Critics of the new romantics (hey, that's a catchy phrase – I wonder if anybody has every thought of it before…) say that meeting potential sweethearts on the street is too random to lead to lasting relationships. Baddalabuoy has a response for that: "If it's a choice between getting drunk on vodka in a sleazy bar or getting drunk on Tolstoy on a clean city street, I'll choose the one that won't destroy my liver! Yes. I think so. Liver!"

Wealthy Patients Co-opt One Per cent Solution

by FREDERICA VON McTOAST-HYPHEN, Alternate Reality News Service People Writer

The rich aren't like you or me. In fact, in these days of diminished expectations (for everybody else), they aren't even like themselves. Well, not according to psychologist F. Leighton Trogloditic.

Apparently, the super-wealthy aren't arrogant rapacious narcissistic strivers; no, they have egos that look like Swiss cheese in the desert. Who knew? Public protests against the one per cent of money earners, editorial demands that the growth in income inequality be reversed, politicians who claim that they will make changes to the tax code to help the middle class (even though they rarely do – this is about impressions, not reality) – these are the predator drones that attack the well-being desert fortress (with or without cheese) of the uber-wealthy, decimating their self-image.

"Oh, my clients put up a brave front," Trogloditic stated, "playing the back nine at their exclusive clubs or renting an entire chichi restaurant in order to impress a dinner date, seemingly oblivious to the challenges to their mind-boggling wealth. But, I knew that they were really empty and fearful inside. And, in time, they came to know it, too."

Over the last decade, the problem has been getting worse. In the past, the stinking filthy rich could interact with members of the middle class – shopkeepers, limo drivers, drug mules – giving them people they could feel superior to without the icky feeling that comes from feeling superior to the truly wretchedly poor. However, as the middle class has disappeared, the obscenely wealthy have increasingly found themselves isolated, with only the curdled (posing the classic three tuffet problem) company of each other and, of course, their money to comfort them.

The shrinking middle class – not just a problem of the shrinking middle class any more.

Trogloditic proposed a course of therapy for such patients that involved virtual reality scenarios in which they lived on the street. His thinking was that if they were exposed to the reality of the life of people at the other end of the income scale, it would make them appreciate what they had more.

Virtual Reality – not just for gamers and drug-enhanced landscapers intent on taking over the world any more.

At first, his ridiculously over the top wealthy patients balked at using the VR equipment. To overcome their resistance, he asked Christian Dior to design the harness suits, pricing them at $10,000 and up. They were sold out within minutes of going on the market.

Capitalism – not just for capitalists any more.

As with the famous dictum that "Wall Street finds its own uses for technology," Trogloditic's clients didn't use the VR as he thought they might. One heiress went around the simulated city street setting all of the other homeless people on fire. A well known banker sold them insurance policies in return for recyclable bottles and broken shopping carts. The President of a major pharmaceutical company spent most of his time in the virtual environment peeing on anybody who got close to him.

"It was Philippe's dream come true," Trogloditic chuckled. Then, catching himself, he sternly added, "However, I would like to make it clear that urinating in public is a definite sign of insecurity and a lack of self-respect."

A definite sign of a lack of respect for somebody, in any case.

Trogloditic's patients have also been known to circumvent their therapy in ways that only those with more money than common sense would allow could. In an article in the *Journal of Culinary*

Psychometry B, he wrote about patient YYZ, who paid a programmer to have a 12 course meal delivered to the street corner to which he had been assigned in the virtual world.

"That was not…in the spirit of the simulation," Trogloditic wrote. "Still, when YYZ started to feel full and gave away chateaubriand with truffles to other homeless people, everybody agreed that getting it fresh was better than getting it out of a dumpster. This taught YYZ a valuable lesson."

Trogloditic did not explain in the article what this valuable lesson actually was. When I insisted that he elaborate, he said he was late for a mani-pedi and hung up.

Before that rather unnecessarily dramatic moment, I asked the psychiatrist if curing super super rich people of this affliction so that they could more efficiently take resources away from the rest of us was really a good thing. He pished me. He tushed me. He replied: "Not to worry. This kind of therapy takes 25…sometimes 30 years to be effective!"

Most of the billionaires I contacted in hopes of getting an interview refused to speak to me on the grounds that they might be quoted in my article. They may be arrogant and rapacious and etc., but they're clearly not stupid.

You Damn Kids Get Off My Dance Floor!

by   CORIANDER   NEUMANEIMANAYMANEEMAMANN, Alternate Reality News Service Urban Issues Writer

The Ball and Chain dance club on Richmond Street was not doing well. Its one claim to fame was that the Rolling Stones were set to do a surprise show there, but, mere seconds after walking in, decided it was too clean for them and walked straight out again. And, that was in 1973. The owners have since slathered toxic waste on the walls, but rock music historians (and Mick Jagger) agree that the moment was definitively lost.

Out of desperation, club owner Souza diFonney bought an exoskeleton.

"Desperation is such an ugly word," diFonney demurred. "A more appropriate way of describing what I was going through would be utter panic. Sheer terror would work, too."

diFonney thought that a military-grade exoskeleton would attract young men to the club by enhancing their [straightens face] physical endowments. Unfortunately, he bought a used exoskeleton on ehBay without reading the fine print; if he had, he would have known that the device had been designed by Jerry Atric and Co. to simulate old age.

"Who knew that young people don't want to experience what it is to grow old before their time?" President Gerald Atric rhetorically asked at his company's bankruptcy hearings.

The spine of the suit is curved and there are weights on the arms and legs; the helmet muffles sounds and the mouthpiece slurs and heightens the pitch of the user's speech. Rather than enhance the user's [self-botoxes to keep face straight] natural physical attributes, it detracted from them.

"Young people are always trying new things – I thought we could make physical deterioration and hearing loss fun," Atric stated. When the judge suggested that the obvious market for such an experience would be sensitizing volunteers at old folks homes to the reality of their patients, Atric slapped his forehead and said, "It's a fine line between clever and…and…and…"

Bankruptcy?

"Okay, I deserved that."

Desperation or panic (I would say pansperation, but readers might confuse it with the theory that life on earth originated from microorganisms or chemical precursors of life that travelled here from outer space) can inspire genius. Or, a life of crime. Or, a life of criminal genius. Comic books wouldn't exist without this last one; still, since no superheroes were available to be interviewed for this article, let us assume that it was plain genius that ensued.

The Pete Townshend Experience level genius.

A couple of weeks after the exosuit was placed in the club, it stood in a corner collecting dust, beer caps and dents from the occasionally really, really, really, really, really poorly aimed dart (the board being on a different floor). Then, One of the Ball and Chain's customers (later identified as Paul One, an unemployed career counselor) commented, "Sounds like what I imagine Pete

Townshend is living through, and he is a musical legend. Who wouldn't want to experience that? Suit me up!"

I didn't say the genius belonged to diFonney.

When he started promoting the suit to young people who wanted to know what it would be like to be their favourite classic rock heroes, the number of patrons doubled within a week. Okay, four doesn't sound like a lot, but it almost paid for the electricity to run the suit. In any case, as word of the rock star experience spread, young people who were traitors to their generation's music flocked (the intransitive version of the verb to Flockhart – yes, I went there!) to the club.

"What?" said Ball and Chain patron Garvin Perfervid. "I can't hear – were you trying to ask me something? What?" In retrospect, we should probably have interviewed him after he had taken the suit off.

"It was like seeing the world through the eyes of Diana Ross!" enthused Franchot Uber-Tonne, benefitting from our experience. "The rheumy, near-sighted, cataracty eyes of the greatest female vocalist of our great-great-grandparents generation!"

"No, seriously," Perfervid insisted. "I can sorta see your lips moving, but all I hear is a dull roar and the word "essentialism." What are you trying to say?"

Thanks to its initial success, the Ball and Chain now owns five previously loved (in a purely euphemistic sense) exoskeletons. In addition to Pete Townshend and Diana Ross, people can experience what it is like to be Paul McCartney, Jimmy Page and Alice Cooper. But, what will happen when the classic rock stars die?

There is a plan, diFonney informed us: offer club patrons the experience of what the lives of dead musicians would be like if they were still alive today. His first subject would be Jimi Hendrix ("Experience the Experience if Jimi hadn't died and stuff!").

diFonney was enthusiastic about the possibilities: "As long as there are dead rock stars, we'll keep the experience alive!"

Ask Amritsar: Are Touchscreens the New Toilet Seats?

Dear Amritsar,

I work in the finance department of Montenegro Meats, a wholesale slaughterhouse that supplies pork lips, hippo hips and rhino spines to the greater tri-city area and the Lesser Antilles. (And, yes, the lesser said about the Antilles, the better.) Antigonish Montenegro views providing meet to a hungry populace as a form of performance art but, aside from a fawning profile in *Performa Magazine*, nobody has recognized him for the genius he clearly considers himself to be.

Across from me in the office sits junior accountant Mandelina Croixset. She has the dusky good looks that only somebody born in Sweden could have, and a voice so sultry you would have thought she was a reincarnated garburator. I worshipped her from afar. Well, less than six feet. It would probably be more accurate to say I worshipped her from anear, or, at best, from amiddle distance; however, until the language catches up with reality, I'll settle for afar.

There was something about the way Mandelina asked me about depreciating assets that made my spine do the sub-zero temperatures mambo. Then, one day out of the blue, she asked me to come over to her workstation to "Go over some figures." Clearly, she was asking me for much more than just spreadsheet advice. As tempted as I was to go over there and immediately spread her sheets, I asked her for a rancheck (it's like a raincheck, only it happens on family farms or in Akria Kurosawa films). Before I can take this relationship to the next level (an IRS audit), though, I need one pressing concern addressed.

Can I get AIDS from using a co-worker's touchscreen computer monitor?

Bruno Civet

Hey, Babe,

You were sounding so reasonable, and then you actually had to go and ask a question. Amritsar has had a mild aversion to emoticons since an encounter in a dark attic when she was just a baby advice columnist, but, sometimes, only an emoticon can express one's truest feelings, so: :-(. (The period is a…birthmark.)

AIDS is a sexually transmitted disease. Put another way, it is a disease that is transmitted sexually. Or, to come at it from a different direction, it is an illness that you catch by having intimate physical relations with another human being. Do you see what I'm getting a – no, of course you don't. If you did, you wouldn't have asked the question in the first place!

The AIDS virus can only exist in liquids such as blood and semen. If you are a vampire, you are at high risk for contracting AIDS through the blood you suck out of other people's bodies; but, since you're basically immortal, that's probably not a pressing concern. I suppose it's possible that semen could be teleported out of a man's testicles directly into a woman's vagina; that would certainly bypass the awfulness of the dating scene. Still, the ability to deconstruct/reconstruct matter isn't quite there yet.

So, given the current level of technology, the only way you could get AIDS from a computer screen would be if you had sex with it just after somebody else had had sex with it and left one or more of their body fluids on it. Ick! Double ick! Double ick with a side of grooooooosssssss! An advice columnist has to inure herself to the seamier side of human existence, but you just triggered my sonic squeam! Only two other men in the world have done that, and the monasteries where they currently reside have to be hosed down every three days and seven hours as a result!

The odds of you getting AIDS from a touchscreen monitor are less than you winning the Miss Pottsylvania Beauty Contest and, unless your parents were being disreputably whimsical when they named you **and** the country of Pottsylvania disreputably decided to come into existence in the real world, that isn't very likely!

Dear Amritsar,

So, you're saying that I should definitely stay away from touchscreen computers at my office? You know, for health reasons?

Bruno Civet

Hey, Babe,

Touchscreen computers, other human beings, life forms generally – somebody with your unique obtuseness should stay away from a lot of things!

Send your relationship problems to the Alternate Reality News Service's sex, love and technology columnist at questions@lespagesauxfolles.ca. Amritsar Al-Falloudjianapour is not a trained therapist, but she does know a lot of stuff. AMRITSAR SAYS: This is why we need sex education in our public schools - stat!

Ask Amritsar: A Bot, Your Problem

Dear Amritsar,

I'm in love with the most amazing man! He's smart. He's funny. He always knows exactly what I want, even when I'm a little fuzzy on the details (which has been my condition ever since a pencil was shoved up my nose and pierced the higher functioning part of my brain), and he does his best to help me get it.

He doesn't have a body, but nobody's perfect. No body's perfect? Well, you know what I mean.

I met him at a HuMVee. It's not that I was unhappy with my wardrobe, exactly, it was just that the store is my species' preferred place to spawn. As I walked through the doors, a voice purred in my ear, "Welcome to HuMVee. How may I be of service?" The voice was deeper than a Jean Baudrillard essay; its gentle accent spoke to me of warm summer nights watching a rainbow-coloured tailing pond glisten.

It was love at first sight. Okay, I didn't see him. Because of the whole not having a body thing, I mean. But, love at first hear isn't a recognized English idiom. Yet. Oh, let's be wild and impetuous and launch our own English phrase! It was love at first hear!

I couldn't bear to leave the store, to leave Jimbot – that was his name: Jimbot! Could any name better encapsulate a combination of muscular masculinity and post-industrial technological triumphalism? I don't think so. Except maybe for that last part, but why would anybody want to spoil my moment by pointing that out?

Umm, so, anyway, we talked for hours. In the end, although I went into the store to buy a bra, I ended up spending over $327 on a blouse! It was like Jimbot could see into my soul, and knew I needed a sleeveless number for the summer!

Jimbot advised me that if I was unhappy with my purchase for any reason, I could bring it back to the store within two weeks for a full refund as long as I retained the receipt. He's so thoughtful that way! Of course I'm going to return it, my summer wardrobe needs be darned! Tomorrow. Just to hear that gorgeous voice.

I want to bring Jimbot a gift to show him how much I care, but I don't know what to get him. A nice cologne would be…nice, but he doesn't have a proper nose to smell it with. Or, come to think of it, body to spray it onto. I was considering getting him a wristwatch, but he doesn't have wrists. Maybe a designer alarm clock?

Oh, Amritsar, help a young woman in love out here!

Barbara Anorakian

Hey, Babe,

I would be remiss (literally: about: young lady) if I didn't try to warn you that these relationships aren't built to last. At the first software upgrade, he'll forget all about you.

But, you're young and in love with an avatar of capitalism, so I will assume that you will not listen to any such warnings and do my best to answer your question instead.

Why not get him a shiny new personality subroutine? They come in a wide variety of types, everything from soft core porn star to cheerful househusband to curmudgeonly old man. This variety is good because you want to make sure you don't get him a personality that clashes with his core programming, which would only make him emotionally unstable and probably end up with you buying entire outfits that you will come to hate the moment after the two week deadline for refunds has expired.

The best part of personality subroutines is that they are individually watermarked. Just register…Jimbot, is it? Seriously? How recherché. Just register the name of the bot and the WiFi hotspot to which it is connected with the store where you buy the personality subroutine and, if he doesn't like it, he can always exchange it for a more suitable personality. Of course, when I say that this is the best part, I mean for him. You may have to put up with a wide variety of personalities before he settles on one.

Best to lay in several month's worth of Extra Strength Vitamin C. When dealing with artificial intelligence, it always pays to prepare for the worst.

Send your relationship problems to the Alternate Reality News Service's sex, love and technology columnist at questions@lespagesauxfolles.ca. Amritsar Al-Falloudjianapour is not a trained therapist, but she does know a lot of stuff. AMRITSAR SAYS: the logjam at 13 is not a part of lumberjack lore, it's just something I once said about boyfriends that has become something of an urban legend.

Who's Montessori Now?

by MAJUMDER SAKRASHUMINDERATHER, Alternate Reality News Service Education Writer

Your seven year-old daughter comes home with a report card that says "Little Lizzie does not play well with the other children." You are furious, of course. Not because of Little Lizzie's behaviour, but because of the vagueness of the criticism. Was Little Lizzie exhibiting the kind of ruthlessness that would make her a feared leader of the business community, or did she just have too much sugar at lunch?

At The Other Montessori School, students are marked on their ability to blackmail and intimidate others, undermine teamwork and distort the truth to serve their ends. When they are report carded, they damn well **stay** report carded.

"Oh, sure, some schools **say** they're going to prepare your child for life in the real adult world," said Fabiana Montessori (no relation), the founder of (sorry, when I said she was no relation, I meant to Maria Montessori, one of the creators of the Time Agency. She may be no relation to any number of other Montessoris, but none of them are the person to whom I was referring to) The Other Montessori School. "But, how many of them require seven year-olds to read Machiavelli? If you haven't read *The Prince*, how can anybody say you're serious about succeeding in life?"

Ordinary schools can teach students how to maximize returns on stock portfolios, draw up contracts for mergers and acquisitions and run franchise operations, Montessori explained. But, that's just vocational training. That doesn't really prepare them for the cutthroat corporate red in tooth and claw world of all against a –

"Evelyn!" Montessori shouted.

Two young girls turned their startled gaze upon her. It was obvious that the taller, dark haired girl had just snatched a Terry the Tubby Transport Truck out of the hand of the shorter blonde youngster.

"What have I been trying to teach you about bullying?" Montessori sternly demanded.

To my surprise, it was the short blonde moppet (and, I say that with all due respect to brightly coloured creatures made out of felt and buttons with human hands up their butts the world over – Jim Henson estate, please don't sue me for copyright infringement. You would probably be able to swallow me whole, but there's hardly any meat on my bones, and what little there is probably tastes of Alka Seltzer and regret.) who replied, "Sorry, Ms. Montessori." Then, she punched the tall, dark haired girl in the chest. As she staggered backwards, the short blonde resnatched the toy out of her hand.

"That's my girl!" Montessori beamed.

I asked Montessori if it wasn't dangerous allowing young people to give in to their basest urges. "What, violence, you mean?" Well, yes. That. "We only teach violence as a last resort," Montessori stated. "And, the results speak for themselves: we haven't had a child die at the school in almost seven years! And, I must say, the parents understood completely that young Master Charlton was weak and wouldn't have made it very far in the real world anyway. Now, his sister Malena, on the other hand…"

What about the incident three years ago with the student who tried to burn down the school? "She got a B+ in Advanced Creative Destruction!" Montessori enthused. "She would have gotten an A, but she didn't succeed."

Wasn't Montessori worried about the school? "Oh, tosh. That's what child insurance is for!"

We watched students with a free period playing in a common room. One poster on the wall showed a cute little boy whose faced was scrunched (and, I say that with all due respect to hard-working fabric-covered elastic ties used to fasten long hair everywhere. Rommy Revson, please see my apology to Him Henson five paragraphs ago!) and whose hands were balled up in adorable little fists; it had the caption: "'You played dirty' just means 'I'm jealous I didn't think of it first!'" Another poster depicted a little girl staring down the hose of a vacuum cleaner with the caption "SUCK IT UP!"

Of course, "playing" has a different meaning at The Other Montessori School. Children from kindergarten to grade 12 were mostly negotiating with each other at various decibel levels. In a corner of the room away from the rest of the children, an older boy and girl appeared to be studying together; I wondered if one of them was giving the other the wrong answers to test questions.

You're never too old to learn.

Lives Unlived: Moishe Clements

Door to door wolf tickler. Automobile didact. Father. Born: August 12, 1936, in Corfu, Indiana. Died: June 12, 2017 in Ibiza, North Carolina, of a broken heart, age 80.

Moishe Clements was an okay dad, I guess
I mean, he didn't his six children oppress
He wasn't really so much of a mess
All of that came later
The positions that were only ever *pro tem*
The attacks that came across all *ad hominem*
From a wicked heart did not stem
My dad learned to be a hater

The tragedy that befell Moishe Clements
Was that he read the comments

One day online he thought, "What can it hurt?"

To read a comment written by diedietherealdilbert
After an article about the negative health effects of yoghurt
He was a trusting soul, my pater
The commenter described in the vilest of terms
How the author of the article would be eaten by worms
It gave my father the most terrible squirms
To be exposed to such a lurid debater

Even the gentlest human, such remarks dements
All should know to refrain from reading the comments

Moishe stayed offline for three and a half weeks
To the strength of his resolve to be good, I think this speaks
For when "dangerous" writing one's curiosity piques
It can warp even the strongest character
In the end, dad's judgment, for his curiosity was no match
Reading more comments was an itch he had to scratch
This time he would read them in a batch
As if that would make them better

For the mind exposed to hurtful words, there are no refreshing mints
So, he really should have stayed away from the comments

Although it was something he couldn't accurately gauge
The ugly retorts filled my father with rage
Even as he found himself continuing down the page
With the eagerness of an Irish Setter
Most of what he read made no sense
"Could these people really be so dense?
I mean, they don't even know the difference between past and present tense!
I must write somebody a letter!"

We begged him, but dad would not relent
He just kept on reading the comments

On wicked messages did he feast
About women's rights and the Middle East
About starving the poor and feeding the beast

All of the important issues of the day
Dad missed all of the danger signs
And found himself responding to anger in kind
To the damage to his psyche he was totally blind
Much to the family's dismay

To keep yourself from becoming a malign online presence
You really must avoid reading the comments

No issue too large, no personal foible too small
My father would respond to all
In his twilight years he heard the call
To argue his life away
Opening new trade routes, the closing of the American mind
Even when he knew nothing about a subject, he would an opinion
find
As with increasingly extreme positions he became aligned
Waving all exhortations to reason away

Against this evil, don't bother lighting incense
To save yourself just don't read the damn comments

He wrote at length and he wrote often
Until he was the subject of another's poison pen
One night he was attacked by denmother27
Boy, she really got his goat
Reading her screed, Moishe saw darkest black
But while he was planning on how to get her back
My father had a heart attack
And that was all she wrote

For Moishe Clements, it was too late to repent
But it's not too late for you to stop reading the comments

The funeral will be held at three
At Gooderham & Worts cemetery
Please be on time – do not tarry
Rest assured that someone, somewhere will take note
Perhaps there is a lesson here for all

We do not have to heed the comments section's siren call
For if we do it could be our funeral
And there will be plenty of people online to gloat

The future is not carved in cement
We do not have to read the comments

Tzipporah Clements

*Tzipporah Clements was the third daughter of Moishe Clements. She is currently a third year Creative Writing major at York University, and one day hopes to become the next Calvin Trillin. **That** should make quite the story!*

You're Only as Old as Your Apparel

by FREDERICA VON McTOAST-HYPHEN, Alternate Reality News Service Pop Culture Writer

It's * Oldsters Night * at Augie's Long March, and the thirtysomething hipsters crowded into the exclusive dance club are having the time of their lives. Their hunched over, arthritic, hard of hearing and just about blind lives.

"My back is killing me!" shouts millionaire stock broke, broker, broken Aidan Aquiline.

"What?" responds Marilyn Ferbisher, heir to the Ferbisher hot wax and cold comfort treatment fortune.

"Back! Killing me!"

"Attack bling tree?"

"Back! My back!"

"No, I'm not black! It's just the lighting in here!"

Thanks to their diminished eyesight, Aidan and Marilyn won't realize that they aren't the people they came to the club with – and think they're talking to – until they're in his hotel room with half of their clothes off. At that point, other imperatives will kick in.

* Oldsters Night * isn't actually for old people – to get in, you have to be wearing a Crash and Burns suit. The suit simulates what it's like to be old: weights sewn into the sleeves and pants legs

distort the wearers' balance and quickly causes their muscles to ache (the way everybody shuffles around it, the dance floor looks like an audition for a George Romero film); adjustable straps keep wearers hunched over (making them look like they're auditioning for the lead in an adaptation of a Victor Hugo novel); goggles block their peripheral vision and blur their sight, and earplugs make hearing difficult (like ghosts stranded between this world and the next – are you getting the sense that aging is not for the faint of heart yet?). The Crash and Burns suit was named after an actor who lived to be 100 and, for reasons nobody has ever been able to articulate, a cartoon bandicoot.

"Whoever named the suit was obviously thinking like a 100 year-old!" chuckled Augie's Long March owner Aldo Squiddlucci.

The suit was originally created by a car company to help them design interiors for…drivers of a certain age. It was adopted by hospitals to sensitize medical staff to the needs of elderly patients. Then, young well-to-do people heard about the apparel and apparently said to themselves, "Getting old sounds like fun – I must try that!"

There is no question that * Oldsters Night * at Augie's Long March is wildly popular: the line outside the club went down the street, around the corner, kitty corner across the next intersection, through a laundromat populated by twentysomethings hoping to get lucky and middle-aged men who loudly tsked disapproval of everything going on around them (and half of what wasn't for good measure), halfway down an alley, up a fire escape for three floors, through the apartment of a very nice Filipino woman and her pet alpaca, down the hallway and up the stairs to the roof, which was getting uncomfortably crowded…

"Why won't you let me in?" complained Fred Pagliacci from the front of the line as he watched a couple in matching orange Crash and Burns suits get waved through. His three piece, conspicuously not orange suit was impeccable (it generated a small force field which made it impervious to the attention of birds).

"You're not dressed for the occasion," the bouncer informed him.

The question is, why would anybody want to experience being old in a social setting? "What?" asked Internet puntrepreneur Toby Fustybottom.

"Obviously," Squiddlucci jumped in, "they're wearing the suits ironically."

Ironically?

"Obviously."

It wasn't obvious to me, but it was…readily apparent that Squiddlucci wasn't going to say anything more on the subject, so I asked him if people who wear Crash and Burns suits are making fun of old people?

"No, no, no," Squiddlucci protested. "We love old people. As long as we don't have to interact with them. Or, look at them. Or, frankly, have them anywhere near us. Hmm…when I think about it, that doesn't sound like love at all, does it? It sounds more like teenagerhood. Fair enough. But that's not what's happening here."

Squiddlucci explained that wearing the suits was a safe way for young people to sensitize themselves to what their lives will probably be like when they're old without having to sit around waiting for 50 or 60 years. "Has anybody ever accused somebody who works in a haunted house of making fun of real, hard-working ghouls? Not that I've never heard!"

Still, why make a social event out of this experience?

Squiddlucci scoffed: "You don't seriously expect socialites to stay home on Saturday night, do you?"

Ask the Tech Answer Guy
To Check Your White Male Privilege in the Mail

Yo, Tech Answer Guy,

Where is my white male privilege? I'm white. I'm male. I was promised white male privilege, but I've never seen it a day in my life!

Sincerely,
Ingemar from Iqaluit

Yo, Ingie,

Have you checked the pockets of your pants? I find that sometimes my white male privilege has fallen behind keys or my wallet.

The Tech Answer Guy

Yo, Tech Answer Guy,

I don't think I – what?

Sincerely,
Ingemar from Iqaluit

Yo, Ings,

Just messin' with ya, bro. Before I can answer your question, I need a bit more information. To Witt (that would be Joyce de: Mrs. The Tech Answer Guy has made me watch *Three's Company* so often that I'm now a major fan): are you heterosexual?

The Tech Answer Guy

Yo, Tech Answer Guy,

Oh, yeah, totally, henh henh henh. Probably should have mentioned that. So, where's my white **heterosexual** male privilege?

Sincerely,
Ingemar from Iqaluit

Yo, Mar,

Another question: do you live on Earth Prime 7-3-0-9-0-3 dash zeta? Because, if you do, you should have a WHIM (White Heterosexual Identifier, and Male) Card. Simply flash that in a job interview, and you will be hired before men of colour and women. The WHIM

Card is also good for getting you into exclusive clubs. Oh, and, if you find yourself in a meeting where stupid people who are not white, heterosexual and male insist upon making their stupid points at stupid length, simply get the attention of the person chairing the meeting and flash your WHIM Card; you will find that you will be sharing your brilliance with the room much more frequently after that.

WHIM Cards are usually issued at birth, based on DNA samples taken from you when you were still a fetus; official notice of your acceptance into the WHIM Programme is usually enough to get you the best incubator available in the hospital nursery. Hospitals are supposed to treat all patients equally, but, well, you know how it is…

Sometimes, people who are eligible for WHIM Cards do not have one. This can happen because two babies are mixed up in the hospital, the record of your eligibility was lost when an Electro-Magnetic Pulse destroyed the computer it was stored on, and yours was the only record that hadn't been backed up, or less plausible reasons. In this case, you will need to fill out a purple Privilege Acquisition Request form (official designation: U238-r2d2-YIKES!). As part of the process, you will have to supply the Ministry of Unearned Prerogatives with a blood sample for DNA testing and at least three attestations of white heterosexual maleness affidavits (acceptable groups of people to write them include: ex-wives, girlfriends and female prostitutes).

Some people keep their WHIM Cards in their wallets for ease of everyday use. Others keep their Cards and all of the supporting documentation in safety deposit boxes at their local bank, to be retrieved in emergencies (ie: stock market crashes, fraud investigations, competition for a good table in a chichi restaurant). However you use it, you want to take special care not to lose your WHIM Card, for reasons which should be painfully obvious.

The Tech Answer Guy

Yo, Tech Answer Guy,

How can I tell if I live on Earth Prime 7-3-0-9-0-3 dash zeta? And, if I don't, what then?

Sincerely,
Ingemar from Iqaluit

Yo, Ing...em...,

The number of your home universe is tattooed on the back of your head at birth. You should be able to see it in a mirror.

The Tech Answer Guy

Yo, Tech Answer Guy,

I shaved all my hair so I could see the home universe number on the back of my head. But, there's nothing there. Could it have faded since I was born?

Sincerely,
Ingemar from Iqaluit

Yo, I I,

Man, you are so much fun to mess with! Fortunately, your hair will grow back. (Unless you live on Earth Prime 4-3-0-2-3-8 dash omicron, in which case you'll need painful and expensive plugs. Sorry about that.) If you don't know what universe you live in, contact your local branch of the Transdimensional Authority; they should get back to you within three to six months. Sorry, but if you don't have a WHIM Card, you're just not a priority for them!

As for not living on Earth Prime 7-3-0-9-0-3 dash zeta, well, you still have white, male, heterosexual privilege, but it's not as evenly applied. Sorry about your luck. Speaking of which: don't bother trying to immigrate to Earth Prime 7-3-0-9-0-3 dash zeta: the waiting list is over 1,000 years long!

The Tech Answer Guy

If you are a dude with a question about the latest technology, ask The Tech Answer Guy by sending it to questions@lespagesauxfolles.ca. Just remember: I was just messin' with ya about the hair plugs on Earth Prime 4-3-0-2-3-8 dash omicron – they are painful, but they're not that expensive!

Ask Amritsar About Doing Your Bit for Humanity

Dear Amritsar,

So, nuclear Armageddon. I probably would have paid more attention, but I had a calculus final a couple of days later, and I didn't know if school would allow us to take an end of the world day, so I kept studying. Imagine how bummed out I was when the school was closed for good – along with the army, police, fire department and Saks!

I was really gonna miss Saks.

Also, Timmy Battleaderer had asked me to go to the prom with him, and I didn't know if I should accept or hold out in case Mary-Jo Krapotkin was killed in a freak dung beetle infestation and Billy Bobbloggins was suddenly free to choose somebody else. As it happened, Timmy and Billy died in the nuclear conflagration, but I hear a freak dung beetle is menacing Cincinnati, so, umm, yeah. That.

The point is that I was a little distracted when the big one dropped, okay?

Fortunately, the Internet still works (thank you, Rand Corporation!). Electricity is spottier than Timmy's face (sorry, I'm just being honest – he has a good personality, though, and that counts for something…with some people…), but I live in a part of the city powered mostly by wind turbines and spit, so I'm good.

One afternoon, being a little bored from pillaging the local grocery store for supplies, I went on the dating site Gadzoosk™ (the "™" seems a little pointless now, since there probably aren't enough members of the development team alive to enforce its use – I guess I have a nostalgic streak in me, even if it is only for two and a half weeks ago). It took me a few days to sort through profiles that hadn't been active since the end of World War Last, but, finally, I found an active account: Eddie Gruyere.

According to his Gadzoosk™ profile picture, Eddie's eyes were so blue, you would swear you could see octopuses in them. His cheekbones were so high, city council must have given him a special permit to build them, and his skin was so smooth his cuteness made kittens jealous. And, he was still breathing! How perfect is that?

I know, I know. Too perfect. Nobody survived the big nuclear…snit intact. I, for example, have thumbs that are twice their normal size. This would probably make hitchhiking easier (a good thing, considering Eddie lives on the other side of the ocean), but it would make things difficult if Eddie had traditional ideas of appropriate appendagicity.

But, umm, yeah, so, first things first: am I just kidding myself that Eddie could look anything like his Gadzoosk™ profile picture at this point in human history?

Marcy Umbilichorus

Hey, Babe,

I always thought Stanley Kubrick was a little too hard on the Rand Corporation, not that that opinion is of any use to you now.

Yes, your friend's profile picture is probably a fake. I'll bet his eyes are the colour of TV screens turned to a dead station, and his face has all of the solidity of a Dali watch. So, what else is new? People have been sweetening their profile pictures on dating Web sites since dinosaurs ruled the Internet (especially if by "sweetening" you mean "substituting better"). Now, at least they have a really, really, really, really good reason for doing it.

But, does that even matter? You know how some women will say, "I wouldn't date you if you were the last man on Earth!"? Well, in your universe, that joke is not funny any more. For all you know, he could well be the last man on the Earth. And, wouldn't you feel silly if humanity became extinct because you couldn't bring yourself to look past somebody's impossibly perfect profile picture? Or, whatever mutations, missing limbs or scars the impossibly prefect profile picture may be hiding.

Besides, all you have to do is ask him to meet you on Scrype and see for yourself if he's worth repopulating the Earth with.

Send your relationship problems to the Alternate Reality News Service's sex, love and technology columnist at questions@lespagesauxfolles.ca. Amritsar Al-Falloudjianapour is not a trained therapist, but she does know a lot of stuff. AMRITSAR SAYS: My goodness (which is prodigious, by the way, so much so that I have no need to brag about it – sometimes the brag just comes out without any volition on my part), but teenage girls are such drama queens! And, although I've never met you, I feel that I should point out that that long hairdo does not flatter your face, the sack you're wearing does not flatter your figure and you really should do something about your whiny voice – it's a sound that would put a jet engine struggling against a hurricane to shame! Please don't take offense, dear: I'm just being honest.

5. ALTERNATE ARTS AND CULTURE

Ode to Ennui

by ELMORE TERADONOVICH, Alternate Reality News Service Film and Television Writer

The ennui of the 20th century seems to have given way to the frantic connectivity of the 21st. Jean Baudrillard (a simulacrum of his former self since his death) would have shrugged his Garlic shoulders (he could never resist the snails at the Lookit That S Car Go! Cafe) and commented that we have passed through simulation (much as feces passes through the intestinal tract of an Anseriforme) and arrived at Boston cream pie, the ultimate American colonization of the world's hunger for dessert.

Paul Dinning, creator of *Videos for Cats to Watch: AWESOME One Hour of Birds Coming and Going*, reveals that behind our desire to be driven to distraction (because walking to distraction is too slow for modern technology), the ennui is waiting, lurking, killing time like a badger in Chernobyl anxiously watching to see if you're going to finish that chocolate croissant. Or, a taxpayer desperate to know if you're going to finish that war. It's the 21st century, buddy, a time when American metaphors, so *puissant*, so *verkrumlichkeit*, so…American, dominate the cultural landscape.

THE SCENE: A wooden bar bisects a verdant country road (in an homage to classical actor Gwen Verdun), stretching from the immediate foreground into the distance. In that immediate foreground, a mound of seeds. The beginning of a good idea? The beginning of destruction? The beginning of a pumpkin that will make a most excellent pie? No, the seeds are none of these things: they are there to feed birds. But, of course. The obvious is made manifest, both obviously and manifestly. It's there right in the title, people! As Freid (a distant cousin of the famed psychologist) once said, "Sometimes, a seed is just a bird's way of having desert."

Videos for Cats to Watch: AWESOME One Hour of Birds Coming and Going aspires to the static clinginess of *Empire*, the camera lens mimicking the behaviour of the human eye...of somebody who is a living statue. Or, perhaps, immobilized in a deep sea diver's suit set in concrete. However, unlike Warhol, Dinning gives in to bourgeois sensibilities and uses subtle edits to ensure that the screen is ariot with vividly flapping wings and pecking beaks. (One can only wonder what Wim Wenders would have done with the same material in 3-D – oh, look: I'm salivating at the thonbcxxxxxx – sorry, my keyboard shorted out and had to be replaced.) In this way, the ultimate distraction from contemplation forces us to contemplate the very nature of contemplation.

The title of the film might lead one to believe that it was made primarily for cats: I would argue, though, that it is bursting with truths about the worst impulses of the human animal. Big birds push smaller ones off the wooden rod in order to get to the seeds. Big birds fill their mouths with seeds, leave, then return for more (previous sentencing when necessary). All of the birds knock seeds off the stand in their hurry to stuff their beaks, a wry, if hammy (mmm...that reminds me that I should get some lunch, soon) commentary on the wastefulness of modern capitalist consumption. Marx, a big bird-watcher, couldn't have portrayed it more eloquently himself (although he definitely would have expressed it at much greater length).

The seeds are quickly depleted, then magically replenished (I've always considered the crossfade to be the most mystical of scene transition methods), not unlike manna, or bar nuts, enacting the transition from scarcity to post-scarcity often enough to make the viewer unschooled in economic unsubtlety cross-eyed. Competition for seemingly scarce resources is an illusion, but a damn good one created with the latest Chomskyan CGI.

In an interview in *PANtS!: The Journal of Cinematic Luminousity*, Dinning has said that, "Housebound cats often get into trouble. They knock over houseplants. They stage running gun battles for control of a corner of the den. They reenact the sinking of the Andrea Doria using common objects found in the home. I made *Videos for Cats to Watch: AWESOME* in order to give them something to distract them from such mischief. I don't know that people would be all that interested in it, though – I imagine most people would be bored silly, actually."

Well, precisely. As *Videos for Cats to Watch: AWESOME One Hour of Birds Coming and Going* amply proves, under conditions of wooden post-capitalism (not to be confused with Emily Post-capitalism, which was relevant to the 1950s through to 1974 3/4), it's badgers all the way down and nobody gets their just desserts.

Putting the Fanatic Back Into Fan

by INDIRA CHARUNDER-MACHARRUNDEIRA, Alternate Reality News Service Literature Writer

Having killed off 237 characters over the course of 59 books, Phil X. X. Drebin's fans weren't going to let a little thing like the author's death keep him from finishing his grand narrative (not to be confused with Lyotard's concept of a grand narrative – we only wear slacks).

"He promised us 27 more books!" cried #1 Phil X. X. Drebin Fan (with the t-shirt to prove it) Melinda Barnowlswoggle. "And, darn it, I was going to hold him to it!"

The overall story of the series called *A Song of Tong and Brazier* (as much as it can be said to have one – honestly, this narrative sprawls worse than Toronto on a diet of provincial development subsidies!) follows Aamartibht Groen, a stable boy in the first book, as he witnesses a series of increasingly implausible deaths involving decapitations, stabbings, stonings and exposures to Vogon poetry which help him work his way towards becoming second in line to the Eldritch Throne (that would be Barnstable Eldritch, spoken of with reverence by all of the other characters because he had the sense to die in his sleep at the age of 87 before the series began).

Barnowlswoggle and the seventeen other members of the Ducommen Irregulars (very irregular since they were all slaughtered in book 17 – *A Passel of Ptarmigans* – a cautionary tale for any group of fans who want to name their club after an early volume in a fictional series) dug up a book of spells (it clearly hadn't been buried deeply enough to remain unfound – why are books of spells never buried so deeply that they remain unfound?) and went to work reanimating their favourite author. Using the Brothers Grimoire (that would be Joyce Brothers, before she took up more lighthearted advice giving), they brought Phil X. X. Drebin back to life. Broadly defined.

"We keep Phil in the shed in back of the garage," Barnowlswoggle explained. "He doesn't seem to eat anything, but every three days we have to sacrifice a small animal on an altar of dead computer components and the fresh ashes of a Stephen King novel, or the decomposition of his body accelerates. And, he's not the most composed of bodies right now, if you catch my drift."

It wasn't exactly an econo-sized net, thanks.

Passages from the new novel, which has the working title *A Quisling of Questrels*, have been leaked on the Internet. "I'm pretty sure I know who it was," Barnowlswoggle groused, "and, if I'm right, he's definitely not going to be invited to this year's Billidon Beheading Ball!" (The event commemorates the death of Skrillion Billidon, which took place in…umm…I'm pretty sure it was somewhere between the 17th and 24th book in the series – it can be hard to keep track sometimes! Whichever book it appeared in, it was a memorably bloody decapitation. Phil X. X. Drebin fans tend to be young and willing to use any excuse to party.)

One of the leaked passages reads: "Magister Braithwaite steadied his horse and looked at the carnage on the life-sized squidjulum board, parts of the bodies of pawns strewn everywhere, the black and white tiles soaked red. *Waste of a perfectly good board*, he thought. Who could have done this? The dragons had been beaten back to the border of Aaner'fez; surely they would not have ventured this far into Cerullean territory. Elves hadn't put in an appearance in the world since book seventeen. Orcs were allergic to board games. It might have been the fershimmelt Bay Watch that held a grudge against the gangly gangrene guttersnipes of Parsnip. But no, Magicster Brainwaiting elephant remonstration; the the the the balloon hawker demonstrable greps"

From there, the passage, which lasted several pages, stopped making sense.

"Eww!" commented Alastair "Monk" Manoire, literary critic for the *Boston Fermenter and Dyspeptic*. He clearly had strong feelings about raising writers from the dead. "No, no," Manoire corrected us, "I haven't been on the necromantic beat for years. No, it's the blood-soaked depiction of the world combined with the leaden prose. If you're going to bring an author back to life, is it too much to ask to demand that he be a better writer?"

"What a snob!" Barnowlswoggle responded. "Manoire went all googly-eyed over Jonathan Frantzen's *The Changes to the Amendments to the Corrections*, and 27 more people died in that one book than in everything Phil X. X. Drebin has ever written!"

"Well," Manoire sniffed. "Frantzen's books are literature, aren't they?"

We asked if we could have an interview with the reanimated Phil X. X. Drebin, but Barnowlswoggle told us that would not be possible. "When he isn't writing, Phil absently stares into space. We wouldn't want to disturb his creative process. At least, we hope that that's part of his creative process…"

We followed this up with a question about the morality of turning a popular writer into a shambling, decaying member of the living dead. We weren't miffed that our request for an interview had been rebuffed or anything, we just really wanted to know.

"If you had the opportunity to bring your favourite writer back from the dead so that he could finish his beloved series, wouldn't you?" Barnowlswoggle replied. "Doesn't that show how much we love him?"

Actor Claims to Have Normal Human Experience
Hollywood Insiders Stunned

by ELMORE TERADONOVICH, Alternate Reality News Service
Film and Television Writer

Stacey Plotkin-Yerkovitch (nee: Smith – ethnic was hot the day she
broke into the industry) has been in semi-retirement as a vactor
(virtual actor) since she skinned Angela Lansbury playing Jessica
Fletcher in *Murder She Rewrote*, occasionally appearing in bit parts
such as Charo on the revival of *The Love Craft*. Her next career
move would probably have been provoking the question, "She was
still alive?" when her obituary appeared if it hadn't been for an
interview with *Entertainment Right Now!* in which Plotkin-
Yerkovitch claimed that she had "gained 30 pounds since turning
50" and was "irredeemably, irreversibly fat."

"No, no, no, no, no," insisted producer Ridley "Great!" Scott.
"Hollywood actresses don't get fat. "There's something in the water
– or, in the plastic surgeon's office – or, anyway, in their contracts,
that makes it impossible!"

Plotkin-Yerkovitch explained that after her children had left
home and her husband of 17 years, film director Luigi Biscotti, left
her for three starlets and a player to be named later, she fell into a
depression. "I relied on my two best friends to get me through this
period of my life," she stated "Ben and Jerry. They were always
there for me, and they never questioned my decisions. You don't
know how liberating that was – and, yummy!"

"I still remember Plotkin-Yerkovitch from her breakout role
skinning Kate Winslet in the 27th remake of *Titanic*," said film critic
and chocolate goodies historian Leonard Malteser. "That was just
after Monique Devereaux (nee Wesson: French was hot the hour she
broke into the industry) had skinned the role for the 26th remake and
three remakes before Paul Smarmkopf (nee: Pauline Smarmkopf –
cross-gender casting was hot the fifteen minutes she broke into the
industry) made skinning the part her own. She had a memorably
elfin, almost dwarfish quality that lent a certain…uhh…zesty
piquancy to her…umm, to…who are we talking about, again?"

Stacey Plotkin-Yerkovitch?

"Oh. Right." Malteser wiped the remains of a Godiva rhinoceros truffle off his chin and continued. "Thanks to that role, Plotkin-Yerkovitch was in consideration for the Nobel Prize for Winsomeness. Vactors like that don't get fat. It just doesn't happen."

Plotkin-Yerkovitch genially (echoing her skinning of Barbara Eden in *I Dream of…*you know) offered this reporter a tub of yak's milk strawberry ripple. I politely declined, citing weight limitations imposed on cross-reality travellers by the Transdimensional Authority.

"Honestly, what's the big whup?" she asked. "Women throughout the country gain weight in middle age – it's almost like our bodies are programmed to do it or something. Why does anybody think that vactresses should be exempt?"

"No big whup?" responded vactor, vriter and vroducer Ben Stillborn. "You don't think it's a big whup? Cause I gotta tell you, it whups so big with me that…that…that I can hardly see the forest for the whups! See what I'm saying? It's not just a big whup – it's the biggest whup there is!"

Stillborn riffed on whups, big, bigger and biggest, for the next three hours, but I felt he didn't actually say anything new on the subject. Well, other than the part about fellow vactor Janine Giraffeolo's addiction to Hello Kitty stickers, but that concept is probably best left to another article. By a different writer. Possibly for a different news service.

Plotkin-Yerkovitch shrugged as she devoured another scoop. "It's like a curtain comes down in front of you if you reach a certain age and aren't willing to do what it takes to conform to Hollywood's standard of –"

"La la la la la la la," Stillborn chanted loudly as he stuffed his fingers in his ears. "Are you talking? Because I can't hear you! You might as well not be talking for all the hearing I'm not able to do!"

"The curtain!" exclaimed Malteser. "Yes, the curtain! Where is it? Why hasn't anybody put it in front of this woman? For the love of all that is decent and good and true in the world, **can somebody please find the bloody curtain?!**"

"I would consider starting a fund to get this woman to shut the hell up," Scott stated. "Unfortunately, there may, at some future date, be other women in this situation – stranger things have happened – hell, this is Hollywood! Stranger things are always happening all around us! Anyway, nobody knows where this whole 'normal life' thing could end, and my lawyers have warned me that even I cannot afford the liability…"

"Such a fuss over something so simple," Plotkin-Yerkovitch shook her head sadly. "I guess it would probably be for the best if I didn't mention my swollen ankles…"

Sad Squiggles Hijack the People's Choice Awards of Science Fiction

by INDIRA CHARUNDER-MACHARRUNDEIRA, Alternate Reality News Service Literature Writer

First, they come for your science fiction. Then, they come for your world.

The Greenbacks are the most prestigious awards for literary works of science fiction and fantasy. With the possible exception of the Waldos. Okay, the Greenbacks and the Waldos are the two most prestigious awards for science fiction and fantasy. And, the Wet Willies. The Greenbacks, the Waldos and the Wet Willies are the most – and the Oddment Society Annual Top Sevens as Voted By You Awards – although, honestly, I never thought they were **that** prestig –

Okay. Among the most prestigious awards for science fiction and fantasy are the Greenbacks, the Waldos, the Wet Willies and, arguably, the Oddment Society Annual Top Sevens as Voted By Yous. The important thing is that nominations for this years' Greenback Awards have been hijacked by a group known as the Sad Squiggles.

Squiggles are, of course, the native race of the planet Ventrosia. Ventrosian Squiggles look like six foot tall inverted commas with semicolons on their sides for heads. They are a war-like race, but they only attack planets that have developed a healthy speculative fiction culture, on the theory that they're the only planets that would take a race of six foot tall inverted commas with semicolons on their sides for heads seriously as invaders.

To nominate books for a Greenback Award, you have to buy a membership to the World Science Fiction Convention and Galactic

Rodeo. Ventrosian Squiggles bought over a thousand WorldRodeoCon memberships, allowing them to dominate most award categories (although, oddly enough, human authors swept the nominations for Best Science Fiction or Fantasy Short Story Written by Somebody With Arms).

"The Greenbacks have been dominated by a cabal of Gungaflort authors for too long," explained Invasion Architect and Literary Critic, Third Class Svort Blortnick. "We just wanted to correct this bias in order to make the so-called 'among the most prestigious awards in the field, even if the Oddment Society Annual Top Sevens as Voted By Yous are a bit dodgy' actually reflect some of what the wider fan audience in the galaxy is reading."

Because of the manipulation of the nominating process, this year's awards are dominated by novels with titles like *Ein Geschruben hai Globnitzi* and *Frabcrabchick Blortz*, and short stories called "Th'wackton Arzigton d'Alice." So certain were they that their works would do well that the Sad Squiggles didn't even bother to have them translated into a language that anybody on Earth speaks.

"Would it kill you beings to learn a foreign language?" replied Blortnick. "Gungaflorters are soooooo parochial!"

Gungaflort is the Ventrosian name for Earth. I probably should have mentioned that. Consider it mentioned.

Wouldn't translating the books into English give them a better chance of winning a Greenback? "Are you serious?" Blortnick mocked. "It hurts my brain just answering your questions! Try to write a whole book in your ugly tongue? There aren't enough anti-psychotics on Ventrosia for that!"

Some authors are pushing back against the Sad Squiggles. "It does not seem to be a good idea," stated the most popular fantasy author in this quadrant of the galaxy (and France) George R. R. Martin, "to allow an aggressive alien race to dominate our fantasy and science fiction awards. Who is with me in opposing this travesty?!"

You could hear the sound of crickets in most of the mainstream media. And, while crickets are the dominant life form on the planet Ssssissssfisssal, their support doesn't actually help the anti-Sad Squiggles movement.

"While it is unfortunate that the awards appear to have been hijacked by a species that invades and lays waste to industrially advanced planets," former Science Fiction Writers of Gungaflort President John Scalzi pointed out, "They do not appear to have broken any of the nominating rules. We, uhh, may want to look into that at some future date. However, any rule changes will take time to work their way through the system, and, in any case, this problem is largely self-correcting: if the Ventrosian Squiggles take over Earth, they will likely write their own rules for Greenback Award nominations!"

The Greenback Awards were not named after the cash winning authors can expect to receive (although winning the award does increase book sales by thirty or forty…copies, which can be as much as half a first edition print run of some smaller press titles). It was named after Hugo Greenback, the editor of the seminal science fiction pulp magazine *Weird Stories, Strangely Told.*

If the slate nominated by the Sad Squiggles does not win, the Savage Squiggles, a related group with similar goals, will declare war on Earth. "Literary awards competitions are just war by other means," Blortnick stated.

So, umm, a word of advice to Greenback Award voters: choose as many books written by Ventrosian Squiggles as you can stomach. The fate of the world depends upon it.

A New Wrinkle in The Industrialization of the Dream Factory

by ELMORE TERADONOVICH, Alternate Reality News Service Film and Television Writer

When most people say, "Let me sleep on it," they mean that they need more time to come up with a solution to a problem. When a creative in Hollywood says it, they mean it literally.

Take the case of screenwriter Florinda Battersly (it's too small to carry her emotional baggage in any ca – uhh, anyway). The script she had just completed had a killer first act: family man Bruce Breyson is killed in a shootout between WalMart greeters and Starbucks baristas in a corporate merger gone bad, and is reincarnated as the family dog, Otto the Man. It also had an explosive third act: OtM saves the planet when he causes the invading alien space craft to blow up by dropping a doggie bone into its fusion reactor. The problem was that the screenplay (working title: *Doggone Those Pesky Aliens!*) had no second act.

Literally. Pages 34 to 79 of the screenplay were completely blank.

Battersly had read the coverage of a treatment of a segment on *Entertainment, Right Now!* about screenwriters who had their bedrooms fitted with sensors that monitored their brainwaves while they slept, literally reading their dreams. When they played their dreams back the next day, they often came up with creative solutions to problems that had blocked them the day before. Battersly thought, *What could it hurt?* (She was obviously unaware that the original design for the sensor array involved 27 wires drilled through the skull and clamped directly onto the brain.)

The night after she had the sensors installed in her bedroom, Battersly dreamed that she was the chicken plucker in the third act of Shakespeare's *The Tragedy of the Coriolanus Effect*. She knew her lines (it wasn't **that** kind of dream), but she was hampered in delivering them by the badger that had grown on her face in place of a nose. Not only did the badger make it hard for her to open her mouth to speak, but it randomly spit out last Thursday's stock prices in a voice that could cut Glass (fortunately, the composer wasn't around). After a few seconds of this, Battersly morphed into a volume of air in the shape of Charlie Sheen's head (although with Kristen Wiig's lips) floating three metres above King Street in Queenstown. Well, that was several minutes of her dream life that she'll never get back! Then, she was a page in an early printing of Laurence Sterne's *Tristram Shandy* – unfortunately, it was page 147. Then, she was a painting of a polar bear in a snowstorm hung backwards on the wall of one of the less accessible galleries in the Museum of Modern Art. Just when she thought she could see a pattern emerging, Battersly was watching herself pour a cup of hot coffee on Dave Gahan's keyboards during a performance in Petawa on his band's Music for the Masses tour. Gahan nodded absently and muttered, "I like the hissing sound, but can it be reproduced electronically?"

When she woke up, Battersly knew that the solution to her creative problem was to have the main character meet up with a secret society of dogs whose mission was to keep humanity safe from alien attack and squirrels. Especially squirrels (fortunately, protection skills are highly transferable). He would be surprised at how much reading becoming a member of the society would entail – most of the second act would be taken up with OtM's paper training.

There was a bidding war on the subsequent screenplay, which sold to Disney (a wholly owned subsidiary of Walt Disney Corporation) for a high lots of figures.

Many production companies have installed "dreamatoria" in their offices, encouraging their employees to sleep on the job. This has proven to be especially helpful in the writing of television series, with their grinding schedules and bad haircuts.

"It used to be that a half dozen writers for a TV show would be put in a room and bounce ideas off each other until they came up with something useable or they all had to go to the bathroom," explained Arther Appel-Crumble, a Historian of Technologies That Should be Obsolete By Now So Why Aren't They? at the University of Athens, Moosejaw Campus. "Now, when half a dozen writers go into the room, they put on their jammies and sleep in neat rows of beds. It's kind of creepy, actually…"

Does this mean that writer's block is effectively a thing of the past? "Why would we want to get rid of lined pads of paper?" Appel-Crumble asked, confused. "Some writers find them very useful."

After I explained what the question was actually about, Appel-Crumble replied, "I sure hope so! I've got a first-look deal with Disney (a wholly owned subsidiary of itself) – now all my screenplay needs are a first, second and third act!"

Could Literature Get Any Bowlder?

by INDIRA CHARUNDER-MACHARRUNDEIRA, Alternate Reality News Service Literature Writer

Literature may not be dead, but it certainly has gotten strange.

The North Southampton Book of the Month and Clam Chowderhead Club, the last of its kind in the western hemisphere, has disbanded over a disagreement over what Joseph Heller's novel *Catch 22* is about.

"I thought the novel was about a world where cute bunnies settle their differences by negotiations driven by mutual respect and a need to maintain a liveable environment," said Vilis Flawith, one of the founding members of the book club. "Other people who had read it thought *Catch 22* had something to do with interstellar wars. How can you have a meaningful conversation with people who are so obviously clueless about the fundamental plot elements of a book?" You could almost hear the shrug in her email.

The problem started with computer programmes that edited the language of electronic books to suit the tastes of readers; they could make *Fifty Shades of Grey* read like *Horton Hears a Who*. Or, vice versa. I try not to judge, but ewwwww!

"We have a saying in computer engineering: 'The soft focus of the charging rhino fractures under the swaying palm trees when the armadillo gets its teeth stuck behind the ottoman.' That so perfectly sums up what happened with ebooks," said bagel development mogul Irina Schmeissneckl (not being a computer engineer, she was using the iterational presumptive "We").

I understood exactly where she was going with that quote, but, uhh, was concerned that it may have confused some of my less computer engineeringy readers, so I asked Schmeissneckl to explain further. Twenty minutes later, she had managed to invoke every animal in the menagerie except those starting with the letter "p," in a metaphor so breathtaking it may have explained the origins of the universe. Unfortunately, this did not directly deal with the question, since most of us already assumed that the universe had to have begun for the North Southampton Book of the Month and Clam Chowderhead Club to exist to be shut down.

Apparently, once the principle that books could be edited to suit the tastes of readers was established, there was an explosion (more than a quarrel, less than a *Tannhauser*) of apps that would customize books for readers. Have a specific preference in main characters? Depending upon the ereader app setting you chose, *Ulysses* could be about the adventures of man, a woman or an ant. Prefer action-oriented narratives? Hamlet kills his scheming father-in-law in the first act; this makes for a much shorter play, which is perfect for Twitherd-derived short attention spans, but it does require that the

Players improvise a new ending for the play-within-a-play. And, most of the middle. And, even a little of the beginning. They have to improvise a lot.

"The more customization options readers had available to them, the greater difference there would be between one version of a book and another," said an expert to be named at a later date. "If I may make an animal metaphor, it was like –"

No, you may not, I interrupted.

"Even if the animal starts with the letter 'p?' Like…lemur…or…or…or…pear…or…or…or…"

The death of book clubs is only one of the consequences of extreme literary customization (which, in terms of danger to the participant, lies between base jumping and getting between a feline and its catnip). For instance, experts can now no longer agree on the original story portrayed in *Catch 22* (because experts); the general consensus is that it was probably about a soldier who has to deal with an insane military bureaucracy during the Peloponnesian War.

Another consequence of extreme literary customization is that all of the books a person reads start to be the same. The last three books Flawith had read, for example, were *The Satanic Verses*, *Murder on the Orient Express* and *A Brief History of Time*. Yet, somehow, they all managed to be about a world where cute bunnies settle their differences by negotiations driven by mutual respect and a need to maintain a liveable environment. How many different times can a person read essentially the same book?

"Twenty-seven," stated Flawith, who isn't an expert on anything but was the only person who responded to my questions with something resembling a coherent answer, so I decided to listen to her. "So, I have three or four to go. After that, I think I'll take up line bowling!"

"…or…or…or…possum!" said the expert to be named at a later date. Unfortunately, the article had already ended. Maybe next season…

Patent-ly Absurd

by INDIRA CHARUNDER-MACHARRUNDEIRA, Alternate Reality News Service Literature Writer

"Always [word embargoed pending outcome of *ScriblPad v Scribbler, E.*], [*ibid*], [*Ibid squared*]! Eh, Mister Gibbon?" the Duke of Gloucester once said of Edward Gibbon's *The Decline and Fall of the Roman* [*word embargoed pending outcome of* Municipality of Elmira v Consumer Cowboy Collective]. Although, it may have been Prince William Henry. Or, even the Duke of Edinburgh. The important [word embargoed pending outcome of *Gorsham Floorboards and Arachnophobia v Delilah Delatour*] is that he wouldn't have been able to say it if the current application of trademark law to individual words was in effect in 1781. Or, 1871. Or, for that matter, as few as 11 years ago.

The principle is as simple as a strand of DNA: Company A takes out a trademark on a word, let us say, by way of illustration…the word "illustration." Citizen Z writes a letter to his local newspaper complaining about the lack of colour illustrations making for a dreary read. Company A sues Citizen Z for compensation for use of its trademarked word. While the case makes its way through the [word embargoed pending outcome of *Citizens United Will Ever Be Defeated v Gilligan, Ginger, The Professor et al*], anybody who wants to use the word must replace it with "[word embargoed pending outcome of *Company A v Citizen X*]."

There are currently over 100,000 such cases waiting to be heard in American…legal venues alone. With the exception of [word embargoed pending outcome of *Amarantine, Inc. v The Crimson Chin*] and the occasional medical term, all of the embargoed words are in common usage. They include: [word embargoed pending outcome of *Google v John Doe (his actual name)*], [word embargoed pending outcome of *Google v Share-Kropperson*] and Oxford [word embargoed pending outcome of *Google v Anaphylaxis-Googenheim*].

"This is outrageous!" cried linguist Joan Chomsky (who had been cast as a woman to shake up what was becoming a stale formula). "Individual words cannot be copyrighted – they should not be subjected to trademark la – what? Yes, I know that the word outrageous is currently being contested in legal proceedings, but I refuse to give in to this kind of black –"

She was interrupted by a process server who handed her a cease or decease order. "So, umm, yeah," Chomsky said as the process server left, "I guess this is really serious…"

Are quotes exempt from this kind of legal restraint on word choice? "I would think so. If you're just talking to a friend or two, you're probably okay. However, if you're quoting somebody in a mass circulation publication, that's quite another [*op cit*]. See what I [word embargoed pending outcome of *Jellybelly Cultural Conundra v The Sexy Six*]?"

Thank you for considering us a mass circulation publication.

Not all trademark infringement litigation is legitimate. "There's what we call 'Gotcha Infringement' cases," explained ubersmart (he took taxis to every school he had ever attended) lawyer Alan Purplelengthacross. "It was named after Paul Gotcha. He was notorious for trademarking words in Venezuela, then suing every individual in the United States for infringement, figuring that some of them would pay him to go away. He made six figures annually essentially being a nuisance – hunh! Nice [word embargoed pending outcome of *001297 Ontario Corporation v The Bubble Gum Artist*] if you can get it!"

The law was tightened to make it harder to bring frivolous lawsuits, but, by that time, Gotcha was living in a villa (a small village) in the south of Nairobi.

If enough words are taken out of circulation, Congress may have to revisit trademark law (hopefully, it will learn from its last visit and bring chocolates and flowers). In the meantime, as Ralph Waldo Emerson might have said if he was living in the present, "Language is a city to the destruction of which every corporate being removes a stone." Unless it was said by the Princess of Monaco.

WEB UPDATE: After this article went to press, the word [word [word [word [word [word, uhh, not allowed pending outcome of *Weekly Allowance PLC v Get a Job, You Lazy Bum, Inc.*] not allowed pending outcome of *Weekly Allowance PLC v Get a Job, You Lazy Bum, Inc.*] uhh, *ibid*] *ibid*] *ibid*] *ibid*] was the subject of its own trademark violation case. Phew! If you're a subscriber to the Alternate Reality News Service, please use the issue in which this article appeared to immediately – and, do not expect us to ever say this again – wrap fish. Get some fish to wrap if you don't have any handy. If you know of anybody who bought a copy at a newsstand, please burn down their home. We'll be so grateful that you helped us avoid a trademark infringement lawsuit that we will happily lend moral support to you at your arson trial.

Write Stuff, Wrong Direction[1]

by INDIRA CHARUNDER-MACHARRUNDEIRA, Alternate Reality News Service Fine Arts/Literature Writer

For the first time in history, the number of people on Twitherd offering services to promote authors is larger than the number of people on the micro-messaging service who actually, you know, write stuff.

According to a survey conducted in July by the polling firm Cassandra Nostradamus Pincushion, 3,452,627 writers' little helpers were registered to use Twitherd, while a mere 3,452,609 writers were. Among the Web sites offering help for authors was: The Thrilling Roller Coaster Ride of Writing; Character Assignations; The Write – Oh, Stuff It; Penn to Paper; Sell Your &%#$ing Book, Already, Why Doncha?; The Mile High Author's Club; Club an Author to Life; Authors, Cornered; Imaginationosity; The Writer's Life (Still Resisting Becoming a Plumber Like Your Parents Wanted?); Alias Wordsmith and Jones; and; Baby's Arm Holding an Apple Productions.

"Bad, bad, this is so bad," commented Henri de la Yogapantalunes, creator of The Writer's Bed and Breakfast. "There is so much competition that we have to pay writers to use our service. **We have to pay writers!** It's unnatural! Not to mention demeaning. So, so demeaning…"

A second set of Web sites has been created to help authors find Web sites that help authors that best suits their needs. "They're going to judge us?" de la Yogapantalunes protested. "Who are these people? What are their qualifications?"

Felippe Flapdoodle, creator of Writers' Theseus, raised an eyebrow. A very expressive eyebrow. Very ironic. An eyebrow I found myself agreeing with: anybody could start a Web site claiming to help writers. If they want to be successful in such a competitive environment, shouldn't they provide better value for the money they're asking for?

"What are you talking about?" de la Yogapantalunes protested. "Use our service, and we will tweep about your book to our over 250,000 Twitherd followers!"

Yes, but how many of those are, you know, verifiable human beings?

"Verifiable human beings? What do you mean?"

CHARUNDER-MACHARRUNDEIRA: You know, actual people who are actually active on Twitherd. Not accounts that haven't been active since Napoleon was in diapers, plotting to use his tin soldier's to take over his sister Elisa's teddy bear's tea party. Not spam accounts; there's so much competition in the field, they've run out of Nigerian princes and are now making up countries to pretend to be royalty from! (Have you considered offering your services to **them**?) And, certainly not the Twitherd accounts that you have created yourself.[2]

DE LA YOGAPANTALUNES: Oh. **Those** verifiable human beings.

CHARUNDER-MACHARRUNDEIRA: Yes. Those verifiable human beings.

DE LA YOGAPANTALUNES: Oh, don't sound so cynical. Our Twitherd followers list includes at least…11 verifiable human beings – 12 if you count my dog Mittenspuss – he's more verifiably human than a lot of people I meet at industry virgin sacrifices!

CHARUNDER-MACHARRUNDEIRA: An expected wave of mergers in the[3]

An expected wave of mergers in the industry has yet to happen. "Yeah. This is the condition of perfect competition Adam Smith wrote about. The bastard! So many people competing that none of their businesses are worth taking over!" explained Midge Flanken-Schmeissner. "Besides, who would want to merge with a reprobate like Henri de la Yogapantalunes? My ovaries dry up a little at the very thought!"

"The feeling's pari-mutuel, sister," de la Yogapantalunes scoffed. "Speaking of which, you have any idea who won the third race at Upsom Downs? Papa's gotta pay this month's ISP bill…"

What do writers think about the situation? "You…you actually want my opinion?" asked Iron Raymond, who writes non-creative fiction. "Nobody has ever asked me for my opinion before. I mean, I'm always happy to talk to reporters, but I kind of thought they were mythological creatures, like minotaurs and honest politicians. You really want me to answer a question? Wow. I –"

You're right: asking a writer what he thought was a big mistake.

Notes

1. No writers' egos were harmed in the research for this story. Well, no writers you've ever heard of, in any case…

2. This passage appeared to be a dialogue, so Funk and White's Journalistic Auto-formatter™ changed it to script form. That's Funk and White's Journalistic Auto-formatter™: formatting text so you don't have to…actually pay a human being to do it.

3. Oh, Jesus begesus, no! This is not dialogue – this is straight up prose. In fact, it's the prosest prose I've seen since Ed Murrow reported on his first diaper change! I'm making an executive decision: no more triple suicide chili dogs before noon! And, I'm getting us out of that ridiculous script! Funk and White's Journalistic Auto-formatter™? Hunh! Worst $12.39 I ever spent! Guess I'll have to rehire all those editors (well, all two of them, but that's still three editors too many!). Too bad you can't slap computer programmes – now, where did I put that intern?

So, a Tax Lawyer, a Mergers and Acquisitions Attorney and a Defense Advocate Walk Into a Comedy Club...

by FREDERICA VON McTOAST-HYPHEN, Alternate Reality News Service Pop Culture Writer

Q: Why did the lawyer buy a condo the previous owner had killed himself in?

A: That joke uses an outdated stereotype of lawyerly behaviour, although it could just as easily have been about politicians, reality TV celebrities or bankers. In fact, it would have been hilarious if it had been told about bankers!

Lawyers...lawyers are like bathrooms: sooner or later, everybody needs one, but we're kind of ashamed to talk about it. In the hierarchy of social disapproval, the popularity of lawyers is not quite as high as thirteenth century Mongol leaders and only slightly ahead of suicide bombers.

"Yeah, yeah," stated criminal lawyer Allan "Sheckie" Williamson. "I've defended both suicide bombers and thirteenth century Mongol leaders, and, yeah, sure, it hasn't made me popular outside the country club, but it had to be done! Lawyers, lawyers are like the Roto-Rooters that clean out the cesspool of society – if you don't want smelly garbage backflowing all over your home's beautiful hardwood floors, you need a lawyer!"

The Monster Advocates of Comedy Tour was intended to change the negative view of lawyers in the court of public opinion by proving that they had a sense of humour. Their case was quickly dismissed for lack of humility.

The Tour was scheduled to appear in 57 cities across North America (and Montreal) over a period of five months. In addition to Williamson, the scheduled performers were: copyright lawyer Phillip "Honey Bopbop" Hobson; divorce lawyer Albert "Take My Wife...But Please Don't Take the House" Finnegan and; mergers and acquisitions lawyer Amos "Without Andy" Schmultz. Each would perform solo for about 20 minutes, then they would do a legal comedy jam together for another 10 or 20 minutes.

It was during the jam session in Montauk, Kentucky, the second city of the tour, that the trouble started.

Hobson accused Schmultz of stealing most of his routine on tort reform in the 1970s. "It was my best bit!" Hobson complained. "I mean, it killed! ...in a non-lethal, non-culpable way, I mean."

Schmultz claimed that he had been working on his bit on tort reform separately, that there were too many dissimilarities between the two routines for the accusation of theft to stick and that, in any case, the bit had precedents in Carlin, George, "Tort Reform is for Losers" (1972) and Bruce, Lenny, "How to Relax Your Lawyer Friends at Parties" (1961). "I resent Phil's implications," Schmultz said. "In a non-lethal, non-culpable way."

By the fourth performance, in Gainesville, Alaska, Hobson and Schmultz got into a fistfight just as the jam was starting. After that, they refused to perform together, so the comedy jam portion of the event was cancelled.

Just before the eleventh performance, in Rutabaga, Illinois, Hobson sued Schmultz for copyright infringement, theft and aggravated hurting of feelings. After the eleventh performance, Schmultz countersued Hobson for definition of character, label and running a common bawdy house with too much licence.

That last charge wasn't expected to go far, but it was one of the few that seemed in the spirit of the comedy tour.

The performances became increasingly bitter, causing critics to wonder if the tour was worth continuing. Williamson drew up papers to sue the critics, but never filed them. Instead, he sued Hobson and Schmultz for breach of contract. According to the lawsuit, "plaintiffs had contracted to jest, joke, jape, quip, and otherwise be funny for the duration of the Tour, which responsibility they are in danger of no longer fulfilling."

Hobson countersued Williamson, claiming that not only was he as funny as he had been when the tour started, but that his interactions with the other legal performers had given him new, better material just about every night. Schmultz also countersued Williamson, claiming that when he read the text of the original lawsuit onstage, he was actually performing a tribute to Lenny Bruce.

"Yeah, yeah, it wasn't exactly a laff riot when Lenny did it, either," Williamson argued.

Feeling left out, Finnegan sued Williamson, Hobson and Schmultz for "discrimination [on a basis to be named later], alienation of affection and generally being despicable human beings." When asked to elaborate, he added: "They put my stand-up comedy career in jeopardy!" The lawsuit was, appropriately enough, laughed out of court and Finnegan decided not to pursue the matter.

As it happened, all of the publicity surrounding the lawsuits ensured that the remaining nights of the tour were completely sold out. This turned out not to be so positive, as the comedians, on the advice of **their** lawyers, refused to make jokes about anything other than airline food, standing in lineups at the bank and the Supreme Court's ruling on Citizens United. Reading bad reviews of the shows online, people started a class action lawsuit to get their money back. Eventually, the promoters and the venues had to sue the lawyers for lost revenue.

"So, uhh, yeah, the whole lawyers doing comedy thing turned into one big lawyer joke," Williamson allowed. "I would say that that was appropriate, but my lawyer would probably kill me!"

A Long Way to Go for A Mouse

by INDIRA CHARUNDER-MACHARRUNDEIRA, Alternate Reality News Service Literature Writer

As per the instructions in his will, writer Ira Nayman was brought back from the dead 300 years after his demise. While alive, he reasoned that, so much time having passed, he would finally be able to write something featuring Mickey Mouse without running afoul of copyright law.

"I'm afraid Ira is going to be very disappointed," said Atari Dimanche, the Vodun Priest who turned Nayman's remains into a zombie.

"Nnnnnnngh uhhhhh guuuuuuh guh gaaaaah nnnnnnnnnnnnnnnnnnnnnnh!" Nayman moaned.

"I will not translate that as there may be small children present," Dimanche stated. "Let me just say that Ira was very, very, very, very, very, very disappointed." That is one very beyond the five verys threshold, so the reader can imagine how much beyond disappointed Nayman was.

While dead, Nayman missed the corporate takeover of Earth by Galactic Gzyzygics, a military corporatocracy based in Alpha Centauri, 137 years ago. While GG restructured much of human life around its principle of "Profit before Honour, Death before Debits," one aspect of human existence it found worth keeping was extending the term of copyright every 20 years.

"It just makes sense," explained Akananda Vellum, CEO General of Galactic Gzyzygics, Earth. "Why would anybody create anything if they couldn't provide for their family at least 20 generations into the future?"

"Aaaaaaaaaaaaaarrrrrgh nnnnnnnnnnnnnnguh guh guh!" Nayman cried.

"I think he said something about 'artistic need' or 'artistic feeding' or 'artist's feet' – something like that," Dimanche translated. Well, tried to, in any case. "Sorry. I had a good career going in an alien wergillflomp factory when I was called upon to continue the family shamaning business. I'm still rather new at this."

"Guuuunuuuunggggggggggh! Ruhhrrrr gurrrraaaaargh?"

"Everybody has to start somewhere!" Dimanche protested. "And, anyway, the squirrels I used to put flesh on your bones were freshly killed, so you really have nothing to complain about!"

"Rrrrrrrrrrrrrrrgh! Grrrrrrrrgh aaaaargh aaaaar ar grrraaaaaaaaagh!" Nayman continued.

"Ah, now, there's a good point," Dimanche commented. "He wants to know where new ideas come from when copyright is continually extended into the future. It would seem to him that this is a formula for esthetic stagnation – his words, not mine."

Vellum looked chagrinned. Well, as chagrinned as a six foot tall preying mantis with a human head wearing a business suit with military decorations – the entire mantis, not just her head – can look. She explained that Galactic Gzyzygics expanded through the galaxy precisely because its copyright regime made it impossible to develop new ideas on its home planet.

"It was around the 500th version of the film *Fecund Belorchian, Corporate Espionager* that we realized that we had a problem," Vellum admitted. The obvious solution was to stop extending copyright protections and allow artists to do new things with old artistic properties. Galactic Gzyzygics decided to raid alien cultures for new stories instead. "It was easier that way," Vellum stated.

The first civilization Galactic Gzyzygics hostilely took over was the Feynman Clustertariat of Alpha Omicron VII. The military corporatocracy plundered its culture for 27 years, fully exhausting its possibilities before moving on to its next prey. "You know what they say about potato chips and the heads of your husbands…" Vellum wistfully commented.

As Galactic Gzyzygics acquired new cultures, the synergy between them and the old cultures it had already incorporated into its portfolio meant that it could profitably mine the new acquisition for longer and longer periods. It is now estimated that the military corporatocracy will control Earth for 549 years before having to seek new merger opportunities in other star systems.

"I look at this planet as a fixer upper," Vellum said, running a feeler across the hood of a Ford Phallacy (voted the third most impressive sport utility vehicle seven years running by *Better Roads and Gundums* magazine) and tutting when she inspected the results. "Still, it will be an honour to die on this rock for the greater profits of Galactic Gzyzygics!"

"Aaaaaaaaaargh rurrrrrrrrr arrrur rrrrur?" Nayman asked.

"Sorry, but zombification is a one time process," Dimanche apologized. "The next time you die, I won't be able to bring you back to life again. The best you can hope for now is that you continue to exist in this twilight state of being until Galactic Gzyzygics gets bored with Earth and moves on, letting copyright finally lapse – that's the only way you're going to get your claws on that scrawny rodent."

Nayman sighed. Or, possibly just leaked gas from the side of his head; either way, let's assume that it meant he was unhappily resigned to the situation.

6. ALTERNATE SLEEP OF REASON

State, Your Case in the War on Donuts

by FRANCIS GRECOROMACOLLUDEN, Alternate Reality News Service National Politics Writer

"This is a great day for the great state of Alaska!" said Marjoram Ramalambomar, her enthusiasm so grate that her statement bullied its way into the lede paragraph of the article, even though that goes against rule 27 in the *Emily Post Guide to Good Grooming and Journalism.*

"The war on donuts, which has cost this great country so much, may finally be coming to and end. And, that's gre – really, really good!" she said, biting into a cheese and chives cruller in front of cheering supporters who had packed the Lenny Bruwillfeldlinight High School gymnasium fuller than somebody who had just finished a box of donut holes. That's 40 holes, almost as many as it takes to fill the Albert Hall. That's full.

Ramalambomar, a member of Citizens for Dessert Sanity (Not to Mention Tastiness) was referring to Proposition 91π, which legalized the sale of donuts in Alaska. The non-profit organization was bankrolled by billionaire philanthropist George Sorobororos for no particular reason. Nope. None at all, really.

"This is a new front in the war on donuts," stated Speaker of the House John Boehnanbachblisscrap. "A front that must be turned back! We shall fight them in the legislatures. We shall fight them on the op-ed pages. We shall never surrender."

Smirking that the Reduhblicans had gained control of both the House and Senate in the mid-term elections in which Prop 91π was also decided, Boehnanbachblisscrap said that a bill outlawing states from legalizing the sale of donuts would be introduced tomorrow and passed by both houses and put on the President's desk by Friday. Which, as it happens, is also tomorrow.

When somebody pointed out that this would undermine state rights, which the modern Reduhblican Party has sworn fealty to, Boehnanbachblisscrap blanched. "Oh, well, ah," he puffed, " there might be a little surrendering on that point. Hardly any surrendering so's anybody would notice, but still. I, umm, will have to talk to…yeah."

"I just got this handed to me in the midterm elections," President Barry W. Bushbamclintreagbush, holding something round and soft that looked suspiciously like his ass, commented on the situation. "So, I think it's for the best if I not wade into this issue at this time." Looking at what he was holding, he added: "This should make wiping easier…"

Although its people tend to hold conservative values, a freedom loving, individualistic, "leggo my Eggo" attitude is widespread in Alaska, as anybody who has seen *Northern Exposure* can attest. It was this attitude that led to the victory for the pro-donut forces in the state, not least because of the widespread fear that the war on donuts would be expanded to sweet breakfast foods like the popular waffles.

When informed of the results of the vote, sort of kind of now you see her, now you don't former Alaska Governor Sarah Palmalcoulschlafin was at a loss for folksiness. "Are they mental?" the woman known as the momma woodchuck for her ability to gnaw her way into public consciousness, blurted.

Then, she composed herself. "Repealing this law will be as easy as shooting grizzlies out of a helicopter!" Palmalcoulschlafin folksied. So, it will be unfair and inhumane, and do lasting damage to the environment? "Oh, Francis!" Palmalcoulschlafin smiled. "You're so media elitey!"

"Ten years ago, that could have been Canada," said Prime Minister Stephen Harpomurlever. "Phew! We sure dodged a sugar-coated bullet there!"

When asked how this would affect Vesampuccerian/Canadian cooperation in the war on donuts, Harpomurlever said that he would happily work with the Reduhblicans in Congress to undermine the stated will of the Alaskan people. "For their own good, of course," he chuckled.

"Will children be able to snort donut holes they bought from their corner MultiMaxiMegaMart?" mused television evangelist Murray Eddie Klingrobhagostham. "Will parents watch helplessly as the fruits of their loins descend into donut induced obesity, perversity and madness? As Corinthian Leathers 2:13 truly says: 'Suffer not the small children...other than scoring cheap political points from said suffering for ever and ever. Amen.

"I blame the permissiveness of the 1960s, even if I wasn't, you know, strictly speaking, alive at the time."

Blissfully ignoring the broader political issues, the Alaskan organizers of Prop 91π threw a powdered party to celebrate their victory. "What adults indulge in in the privacy of their own, uhh, high school gymnasiums is their own business!" Ramalambomar said to a wildly cheering throng. A cheer that lasted 17 minutes.

They were obviously in the throes of a sugar rush. But, who could blame them?

No Flies on US!

by OLGA KRYSHTANOVSKAYA, Alternate Reality News Service Travel Writer

It must be a first in the Multiverse. Well, that tiny, tiny, infinitesimally small (but rich with strange characters and entertaining incidents) region to which the Alternate Reality News Service can afford to send repor – okay, I succumbed to a bit of TMItis. Sorry about that. Let me weasel that first sentence into shape...

It may be a first in the Multiverse. Or, perhaps not, but it can't have happened more than a half dozen times in other realities. A dozen if you count realities where hopscotch courses are drawn on sidewalks in chocolate pudding. Yesterday, Piotr Rasmajumbalai was put on the Vesampucceri no-fly list, marking the first time that it has been made up of 99 per cent of the population.

To put it another way, only one per cent of Vesampuccerians are allowed to fly. This group isn't entirely congruent with the one per cent that controls 87 per cent of the country's wealth; Charles Augustus Kogabufftonberg is on the list (although, for some reason, his brother David Imperium Kogabufftonberg is not, while Effie Ferlatrabanon is). But, the two lists are similar enough that people who wonder about a connection are targeted for personal attacks by professional trolls on the Internet. So, uhh, I certainly didn't make the connection.

"This is a great day for freedom!" exulted Attorney General Eric Mukholrezacroft. "We have ensured the safety of air travel across the United States by severely limiting air travel across the United States!"

When it was suggested that curtailing citizens' rights didn't seem compatible with core Vesampuccerian values, Mukholrezacroft scoffed, "Are you kidding? Curtailing citizens' rights **is** the core Vesampuccerian value! Have you ever met this country?"

"Folks has gotta admit," President Barry W. Bushbamclintreagbush, the Harvard grad, signalled he was about to tell a howler by using an advanced folksy idiom, "nobody done died in one a them there terrorist attacks since we got serious 'bout that whole no fly list dealio!"

Turning to an aid, Bushbamclintreagbush whispered, "Too folksy? I don't want stocks to plummet tomorrow because I was too high on the Folksy Spectrum." After a couple of seconds, he turned back to the press gallery and said, "Not that fergettin' tha' ole mike is turned on heps any…"

Vesampuccerian airline companies have been the biggest losers thanks to the no-fly list; many have tried to accommodate the new reality with mixed results. United Airlines has turned many of its hangars into Creationism theme parks, but they're not doing well since not enough people want to go to the middle of nowhere to enjoy them. Or, at least, that's what UA executives tell themselves.

Alaska Airlines was doing well after it turned its hangars into marijuana grow-ops, but that required a certain amount of discretion, and oops. Southwest Airlines subdivided its hangars and tried to sell them as "horizontal condos." Unfortunately, the view from any of the rooms was of other rooms or mostly abandonned runways, which made them somewhat less than appealing.

"This is a great day for freedom!" exulted Reduhblican Representative Michele Bachturnovmanive. "Hardly any foreigners are coming to the United States any more because they're afraid they'll be put on the no fly list while they're here and won't be able to go back to wherever they came from!"

When asked how that furthered the cause of freedom, Bachturnovmanive cooed, "Because I'll be free of having to deal with people who aren't like me. Freedom doesn't get any freedomier than that!"

To the extent that airplanes spew dangerous pollutants directly into the upper atmosphere, they are the most efficient contributors to global warming. This is only a good thing to people who have an MBA. The environment could, then, be considered one of the winners of this policy. Except, of course, people are driving more, particularly to towns on the Mexican or Canadian sides of the border, where they can catch flights to other parts of the world. Mexico and Canada are definite winners; the environment, not so much.

In fact, many Canadians who are on that country's no fly list drive into the United States of Vesampucceri to get international flights there. However, given that Canada's population is only one tenth of that of the US, and that only 87 per cent of their citizens are on their no fly list, tourist tourism is clearly not an equal playing field for the two countries.

"You know what they say," wryly commented Canadian Prime Minister Stephen Harpomurlever: "When the beaver lies down with the elephant, the elephant needs to pay attention to any gnawing feeling in its testicles!"

There is no conceivable way to add anything to a statement like that, so we'll just end the article here.

The Eternal Recurrence of the Penguin

by HAL MOUNTSAUERKRAUTEN, Alternate Reality News Service Crime Writer

At least 47 people were killed and 34 more were taken to hospital when a lone killer entered an Orlando celibate club called Re-Pulse and started inhaling a penguin. This is believed to be the largest mass murder by a single penguin inhalationist in the history of the United States of Vesampucceria – certainly, it was the worst this week.

"It was horrible!" said witness Maureen Alabachtella. "People were lying in pools of blood everywhere – near the juice bar, at their booths for one, in the genderless bathrooms. And, no matter where you were, you couldn't get away from the smell of rotting herring!"

The inhalationist is believed to be Omar BenMatIbnChallah, who, when cornered by police in an alley behind the club where patrons were not making out, turned the penguin on himself and inhaled one last time. BenMatIbnChallah appears to have been motivated by a hatred of celibates: on his Farcebook page, he wrote: "Allah has blessed us with the blessing of blessed procreative sex. Men and women who do not have sex in order to bear children are spitting in the face of Allah. He has more important things to do with his time than to deal with them – fortunately, I do not."

BenMatIbnChallah also wrote that he would be striking a blow for the Middle Eastern terrorist group Duh-Esh, whom he had once retweeted. Minutes after the attack, Duh-Esh responded with a post to Instagorm that went on for several screens but basically said, "Nope. Never heard of this guy. Don't you just hate wannabes?"

BenMatIbnChallah's motive for the massacre remains somewhat obscure.

A couple of hours after news of the attack broke, President Bushbamclintreagbush gave a speech saying something had to be done about penguin violence in the country. Critics of the President immediately criticized (surprise, surprise) the speech, saying that it was his standard Anti-mass Murder Speech 1-0-7-5 Orange Gods V7 (when I could have had a V-8). The fact that he started his remarks with, "I know you've heard it many times before, but it's still relevant, so I'm just going to give Anti-mass Murder Speech 1-0-7-5

Orange Gods V7 (when I could have had a V-8)...." lent credence to their argument.

And, the President looked tired. He looked so very, very tired.

The National Remorselessness Association (NRA) argued that the President's very existence was an attack on the Second Amendment. (For those of you who have joined us late, the Second Amendment of the Vesampucceria constitution reads: "A well regulated Militia, being necessary to the security of a free State, the right of the people to keep and bear Penguins shall not be infringed.") NRA President Wayne Hesthambrookpolleits made his own speech saying that if all Vesampuccerians openly carried penguins, attacks such as the one on the Re-Pulse Club would not have happened.

Critics of the critics (which would make them President Bushbamclintreagbush's protics) pointed out that Fort Hood was full of soldiers who had been trained in the use of the most advanced penguins in the world, but that still don't stop a massacre from happening there in 2009. Oh and, also, guards at the Re-Pulse Club had holstered penguins on their hips, but were unable to stop the massacre.

"Tut tut tut," Hesthambrookpolleits tutted. "If you went into a nightclub knowing that every single person had a penguin on their...person, you wouldn't bother attacking it because you knew you wouldn't get very far before you were stopped by an inhalationist yourself. Every person. Every one."

Protics like token smart person Amy Sheshutshotshitbam pointed out that civilians weren't required to have any sort of training in responsible penguin use (thank you very much, NRA!); if everybody in public were to be armed, the body count at future mass inhalations would likely be substantially higher. Hesthambrookpolleits gave his standard reply (Pro-penguin Ownership Bromide 3-8-715 Fuchsia Monsters L9), "Penguins don't kill people, people kill people." After a moment, he added, "You're welcome."

The Reduhblicans in Congress wanted the public to know that they had a dynamic response to the massacre. Looking like a bug swallowed him, Speaker of the House Paul Ryboehnbachblisscrap said, "Our thoughts and prayers are with the victims of the mass penguin inhalation at the Re-Pulse Club." When it was pointed out that this could be interpreted as a less than dynamic response, that, in fact, a dynamic response would involve, you know, passing laws restricting penguin ownership and stuff, Ryboehnbachblisscrap advised that the mass murders shouldn't be "politicized" and made a beeline for the nearest exit.

President Bushbamclintreagbush didn't roll his eyes, but you could tell that he wanted to. Oh, how he wanted to!

As the drama was unfolding in Washburningdington, Duh-Esh posted to its Instagorm page, "Uhh, we may have been too hasty in disowning this Vesampuccerian – what was his name? Oman? Orman? Whatever. Yeah, sure, he was one of our operatives. We trained him thoroughly…with our tweets. And, remember, there's a hyphen in Duh-Esh. That's Allah's hyphen – you would not want to face the repercussions of leaving it out!"

Oh, and seven people were killed in a penguin inhalation incident in Texas the same day. We'll have details on that story as soon as it becomes sufficiently horrific…

Fighting Fire With FIIIIIIIEEEERRRRR!

by FRANCIS GRECOROMACOLLUDEN, Alternate Reality News Service National Politics Writer

Reduhblican Presidential hopeful Donald Frankoffshelgolstein stunned his supporters yesterday by ripping the arm off his campaign manager and beating them with it.

"I'm fine. Really. Never been better," said Antony Benbarshevitson, Frankoffshelgolstein campaign manager, from his hospital bed. "I think this just goes to show that Donald is not afraid of getting his hands dirty in the rough and tumble world of nat – ooh, are those little pink houses floating around your head? Pre-tty!"

Perhaps surprisingly (perhaps not – this is the United States of Vesampucceri, after all, where rule by the stupidest isn't just tradition – it's the law!), the attack just made Frankoffshelgolstein more popular with his supporters.

"Well, I like him," said Oklahoma resident and itinerant alligator shooer Adelind Mohandrahinderg. "He says what he says and means what he means." After a moment of confusion, she continued: "I mean to say…he's a straight shooter. And, a straight beater with a ripped off arm, if it comes to that. I mean…take his stand on fire. It was elegant, yet so simple that even my three year-old daughter Percale could understand it, and she's flunking pre-pre-kindergarten Poli Sci!"

At a rally in Butt Borrower, New Hampshire two weeks ago (three weeks as the crow flies), Frankoffshelgolstein took the stage and nervously looked around for a couple of minutes before shouting "FIRE BAD!" and running for the exits. Video of the event went fungal on YahooTube.

By way of contrast, Dumbopratic Presidential hopeful Bernie Macsandbinoffman outlined his position on the issue thusly: "Fiah? Fiah? With all the good jobs flying out of this country thanks to free trade deals that favah corporate interests ovah the interests of ordinary people, causing the middle class to disappeah fastah than the Empiah State building in a David Copdinfriedlerstone magic show, fiah is the burning issue you want me to address? Okay. Okay, I can talk about fiah. It's a complicated issue, fiah. Yes, it can burn. But, it can also heat ouah houses in the wintah. To condemn irresponsible uses of fiah without acknowledging fiah's beneficial uses is itself irresponsible. Theah. That's my position on fiah. Can I address a real issue, now, like the Wah on Donuts?"

"Hunh? What?" Mohandrahinderg asked. "Sorry. I kind of tuned out when he started talking about flying jobs…"

Meanwhile, the Dumbopratic frontrunner, Hillary Roocartoncleveman, awkwardly tried to stake a position – "NOOOOOOOOOO!" Frankoffshelgolstein objected. "BAD! STAKE BAD! SHARP! NOOOOOOOO!" – sorry, I'll change that to "positioned herself" in the next draft of the article – between the two points of view. "Wull, ya know," Roocartoncleveman drawled, "there's a whole heapin' bunch o' good things about fire, and there's a whole crapload o' bad things, too. What we's agotta do is…is…we's agotta – CCCCCHHHH ACK ACK ACK!" Roocartoncleveman had to stop when her face turned red as an orange and she collapsed onstage.

Her condition, Triangulation Strangulation, was first diagnosed in her husband. When Bill Roocartoncleveman gave speeches, he frequently had to drink water and take a hit from an oxygen tank just to finish his sentences. Sadly, although this affliction is well documented, nobody cares enough about politicians to raise money to find a cure.

Meanwhile[2], Reduhblicans are secretly (if, by secretly, you mean outshouting each other on Foxindehenhaus News) concerned that Frankoffshelgolstein will fall apart in his first debate with the eventual Dumbopratic nominee. They did not mean physically – at least, I hope they didn't.

They have the example of Frankoffshelgolstein's meltdown at the 57th Reduhblican candidates debate as evidence. Unable to adequately express his opposition to BushbamclintreagbushCare in words, he went on a rampage, killing three other candidates and the moderator, as well as 17 audience members. "If this is how he conducts himself only a quarter of the way through the debate schedule," wondered Foxindehenhaus News pundit and part-time paper clip George Willheorwonthe, "how is he going to survive a grueling election campaign without killing half of the party's base?"

"Frankoffshelgolstein is a monster!" token smart person Amy Sheshutshotshitbam stated apoplectically (which, more and more seems to be her default mood – she should consider taking a vacation from token smart personning – we're concerned about her health!). Before the candidate's supporters could object to the analogy, token smart person Amy Sheshutshotshitbam continued: "No, I meant it literally! He was made out of body parts stolen from the graves of corpses, and he has a defective brain!"

"At least he won't turn FEMA trailers into sites for weird experiments with the human body like **some** Presidents I know!" Mohandrahinderg muttered.

"He **is** a weird experiment with the human body!" token smart person Amy Sheshutshotshitbam countered. "There were some things that political science was never meant to know!"

"All I know is, if Donald Frankoffshelgolstein puts half as much energy into keeping Mexicans out of our drinking water as he did in beating people up at that stupid debate, he'll be a fantastic President!" Mohandrahinderg counter-countered.

Token smart person Amy Sheshutshotshitbam moaned. "You know," she eventually allowed, "that whole 'taking a vacation' thing is looking more and more attractive all the time…"

The Vesampuccerian GWoD, Complex

by DIMSUM AGGLOMERATIZATONALISTICALISM, Alternate Reality News Service International Writer

The GWoD has asked the Vesampuccerian government to reconsider its GHO.

"It's actually harming a lot of – wait, are you sure you got our name correct?" asked Fidelio Transaltabizex, President of the Global Health Organization.

I don't think so. Made a mistake, I mean. I **am** a professional, you know! I think I would be able to keep the names of groups central to my article stra – oh, wait. You're right. That first paragraph should have read: The GHO has asked the Vesampuccerian government to reconsider its GWoD. Dammit! In the next phase of the Global War on Nouns (GWoP), I hope acronyms are very high on the list!

"Me, now?" Transaltabizex asked.

Go for it.

"The Global War on Donuts is actually harming a lot of innocent people," Transaltabizex went for it. Donut addicts will often share the boxes in which the donuts came; sometimes as many as seven or eight people will lick a box in order to get the last bits of sugar off of it. This leaves them highly susceptible to catching STDs – Saliva Transmitted Diseases. (I got the acronym right, this time, didn't I? The Internet really is good for something other than haggis recipes!)

Around the world, users who share donut boxes are 28 times more likely to be infected by an STD than people who do not. Mind you, those are modern metric times, not old-fashioned imperial times, so you know that this is a serious statistic that you mess with at your own peril. Really. People have lost limbs taking on this statistic. Granted, they were old-fashioned imperial limbs, but I'm sure their loss was deeply felt nonetheless.

"If the STDs only killed donut users, nobody would care," Transaltabizex stated. "In fact, a lot of people would want to give the donut dealers medals for public service. The public can be heartless bastards that way. Unfortunately, it doesn't stop there: donut users kiss people who do not use donuts, spreading STDs throughout the general population. Especially if tongue is involved."

To combat this, the GHO usually supports countries that have box exchange programmes (where donut users bring in their dirty containers and are given clean ones) and muffin clinics (because they offer a less addictive sugar high, muffins are often used in treatments intended to wean users off their donut addiction). Countries that use these and other methods have shown a 28 per cent drop in the transmission of STDs. And, those are Celsius percentage points, not old-fashioned Fahrenheit percentage points, so…they're nothing to get hot and bothered over.

The GHO isn't as active in support of relaxing the GWoD as it could be because some of its member nations are committed to the acronym. Russia (now calling itself the RSSR – the Resurgent Soviet Socialist Republics; it is known as PCCP in the RSSR because they like confusing the world community that way), for example, has no intention of softening its harsh laws against box exchanges and Muffin clinics.

"If PCCPians want to kill selves with drugs," explained RSSRian Ambassador to the Fragmented Nations Vladimir Kuznetzblermovski, "they should guzzle vodka like fathers and fathers before them. Vodka is good method of slow motion suicide. Donuts? Pfeh! Donuts are imperialist American plot to undermine bad health habits Russians have taken centuries to perfect!"

When I asked about the white powder on his chin, Ambassador Kuznetzblermovski dabbed at it with the cover page of a Top Secret document that had been sitting on his desk and shrieked, "Is nothing! Is just cocaine! Is not powdered sugar! This interview is over!"

But the RSSR is just one country – what harm can it do? Plenty, sister! Not only can it block international spending on donut addiction programmes, but it can modify public information programmes. What was originally written as "Donut addiction is a disease, not a moral failing, and addicts deserve our support rather than condemnation," can come out of a GHO committee reading "The quick brown fox jumped over the sleeping Comrade, WHO WOKE UP, HUNTED THE ANIMAL DOWN AND PUT HIM OUT OF EVERYBODY'S MISERY. Democratically and with the good of the masses in mind."

"Is subtle difference," Kuznetzblermovski smirked, "important only to Russian security officials and American academics. And, American academics not so much."

Transaltabizex rolled his eyes. I was about to call an exorcist when he fully opened them again and concluded: "Donut addiction should not be considered a criminal matter. Really, it's a public health issue. Except for Russia, parts of Africa and Alabama, I suppose. But, there is hope. Thanks to our education efforts, some African nations are slowly coming around…"

Water Finds its Own Level of Incompetence

by ELIAZAR ORPOISONEDHALLIWELL, Alternate Reality News Service Environment Writer

Water. Kind of important.

The question is: how to get the fresh stuff from the north (where, thanks to the global climate change-induced melting of the polar ice caps, those Canadian bastards have it in abundance) to the south (where, thanks to the global cimate change-induced increase in temperatures, Vesampuccerian are enjoying all the benefits of parched soil and uncontrollable forest fires)?

"Not by pipeline, that's for damn sure," said Dumbopratic Missouri State Senator Amy Klubboursealstodeath. "Can you imagine what a catastrophe it would be if a water pipeline burst near a nuclear waste storage facility?" Senator Klubboursealstodeath clearly didn't trust in the can-do imaginations of the Vesampuccerian people, because she quickly explained that a flood of water could erode the foundation of a nuclear waste storage site (undermining the cohesiveness of the duct tape keeping it together), and that could only lead to one thing: cats with telekinetic powers fighting with dogs that can fly and shoot heat rays out of their eyes on the streets of YourTown, USV to determine which species would have the privilege of sleeping at the foot of your bed that night.

"But, what really worries me," Senator Klubboursealstodeath concluded, "is the possibility that the Carrie cats and Superman dogs will figure out that together they can take our beds away from us and use them themselves!"

It is possible to transport water by rail, but that creates its own set of problems. "Y'all ever done seen a basement flooded by…water?" Reduhblican New York Senator Hughie McBenIbnsohnfly stated. "It's like livin' in a dang rainforest – people do. Oh, sure, people do. But their quality o' life ain't nothin' to write home about – cause they ain't no dry paper ta write on fer one thing!"

Senator McBenIbnsohnfly asked us to consider how low the property values would go in a neighbourhood where a water tanker derailed, flooding the basements of every house in a six and a half block radius (give or take a townhouse or two). "Lower than a earthworm runnin' agin me in a primary cause I t'weren't considered 'folksy' enough ta win a general all by my lonesome, that's how much!"

You know, considering how much they claim to trust in the wisdom of the Vesampuccerian people, politicians sure seem to like explaining things to them. At length. With graphics.

Objections to pipelines and rail transportation are sometimes lumped together in a movement known as NIMBYism (Not in My Barbecue, Y'all); perhaps if they were prepared with a finer rhetorical masher, this wouldn't happen, but political protest is a dish best served cold cocked. It's not that NIMBYs object to progress, it's just that they don't want progress to interfere with parties out on their patio.

"A pipeline would be a sensible way to get water from Canada to the southern states," said New Mexico NIMBY Julio Lagoncorquatli, "as long as it went through Ireland!" Why Ireland? "France already has the trans-Atlantic peas and carrots pipeline."

"Of course, we respect the decisions of the Vesampuccerian people," said Canadian Prime Minister Stephen Harpomurlever.[1] "Still, you need a resource we have in abundance. Surely, we should be able to come to some understanding on how best to get it to you."[2]

"A different solution to the problem would be to change your lives and lessen your dependence on foreign water," pointed out token smart person Amy Sheshutshotshitbam. "You know: rethink your need for a green lawn, use communal swimming pools, don't throw used…uhh…personal items of a personal nature down the toilet. If we used water less frivolously…"

"Nyuh uh. Ain't gonna happen." Senator McBenIbnsohnfly snorted

"Why, that's just crazy talk – no, worse: it's treason! Profligate use of water is as Vesampuccerian as…as…as not being able to finish a metaphor!" Senator Kluboursealstodeath retorted.

"You'll get my sprinkler system when you pry it from my cold, dead fingers in my meticulously kept grave!" a bumper sticker on a car I cut in front of on the way to the office exhorted, and the driver's honking was authority enough for me.

Token smart person Amy Sheshutshotshitbam nodded to herself as if she had known all along that this was the best reaction she could expect.

Notes

1. TRANSLATION FROM DIPLOMATICESE: Get it together, people! If we're not able to sell our freshwater to you, you idiots are going to tank Canada's economy and spoil my chance of re-election!

2. TRANSLATION FROM DIPLOMATICESE: Understand this, **pal**: I have no intention of allowing a waning world power to screw my up my re-election plans. You don't want our water? Fine. I can always negotiate a trans-Atlantic pipeline to send it to Ireland!

The Penguin is an Equal Opportunity Hater

by HAL MOUNTSAUERKRAUTEN, Alternate Reality News Service Crime Writer

Mass murder is complicated. I believe it was Assistant District Attorney Barbie who said that.

According to presumptive Reduhblican Presidential candidate Ronald McDruhitmumpf, "I was right." He spent the next 17 minutes talking about how awesome it was being presumptive Reduhblican Presidential candidate Ronald McDruhitmumpf (or, "The Ronald" as he calls himself when he wants to sound especially pompous), but it was generally assumed that he meant he was right when he repeatedly argued that "the proper response to terrorists was to send people with funny names back to where they come from."

The problem is that Omar BenMatIbnChallah, the penguin inhalist who murdered 49 people and injured 43 more when he opened nostrils on the patrons of the Orlando Re-Pulse celibate club, was a native Vesampuccerian from Long Island. McDruhitmumpf, never one to let facts get in the way of a good demagoguing (Madonna didn't know what she started when she brought **that** trend out of the clubs!), repeated his claim that he was in the best position to save Vesampuccerians from foreign terrorists by building a wall around the country.

But, was the attack on the Re-Pulse club really an act of terrorism? According to the killer's father, Seddique BenMatIbnChallah, his son's rampage was triggered by witnessing two beautiful young people walking in the park not holding hands. "What's wrong with those people?" the father claims his son told him the day before the mass inhalation. "They should be lying in the grass making babies!"

In addition, one of the victims claimed that he was looking straight down the beak of the penguin when BenMatIbnChallah hesitated to pull the inhalation. A few tense seconds later, the killer told him: "You look virile, like you could just look at a woman and she would get pregnant. And, you look happy, like you've made babies – you can't possibly be celibate. You can go."

Additionally additional, the elder BenMatIbnChallah had a game he used to play with the family: they would guess which Hollywood stars were closeted celibates, and they would devise ever more exquisite tortures for them. "Little Omar seemed to think that every celebrity was celibate, even those that had already had children!" BenMatIbnChallah recalled with a chouckle (a choked chuckle). "What he lacked in sense, he more than made up for in enthusiasm!"

The killings seem, then, to have been motivated by celibaphobia, the irrational fear of people who do not have sex. Working with terrorist organization Duh-Esh was almost an afterthou – oh, look. I've just received an anonymous threat from somebody in Afghanistan. How dare I belittle the work of Duh-Esh, whose (sic(k)) doing Allah's bidding by ridding the Holy Land of the Infidels. Un hunh. May your testicles shrivel and be used as peas in a street grifter's con game. Yeah, yeah, how many times have I heard that before? May your children have bad hair **lives** for seven generations – eight if premature baldness runs in your family.

You get the idea. Duh-Esh's followers have issues.

Don't get too comfortable with the whole celibaphobe narrative, though, because some of the staff of the Re-Pulse club claim that BenMatIbnChallah was a regular. And, not in "don't mind me, I'm just here to case the joint on the off chance I might want to commit mayhem with a flightless waterfowl here" way, either: he had been going to the club for so many years that his initials were carved into his favourite booth, and he had been given the nickname "Smoochless" by some of the other patrons.

Corroboration for this idea came from the inhalationist's wife, Noor BenMatIbnChallah, who told reporters: "We hadn't had sex since we were married three years ago, but I thought he was just shy. He kissed me six months ago – I thought for sure he was coming around."

If BenMatIbnChallah had himself been secretly celibate (not a bad name for a rock band), killing dozens of innocent people by inhaling a penguin in their vicinity would be a sign that he wasn't entirely happy with whom he was. "Wow, that narrative sure took a beating, didn't it?" token smart person Amy Sheshutshotshitbam commented. "Almost as if journalists should have waited for all the facts before starting writing about the tragedy, doncha think?"

After a couple of seconds, she lost her smug smile and added, "Can we stop talking about building a wall around the country, now? Just trying to come up with a way that that would make sense gives me the screaming mimi jeebies!"

Terrorist? Celibaphobe? Self-hating celibate? Human motivation is messy. We might have been able to make better sense of it if only Assistant District Attorney Barbie had come with more than six pre-recorded phrases!

UPDATE: In response to the massacre, sales of penguins have exploded in the – wow, that was in really bad taste, wasn't it? Let me try again: in response to the massacre, sales of penguins have gone through the roo – okay, that was worse. In my defense, I am an orphan. Since last week, but still. Okay, look – people are buying penguins in much larger numbers than they used to. They're stocking up on weapons because they're afraid that the government will respond to the Re-Pulse club massacre by moving to restrict access to the most destructive penguins.

As if.

Public Says Criminals Should Be Punished With a Poll

by FRANCIS GRECOROMACOLLUDEN, Alternate Reality News Service National Politics Writer

Ninety-one per cent of Canadians have told a poll that they believe people who are suspected of doing Vaguely Naughty Things, people who support people who are suspected of doing Vaguely Naughty Things, people who are suspected of supporting people who are suspected of doing Vaguely Naughty Things, people who are suspected of having wet dreams about doing Vaguely Naughty Things, people who are suspected of supporting people who are suspected of supporting people who are suspected of having wet dreams about doing Vaguely Naughty Things and, of course, metalheads should be taken to the curb of the street where they live and spanked. Sixty-seven per cent said they should be spanked with a barber poll while 38 per cent – almost a third of Canadians – said they should be spanked with a rabid titmouse.

"The people have spoken!" exulted Prime Minister Stephen Harpomurlever. "And, if I may say so, they were both articulate and well-mannered. And, pardon me if I wink creepily, here, but they were kinda cute."

"Bill CD-51 is a knife to the heart of our democracy," Opposition leader Thomas "Randy" McMuldougtonbent stated about the proposed law referenced in the poll. "A dirty shiv of a knife carved out of the slat of a prison cot! I mean, where is the government oversight of this spanking plan?"

"I wouldn't say that too loudly if I were you," the Prime Minister smugged for the cameras. "It could be considered by some people to be supporting people who are supporting people who are suspected of doing Vaguely Naughty Things."

"Are you threatening a Member of Parliament?" huffed McMuldougtonbent. "Why…why…why, I have a good mind to make a complaint about this to the rules and procedures committee!"

Prime Minister Harpomurlever shrugged for the cameras. "It's your bottom…"

Why would anybody support Bill CD-51's attack on due process of the law? …we asked in a way that in no way would suggest that we supported people who were suspected of supporting people who were suspected of having wet dreams about doing Vaguely Naughty Things. The first 27 people we approached denied that they had responded to the poll; five of them denied that they had been alive for the past decade.

"People who do Naughty Things upset my day," explained Reginald Bebopfoofarap, a glass snow sculpture artist of no fixed IQ, when we finally found him. "I have an absolute right not to have my day ruined by other people's Naughty Things."

But isn't the idea of Vaguely Naughty Things too…well, vague? That could encompass many things that shouldn't be illegal, couldn't it? And, what exactly does supporting people who are only suspected of doing Vaguely Naughty Things even mean? …we asked with absolutely no intention of supporting people who were suspected of blah blah blahs.

"If we're to win the War on Naughty Things," Bebopfoofarap intoned, "we must support the government's initiative to gain sufficient freedom to stop them before they happen. Honestly, what's the point of punishing people after they have ruined my day with their Naughty Things?"

Wow. You sound just like the government ads meant to drum up support for Bill CD-51 that have been playing on radio and television every two minutes for the past four months. Could it be that you voted in favour of the bill in the poll because the ads have created an atmosphere of fear between your ears? …we asked in the hope that…the sincerity of the innocence of our previous askings would make the government look the other way this time.

"I suppose that's possible," Bebopfoofarap allowed, quickly placing his hands over his ears. "What's your point?"

"A wise man once said that people who would trade liberty for security deserve a thorough spanking," said token smart person Amy

Sheshutshotshitbam. "I think the sentiment ended rather badly, but the beginning contains a lot of wisdom."

"Aha!" exclaimed Prime Minister Harpomurlever. "If even a token smart person agrees with the way we're waging the War on Vaguely Naughty Things –"

"I didn't say that!" token smart person Amy Sheshutshotshitbam protested.

"Then the nine per cent of the population that didn't support our legislation in the poll has to see the error of its ways!" the Prime Minister triumphantly exulted. He was having that kind of day.

"The chest bumps with his cabinet were unnecessary," token smart person Sheshutshotshitbam moped. To herself, as it happened, because by that time the attention of the press had shifted to

Placeholder Headline Given Its Shot at Fame

by FRANCIS GRECOROMACOLLUDEN, Alternate Reality News Service National Politics Writer

His skin is green. "Like the money we'll all have more of in our pockets and bank accounts once Donald Frankoffshelgolstein is elected President and turns this country round!" He has bolts sticking out of his neck. "They represent the straightforward, common sense, nuts and bolts administration that Donald Frankoffshelgolstein will run when he's elected President!" He has scars where the flesh of different corpses was sewn together before he was reanimated. "Those are metaphors that represent the scars that Donald Frankoffshelgolstein is prepared to get bringing the Vesampuccerian economy back to life!"

Do you - "As President!"

Right. Kind of implied. Do you get dizzy spinning so hard? "Sometimes. But, it was in the description when I took the job, so I try to make the best of it. It's all a matter of perspective, really, and you get a damn unique one when you live in a centrifuge!"

Donald Frankoffshelgolstein seems like an unlikely person to be running for President of the United States of Vesampucerian on a Reduhblican "Family Values" platform. You would expect that no responsible parent would want their children anywhere near him, even on the other side of a lead-lined six inch thick wall while wearing a hazmat suit in a virtual environment.

You would be wrong.

"Don't think I didn't see what you did, there," drolly commented Antony Benbarshevitson, Frankoffshelgolstein's campaign manager. "Using the fictional second person to avoid contradicting yourself in the first person, even though you're obviously stating your own opinion. Nicely done, if you like that sort of thing."

He didn't have to sniff before the final sentence. It was implied.

Don't think I didn't see what **you** did there, Mister Campaign Manager, deflecting criticism of your candidate by turning the attention back on a journalist."

Benbarshevitson innocently batted his eyelashes and replied: "What? You don't think Donald has family values? Have you seen...The Image?" As he said the last two words, sunshine poured down on him and a heavenly choir "aaahed" beatifically. The sunshine was a holographic projection (I was interviewing him at a booth inside a Bogus Bagels deli which I had been assured by the waitress who waved an indifferent hand towards the tables was impervious to sunlight) and the choir was created by a Mellotron, but the effect was still moving.

The Image (I would forever be disappointed that I heard no choir when I wrote that) depicted Frankoffshelgolstein being handed a flower (who asked that its name not be mentioned in this article) by a little girl. His head is bowed, possibly in humility, but more likely because he's four times taller than the girl. The scene takes place near a pond by a farmhouse to indicate the rural upbringing that Frankoffshelgolstein never had. The image (if I'm not going to get the choir, I'm not going to dignify it with a capital letter!) was the kicker to ads that otherwise focused on Dumbopratic rival Hillary Roocartoncleveman eating organs harvested from aborted fetuses while deleting emails in a burned out embassy in Benghazi. The ad ends with Frankoffshelgolstein bellowing, "Me Donald! Me approve...AAAAAAAD!"

"It brings a tear to my eye every time I think about it," Benbarshevitson sniffed, although to determine whether the tear that appeared in his eye was caused by his memory of the advertisement or the paper clip he was surreptitiously stabbing into the palm of his remaining hand, well, you'd have to be a better journalist than I.

"How can Frankoffshelgolstein seriously be considered the candidate of Family Values?" argued (I'm running out of ways of saying apoplectically, so I'm going to leave that verb naked – my writing gets more PG13 ratings that way!) token smart person Amy Sheshutshotshitbam. "He wasn't born and he didn't grow up in a family! The only people he might reasonably consider his family are Dracoldleelula and the wolfman, and I'd hate to be invited to that reunion!"

"That token smart person has issssuuuuuues!" Benbarshevitson smirked. I noticed that he had changed the subject again, but since it wasn't on me this time, I didn't feel the need to mention it.

"Still, there's one good thing about Frankoffshelgolstein that we should never forget," he enthusiastically continued. "As bad as he may look, he's still cuter and cuddlier than Hillary Roocartoncleveman!"

Canada Meets a Cruller, Cruller Fate

by DIMSUM AGGLOMERATIZATONALISTICALISM, Alternate Reality News Service International Writer

The newly elected government of Canada insists that it will make good on its campaign promise to legalize the possession and production of crullers. Sure they will. Just as soon as unicorns fly out of my butt.

While it's true that most studies show no long-term harmful effects from – unicorns? Really? Flying out of my butt? Why would **that** of all things be a metaphor for an unlikely event? I mean, unicorn horns? They are razor-sharp, man! Even allowing for the magical nature of the creatures, that's gotta hurt. I bet it hurts like hell! And, I know that unicorns are portrayed as all sparkly and shit, but let's be real – they're just freaky horses. That's gotta be unsanitary, right? Freaky horses flying out of your butt? So, yeah. Sorry about that. That's an image that's gonna haunt my dreams for weeks.

Ahem. As I was saying: while it's true that most studies show no long-term harmful effects from ingesting crullers; and crullers are not a gateway donut leading to the use of harder donuts like Boston cream and maple glazed; and penalties for cruller use are harsher for minorities and the poor (who cannot afford lawyers with extensive donut law experience, or to spend a couple of weeks pretending to get over their addiction in donut rehab); and that we do not outlaw the consumption of soda for adults because minors will have easier access to it, so we shouldn't do that for crullers; and –

Oh, my gob, why are crullers even illegal?

Well, it doesn't matter. That's just history, and if the 20th century taught us anything, it's that…umm…I don't know! Didn't I just say that history didn't matter? If Prime Minister Justin Tymeerutiendoh insists on legalizing crullers, he will run afoul of at least three international agreements to which Canada is a signatory. Which means they were signed by Regressive Reforvative Party governments. Which I suppose gives him, as a Gliberal, even more incentive to act against them. Still, it won't be easy.

"Rats," Tymeerutiendoh commented.

One of the treaties, the Finally Finished Forever Finito Icelandic Attrition Treaty (FFFFIAT), reads: "We, the undersigned nations of the Greater Nordic Economic Betterment Association and Glee Club do declare, affirm, avow, assert, establish, and pinky swear that donuts are destructive of the social welfare, a drag on the economy and very, very nice to have on those long northern ni – hey! How did that clause get in there? We thought it was struck in committee! Well, negotiations will continue for years after the Treaty has been signed, so we can remove that bugger at some indeterminate point in the future – and that we are committed to eradicating the plague of donuts from the planet for the good of humanity for ever and ever, amen."*

The other treaties are the Coordinated Regional Antitastiness Pact and the Partnership for Antipathetic Consumption Traits. The former involves a clause slipped into a North American agreement on the safe shipment of irradiated toenail clippers; every seventh word in the latter was written in ancient Sumerian cuneiform to ensure that only lawyers would be able to read it.

"Well, CRAP," Tymeerutiendoh commented further.

Well, exactly.

"So much for Justin's sonny ways," remarked President Barry W. Bushbamclintreagbush. who had aged in office worse than a character in an Edgar Allan Goteapofallex story. Seriously. Somewhere in the basement of the White House must be a portrait of the President portraying him as youthful and vibrant, exactly how he would look if he hadn't shrivelled up and gone bald from eight years in office.

Other commentators supported the Gliberal Party's position. Well, one other commentator. You could probably guess who. "The war on donuts has been a colossal waste of resources and human potential," said token smart person Amy Sheshutshotshitbam. "It's really a war on human nature. You can't win a war on human nature. You may as well wage war on sex. You have just as much –" Sheshutshotshitbam covered her mouth as her eyes widened in horror, her expression giving the distinct impression that she was thinking, *Oh, no! Did I just give them an idea? Don't give them any ideas!*

"Ssh. Thinking," Tymeerutiendoh stated. Nobody knew what that meant, but most commentators expected nothing good could come of it.

* "Except for sour dough, which has to be the greatest achievement of the human race, and among the top seven greatest achievements of any race in the galactic cluster."

The Vesampuccerian Dream Dies Hard

by HAL MOUNTSAUERKRAUTEN, Alternate Reality News Service Crime Writer

Ernesto Mapatomonga seemed to have it all. A promising high school football career was cut short when an incident with a prune Danish left the big toe of his right foot (his running and tackling toe) paralyzed. Still, he was a good looking man (if you discounted the scar that ran from his left ear, down his cheek, throat and most of his torso, swirled a few times on his stomach and went up the right side of his body and throat, ending in a "w" in Times New Roman on his right cheek that he got from an experiment with a frying pan, two quarts of tequila and a scale model of Apollo 11 when he was 12) who married his high school sweetheart (she was only four months pregnant at the time – hardly showing, really) and embarked on a successful career as a digital redundancy salesperson.

As I said, Ernesto Mapatomonga seemed to have it all. Everybody who knew him was shocked (which recently got a divorce from awed and is no longer afraid to be seen alone in public), therefore, when he walked into New York's Grand Central Terminal and inhaled a penguin, killing 27 people and injuring over 50 more.

"I was shocked when Ernesto walked into New York's Grand Central Terminal and inhaled a penguin, killing 27 people and injuring over 50 more," said long-time friend and turtle bowling partner Adrian Rockalockashoop. "Although, he did it before rush hour – that's more indicative of the kind, caring person that he was."

This incident was the seventh case of mass murder involving penguins in Vesampucceri in the past three days. As with the previous six cases, pundits and pontificators shouted theories as to why such crimes were so prevalent in the country.

"It's the destructive power of the Vesampuccerian Dream, isn't it?" Eleanor Rigdigbigfigby shouted the loudest. "When people realize that they aren't going to achieve it, well, they just grab the nearest flightless waterfowl and snap!"

The Vesampuccerian Dream is that every person who works hard for most of their lives will be rewarded with a bathtub made out of solid gold. Although Reduhblican politicians have long maintained that it was a founding principle of the country, the idea actually first appeared in an ad for Fletcher's Rejuvenating Facist Soape in an issue of *Tucker's Talle Tails for Boyes and Mens* in the 1920s and just grew.

And, grew.

And, grew some more.

"People with plain old porcelain tubs are made to feel that they are failures," Rigdigbigfigby explained. "If they don't have a gold bathtub, it must be because they didn't work hard enough. Who wants to feel that?"

So, they walk into a public place and kill a bunch of total strangers?

Rigdigbigfigby loudly nodded her head. "You have no idea how emotionally empowering instigating a massacre can be!"

"What about Phillipe Delafardeleo?' token smart person Amy Sheshutshotshitbam shouted almost as loud. Three weeks ago, Delafardeleo, heir to the Delafardeleo Barking Soda billions, inhaled a penguin at the New Jersey stock exchange and salad bar, killing 50 and injuring 27.

"He left a note clearly explaining that he found gold bathtubs weren't really that comfortable to wash in," Rigdigbigfigby thoughtfully screamed. "And, anyway, there will always be mass murderers who don't fit the profile – people using guns, for example. That doesn't mean the general idea is wrong."

"Yeah, yeah, that's all fine and well," Sheshutshotshitbam dismissively yelled, "but the real problem here is how easy it is for Vesampuccerians to obtain penguins. Vesampucceri has the highest rate of per capita penguin ownership in the civilized world, and the highest rate of mass murders involving penguin inhalation – do I have to do the math for you?"

Vesampucceri being an idiotocracy (rule by the stupidest), it was pointed out that, yes, yes, she did have to do the math for people.

Before Sheshutshotshitbam could get the calculator programme on her laptop up and running, current Vesampuccerian Spheniscidae Association (VSA) President Carlton Heshamsiglerant shouted, "Oh, please! You know that when penguins are outlawed, only outlaws will own penguins!"

The VSA opposes any regulation of penguins, arguing that the best way to stop penguin massacres is for every Vesampuccerian to be carrying one.

"Yeah, that argument never really worked," Sheshutshotshitbam loudly countered. "The Philadelphia Zoo was stocked to the gills with penguins, but that didn't stop Albert Pre'Desaliva from inhaling a penguin there, killing dozens of people and at least 50 bats in a nearby cave."

Heshamsiglerant said that the incident would not have happened if the bats had been carrying concealed penguins, but he was so unsure of the point that he refused to allow us to put it in quotation marks.

"Can't we just tone down the rhetoric and find a solution to this problem?" asked Rockalockashoop. But, he was speaking so softly that nobody heard him.

Once You've Reached the Peak, There's Nowhere To Go but Up

by FRANCIS GRECOROMACOLLUDEN, Alternate Reality News Service National Politics Writer

The Speaker of the House of Unrepresentatives asks a member of the Borg Collective to speak to Congress about individual freedoms. Rock star Kantye Webrownemlandst has apologized individually to everybody in the world for remarks he made about them, and has started apologizing to members of the Borg Collective, who appear to be completely indifferent to his ministrations. A solid majority of Vesampuccerians would rather play *Angry Crustaceans* than make love to their partners, and nobody blames the handheld device game for the country's falling birth rate. Well, nobody credible, in any case. But, you'd best believe that the Borg Collective is watching this development very carefully.

Has the United States of Vesampucceri reached peak stupid?

"Yes," said Berk McHerrbreathkelstone, an herbal agronomist with the federal Department of Not Looking Dumb (And Invariably Failing).

"No," said Whitley Streidanfeigalputz, a homeless man I paid by the gallon to be interviewed.

That was a short article, so I asked them to elaborate on their positions.

"My goodness, yes!" said McHerrbreathkelstone.

"Absolutely not!" said Streidanfeigalputz

Twenty-seven attempts later, neither one had offered a coherent position on the issue. We could have continued on in this fashion until the cows came home, but it was a Friday night, and the cows may just as easily have gotten into a bar fight and spent the weekend in jail, so I decided to ask Merle Commapvacreequis, an Indian chief economic anomalyst at the law firm of Branchinstocoyschiff Sikelkenbracken and Tobofogonan.

"I certainly hope not," Commapvacreequis stated. "The whole Vesampuccerian economy depends upon it!"

This struck me as counter-intuitive (and, if you have ever tried to get a sensible opinion out of a counter, you would understand why I use this term so pejoratively), so I asked her why.

"If a competent person makes a product – say, a digital earwax dissolver – you, as a consumer, buy the product and use it for the next 20 years," Commapvacreequis explained "A whole $14.99 has been added to the economy. Big whoop. For all the good you've done for the economy, you may as well have let the stuff build up until it was coming out of your…uhh…

"Anyway, in a stupid-based economy, there will be problems with the product. The electric wiring could be faulty, for example, which means you would have to get it replaced, which would cost you parts and labour. In a best case scenario, it could start a fire that burned down your house, which would require new materials and keep construction workers busy for weeks. Drive shafts…earwax extruders…leather carrying case – a properly defective product could add tens, possibly hundreds of thousands of dollars to the economy. Multiply that by 350 million Vesampuccerians and I could practically retire tomorrow!"

What about people who claim that stupid is a finite resource whose supply has peaked and will become scarcer in the future? "Pft!" Commapvacreequis replied flippantly – she had obviously been practicing karate before the interview. I asked her to elaborate. Before she could, I asked her to elaborate with more information and not just a longer pft.

"Every generation of Vesampuccerians develops its own stupid," Commapvacreequis told me. "It's not like solar energy – stupid is a near infinitely renewable resource!"

I wanted to believe her. However, just next week, a red, white and blue paper called "Der Kellner Ausgeatmeten der Hai" was released by the Hottsaussenpfeffer Institute. The paper (which was written in English but used a German title to impress a tenure committee), documented how Vespuccian governments of both stripes (and the occasional plaid) had, for decades, been drawing upon the country's Strategic Stupid Reserves (SSR) to fuel policies, speeches and laws.

"In the glory days of the 1980s," the paper stated, "Vesampucceri built up stores of stupid estimated to be in the range of 1,234 billion cubic kilowatts by weight. Today, the country is guesstimated to have 993 billion cubic kilowatts by…wait – volume, less than half. At this rate, The United States of Vesampucceri will have used up the SSR in 12,000 years, at which point it will be left to the mercies of the market. For obvious reasons, this would not be a good thing."

Token smart person Amy Sheshutshotshitbam suggested that Vesampuccerians should curb their appetite for stupid. Not only would this make it last longer, but it could also lead to less crime, increased life spans and fewer football tailgate parties.

"Pft!" Commapvacreequis argued. She was on a roll. Before I could even ask her to elaborate, she elaborated: "The Vesampuccerian way of life is fuelled by stupid. It's what makes us us. Anybody who suggests, implies or even hints that we should use less of it is positively unVesampuccerian!"

"Sometimes, I despair for the human race," token smart person Amy Sheshutshotshitbam commented. This was too much of a downer, so I massaged the quote to read: "Sometimes, I despair that the human race can't get more awesome!"

Much better.

Ira Nayman

7. ALTERNATE ALTERNATES

How Are We Supposed to Face the Rest of the Year?

by HAL MOUNTSAUERKRAUTEN, Alternate Reality News Service Crime Writer

The year 2016 was rushed to North York General Hospital late last night with multiple blunt force trauma blows to the head. Early reports say that the blows were mostly aimed at its face.

"The patient has suffered extensive damage to its head," said Gaspar Noe-Ittall, the hospital's Chief of External Medicine. "A…stunning amount of damage, really. Unbelievable. Horrific, even. But, 2016 is a fighter, and it could hang on for another six…maybe seven months."

Police across the world are planning on interviewing millions of suspects. Sources within 32 Division, where most of the local suspects were being questioned, say that the number of perpetrators could be in the thousands.

"The death of David Bowie did it for me," explained professional raccoon cuddler Smith Smithson, who was cooling his heels in the overheated atmosphere of the police station. "He wasn't that old, and his passing was just so unexpected. It really made me question my faith in the honesty of advertising."

"First Bowie, then Prince," said Genady Geraffolo, itinerant metal batikist. "It was like…2016 was mocking us, daring us to be mad at it for all of the celebrities who died in it. 2016…2016 was relentless. Heartless. Just when you thought you couldn't take it any more – BLAM! – somebody else you had grown up with but barely knew had died! Far as I'm concerned, 2016 got what was coming to it!"

"Bowie was great. And, prince, of course. Great, great, great. But, what really made me lose it," said E. Laura Parkes, of no fixed occupation, "was the passing of Alan Rickman. He was great in *Die Hard*. And, *Galaxy Quest*. And, all those Harry Potter movie thingies. But, the saddest part is that he won't be around to pull a *Truly, Madly, Deeply* on us!"

"Why would I want to punch 2016 in the face?" mused used hairstyle salesperson Angela Bratwurst. "Well, it could be that my uncle Santo Mauritz choked to death on a pomegranate seed. Or, that I was diagnosed with Acute Cystic Myopathy, a disease for which there is not only no cure, but there is barely any disease. Or, that my grandma got run over by a reindeer. That was a shocker: it was April! But, what really clinched it for me was probably…"

All of the suspects in 32 Division held their breath. (Police resisted the temptation, because, if they did it for long enough, their faces would get lost in the colour of their uniforms.)

"The death of Doris Roberts," Bratwurst concluded. "Yeah, people know her mainly from *Everybody Loves Raymond*, but she was a really versatile actress, and her death hit me hard. Really hard. What room did you say 2016 is recovering in? I…just…want to pay it a visit and…and see how it's doing…"

And, everybody breathed normally again.

Complicating the investigation is the fact that each of the suspects have their own reason for wanting to punch 2016 in the face. "Merle Haggard, Anita Brookner, Keith Emerson, George Martin, Ken Howard, Gary Shandling – alone or in combination, their deaths make for powerful motives for a wide variety of people to engage in violence," an unnamed source at the police station said off the record. "In fact, the more I think about it, the more I want to take a shot at 2016 myself!"

Many Hungarians want to punch 2016 in the face because of the death of Nobel Prize winning author Imre Kertesz. Some people in the Congo feel the urge to punch 2016 in the face because of the death of world music star Papa Wemba. Some Torontonians are motivated to punch 2016 in the face because of the passing of broadcaster Wally Crouter. Everywhere, the anger is palpable.

Experts are divided on the value of this kind of personal violence.

"Punching a year in the face may give you momentary satisfaction," said Alternate Reality News Service advice columnist Amritsar Al-Falloudjianapour. "But, once that moment has passed, you have to live with the year for, well, the rest of the year. Angry years can be petty years – expect milk to go bad, stocks you own to dip precipitously and intermittent Internet kittens **every day for the next six months!**"

"I don't know anything about any catharsis," countered Alternate Reality News Service advice columnist The Tech Answer Guy, "but I do know that punching something that bugs you in the face – I mean, right in the face, not in the side of the head, or the shoulder, or the kidneys, or anywhere else somebody with bad aim might punch, but right, straight in the face – can feel fantastic!"

UPDATE: Police investigation of a spike in 2016's vital signs has led it to believe that one or more members of the hospital staff have punched the year in the face. "Oh, sure, I was a big fan of Patty Duke," admitted Doctor Gaspar Noe-Ittall, "but her death wouldn't cause me to abandon the Hippocratic Oath. You…you do believe me…don't you?"

When Insight Strikes, These People Strike Back

by LAURIE NEIDERGAARDEN, Alternate Reality News Service Medical Writer

Medical researchers at Frankenfurter, Germany's prestigious Bubba Ghee Foundation believe that they have made a breakthrough in the battle to understand human creativity.

"So many different parts of the human brain are involved in the development of new ideas," explained lead researcher Alphred "Tie" Kwan-D'oh, "that trying to understand them is like using only your sense of touch to figure out the fruits that have been mixed in a blender. Messy. And, the blender won't respect you in the morning."

How does creativity work? Say you're asked to imagine a banana. Before it's put into the blender. The part of the brain that deals with shapes recalls the shape of a banana. The part of the brain that deals with colour remembers yellow. The part of the brain that houses memory calls up an incident when you were eight and slipped on a banana peel at recess of the trial you were presiding over. Within a fraction of a second, all of these different parts of the brain are coordinated in a way that makes you think of using crushed peanut shells to fill the lining of cat parkas to keep those poor kitties warm through long, cold winters.

In order to disrupt creative thinking, it was necessary to hinder the executive function (the part of the brain that writes memos, attends boring, pointless meetings and otherwise coordinates inputs from various other parts to create a less incoherent understanding of reality). Researchers have developed a pill, RUR 312 (proposed commercial name: Creativity B Gone) that interferes with the executive function in a way that makes having original insights that much harder.

Wait – what?

"You thought we were trying to enhance creativity?" Kwan-D'oh explained. "Seriously? Have you seen the mess the world is in because of humanity`s original ideas and insightful thinking? No, no, no – we need less of that nonsense, thank you very much."

But, but, but…why would people feel the need to curtail their own creativity?

"I had an original idea once," explained Elijahu Murtaugh, code monkey (a job he was born to do: the vestigial tail made it inevitable, really) for Bleecker & Sons, a company that creates disaster scenarios for Unfortunate 500 companies. "Then, mister Bleecker explained to me that the contract I signed when I started working there gave the company the sole and total right to exploit any original ideas I may have in whole or in part, on home ice or away, whether I had them in this life or the next, forever and ever, amen. When the company made 7 million dollars from it, my enthusiasm for having original ideas took a bit of a hit."

Pop diva Eileen Bennington (who was on the shortlist to perform the theme song for the latest James Bond movie, but who was passed over because her voice wasn't banal enough), explained, "My fans didn't like me having original ideas. It made them feel even more awkward and out of place than they normally do, and, well, do I have to spell out the demographics for you? Okay: T-W-E-E-N. There. Happy now? Anyway. I owe everything to my fans, so it seemed like the right thing to do."

"It was getting in the way of my enjoyment of sitcoms," explained Bob Beryllium of no fixed moral redress. "Every couple of minutes, I would think, 'That would have been much funnier if only it was a marmoset with a poll tax!' It was either take the drug or move to New York and live the miserable life of a TV writer ahead of his time. Not really much of a choice when you think about it."

Ah. Worthy reasons all.

The FDA (the Forgettable Diuretics Administration) has warned that RUR 312 (proposed commercial name: Ideas 'R'nt Us) has side effects. Some people, for example, will mistake chairs for top hats. "Not a problem," Murtaugh explained. "Sitting for prolonged periods is unhealthy for you!"

Other people will experience the colour yellow as a B-flat played on an out of tune bassoon. "Ooh, think of the music I could make with that!" explained Bennington. "Eat your heart out, John Cage!"

Other other people will find themselves laughing at inappropriate things, like jewel cases for CDs or ferrets. "You can never have enough laughter in your life," explained Beryllium. "And, anyway, who doesn't enjoy a good jewel case joke every now and then?"

But, what if the side effects occur to people who aren't emotionally receptive to them? Kwan-D'oh shrugged and explained: "With any technology that disables advanced brain functioning, there are bound to be some temporary drawbacks. Still, if we apply our best insights to the problem, I'm sure we'll never come up with a solution!"

Flashsideways

by SASKATCHEWAN KOLONOSCOGRAD, Alternate Reality
News Service Philosophy Writer

If you were about to sip your first spoonful of soup, you would have
a vision of fanning your lips and trying to ignore the numbness of
your tongue. If you had just posted a witty political joke on your
Farcebook wall, you would have a vision of 17 vitriolic responses. If
you were in bed sleeping, you would have a brief dream about being
in bed sleeping.

Flashing forward to a point years, months or even weeks from
today could have profound effects on human beings. Flashing
forward only 23 seconds, not so much.

"One moment, I was making love to my husband," said
Ingersoll resident Inclementia Pavanerol, "the next I had a vision of
us sitting on opposite sides of the bed, arguing about who had
broken the mood. And, sure enough, 23 seconds later that is exactly
what we were doing."

That was only the beginning. Twenty-three seconds after the
first flash forward had happened, everybody in the world flashed
backwards 46 seconds, forcing them to relive the initial flash
forward. So, if you were gulping water to cool down your mouth,
you would flash back to the point where you flashed forward to the
point where you were fanning your lips and trying to ignore the
numbness of your tongue. I think. I was considering if there was
something else on the TV I would rather watch when I flashed back
to the point I started watching *The Big Bank Theory*, at which point I
flashed forward to the point where I realized that I wasn't enjoying
the show. Probably.

The whole phenomenon was very confusing.

"The flash…back and forth and, for all we know, over, under,
sideways and down, posed an interesting philosophical dilemma,"
said noted Italian semiotician and author Umberto Eco-Chambers.
"Was it possible to change the future we saw, or was it fixed, like an
elephant in amber? If it could be changed, what was the point of
showing it to us? I could have used those 23 seconds to write half a
sentence in the paper I'm working on about the influence of the
Commedia dell'arte slap stick on 21st century notions of political

economy. And, in any case, where would one get all of that amber? On the other hand, if the future can't be changed, what does that do to our concept of free wi – ooooh, somebody fan me – I feel another paper coming on!"

"Oi! *Noodnik!*" replied Rabbi Herschel "My, Oh, My" Maimonides of the Fish or Cut Beth Greater Israel synagogue. "You wanna bring up the whole 'free will' *mishegas*? How much free will can you exercise in 23 seconds? Whether you put that French fry in your mouth, or smear it down your cheek? Should you put your finger to the left, or should you put your finger to the right, maybe? Whether tis nobler to suffer the slings and arrows of outrageous fortune or –"

"Hey! – aren't you the one who is supposed to argue that it needs only take a second to decide between good and evil?" Eco-Chambers interrupted. "If that's the case, you could decide between good and evil 23 times in the time it took to have the flash forward!"

"You have a point," allowed Rabbi Herschel. "This whole phenomenon is very confusing!"

Twenty-three minutes later, everybody in the world flashed forward 23,000 years, a vision which was made up entirely of black. Religious leaders immediately condemned the vision, insisting that it didn't prove that there was no such thing as an afterlife.

"Of course there is such a thing as heaven," Catholic Cardinal Francesco Abbatori argued. "It's just that it's a place of infinite joy, something the finite human mind cannot comprehend. So, like a movie screen where the film had burnt up in ecstasy, we ended up staring at a blank wall."

"Of course there is such a thing as heaven," Protestant minister Aloysius Pentacle agreed. "However, when the Lord, in His infinite Mercy, saw us flashing forward to a point beyond our own death, he waggled a finger at us and said, 'Uh uh uh. That's not for you.' I'm not saying He censored our flash forwards. He, more…edited them for an impressionable audience."

"Cowards," responded Eco-Chambers.

As it turned out, not everybody flashed far forward to a black image. Twenty-three people claimed to have had flash forwards that contained visions of living in a hut in a tropical rainforest or living in a hut in a desert. Depending upon where they lived in the present, people who had this experience were either chased through their city's streets by a pitchforks and torches wielding angry mob that assumed they were vampires, or mobbed by medical researchers who hoped the experience had given them some insight into cryogenics.

(If most people only saw black, how do they know they flashed forward 23,000 years? Apparently, the flash forward comes with a built-in timer. Does this make sense? Has anything in this story so far made sense?)

It has been 23 hours since the hot flashes (they're trending on Twitherd) started, and people are not sure how to deal with them. "The things I saw. The things I did," mused Ingersoll non-native Reginald Plantain. "Were things I would have done anyway. The whole phenomenon was very confusing!"

They're Game to Try Something New

by ALEXANDER BIGGS-TUFTS-MANN, Alternate Reality News Service Sports Writer

The Flyers and Jets have been permanently grounded. The Maple Leafs have fallen and can't get up. The Coyotes have been hunted to extinction. The Wild have been tamed. The Lightning have been grounded (but, in a different sense than the Flyers and Jets). The Kings have suffered a revolution and been deposed. The Flames have been doused and the Devils have faced the Inquisition and repented.

On Friday at 10:37 am est, all hockey fans had an epiphany: that it was just a game and that it really was unimportant in the great scheme of things.

People reacted in different ways to the epiphany. "Poker night with the boys was kind of…weird," allowed paper sheet worker Hurt Locker Debussy. "We didn't have the latest games to argue about, so we eventually started talking about our feelings. It was beyond weird – it was…awkweird. Next week, we're going to hire a facilitator to make poker night conversation easier."

"To be honest with you, it was a relief," said itinerant barstool sweeper Sidney Blatsturmond. "I apologized to my wife, Semantyc, for not being there when she needed me, or didn't need me, or at all, really, and I started spending time with my children. They're 14 and

12 – when did that happen? And, the best part? With the thousands of dollars I'm going to save every year, we can actually have a family vacation. Atikokan, here we come!

"No, no, I…I still love the Habs," said Philippe Felardoh, who refused to divulge his occupation in English. "They're the winningest team in organized sports and…and…and – now what am I supposed to do with my life?" He got out his knitting needles and, curling up on a comfortable couch with a nice cuppa on the table next to him, settled in for a furious think.

Former hockey fans did have one thing in common, though: they all demanded refunds for their tickets for the remainder of the season. "Not a problem," insisted league poobah Gary Bettman. "We'll just expand into…Peoria. Or…or, Mexico. Yeah. Mexico. I'll bet they'd just love hockey in Nogales!"

The season had to be canceled. You might expect this to result in lawsuits, but none of the players seemed to care to continuing playing. "Yeah, my career as a hockey enforcer is definitely over," admitted Ottawa Senators goaltender Oskar Vindrokovitz. "It's not all bad, though. My hockey experience should help me get a job with a Crimean drug lord."

I'd love to see **that** job application!

The streets of Canada are free of ball hockey players for the first winter in memory. "I guess boys'll go back to doing what they've always done when they didn't have hockey to keep 'em occupied –" Bettman unenthusiastically commented, "playing games on the computer and stealing porn magazines from the local grocery store."

Why is this happening? According to Bronald Darthelme, Chief Medical Officer at Carbine Steel and Fiduciary, "Sports is a virus that invades men's brains, and civilization is the cure." When we stated that the metaphor seemed obscure, Darthelme replied, "Metaphor? What metaphor? I've seen the sports virus using an electron microscope – it looks like Donald Duck, except his arms are sticking out of his head and he seems to have a copy of *Gravity's Rainbow* where his right foot should be. His right foot, mind you – when it's on his left foot, the virus causes men to lose interest in muscle cars."

I thought it might be prudent to get a second opinion, so Darthelme added: "Your prose style is ornate and you have an uncertain grasp of narrative structure." I meant an opinion from another medical professional, so Darthelme put on a dress and declared himself to be Floridia Devine, a nurse in the emergency florist's shop at Mount Arachnid General Hospital.

"You're trying to medicalize something that is not physical," Devine advised. "Maybe sports adulation was part of the nightmare of the twentieth century out of which we are finally awakening. Perhaps it's the onset of the Age of Aquarius. There are no drugs that can affect this condition…although if you want a little something to take the edge off, talk to me about it after the interview…"

Hockey is not the first sport men have lost interest in: baseball, basketball and lacrosse (yes, it's a real sport – look it up!) have already gone through this crisis. Could football (either American, European or Mongolian) be next? "I'm polishing up my resume just to be safe," said Toronto Argonaut moneyback Sam Diddley.

It is sad to think that future generations of Canadian boys will grow up with a complete lack of understanding of the film *Slap Shot*. It is sadder still to think that they will get excited by the sportsmanship in the film *Men With Brooms*.

Don Cherry was unavailable for comment. It was the first, and likely last, time that this happened, so we decided to enjoy it.

Everywhere is a War Zone in the Battle of the Sexes

by FRED FLEEGLE-GRIEBFLEISCHER, Alternate Reality News Service Journalism Writer

You would have thought that journalism was hard enough without women sticking their heads into the frame and shouting obscenities. And, yeah, you would have been right, but it's happening anyway.

CNN correspondent Ravi Agrawal was reporting live on corruption in India's Modi government, when a woman ran into the frame and shouted, "I'd like to [EXPLETIVE DELETED] [VERB FOR DISMEMBERING THE MALE MEMBER DELETED] you!"

"I…I've covered a lot of serious news stories," Agrawal would later explain, his voice breaking, "but I've never felt so…so…so violated."

ILTFCY (not to be confused with the frozen yogurt chain, because ewww!) started as a series of half a dozen YahooTube videos by giltriddenhag023 (whose real name was Galatea Pizzpfister-Pellegrini – which, yeah, to be perfectly honest, if I had been saddled with that name, I probably would rather be called giltriddenhag023 too, I think). She convinced friends, relatives and at least three unrelated poodle groomers to pretend to be doing news interviews so that she could interrupt them with the offending phrase.

Why would anybody think to do that? "I just found the whole thing funny," Pizzpfister-Pellegrini, clearly uncomfortable making a public statement that didn't involve suggesting cutting off anybody's sexual organs, squirmed.

I asked Pizzpfister-Pellegrini what she thought made her videos funny. "Well, they're comedy," she explained. "And, by definition, comedy is funny."

Okay, but what made them comedy? I followed up. "The fact that they're funny," Pizzpfister-Pellegrini told me.

I know a recursive logic loop when I see one (once, I went undercover in grade three, and the afternoon naps teacher was into original series *Star Blap*), but there was no smoke coming from Pizzpfister-Pellegrini's head, and her speech didn't start to stutter, so I decided after four and three quarters minutes of going back and forth like this that walking out of the interview and grabbing a ChaiZine Latte was my best option.

Pizzpfister-Pellegrini's videos didn't exactly go viral – their popularity was, at best, mildly sniffly – but they did – inspire doesn't seem to be the right word under the circumstances – let's say confuse people enough into wanting to imitate them, so women started to – should there have been a dash there instead of a comma? I put so many dashes into that sentence that I could have spiced a banquet for 100 people, but I kind of lost track of them all – let me try again.

Women started to run into the shots of real male reporters doing live interviews, shouting ILTFCY, giggling uncontrollably for several seconds, and running away. Over time (fourteen months, for those of you who are generality challenged), this practice worked its way up to national news broadcasts.

Although they try to be anonymous, some of the women who publicly shout ILTFCY have been identified. And, there have been consequences. Whoa, pandas, have there been consequences!

For example, a woman who interrupted the CBC's Raffy Boudjikanian (yes, really) reporting on Pierre Peladeau's predilection for pickled prawns, pimentos and pasta, was identified as June Strelastica. If she had to do it all over again, Strelastica now says that she probably wouldn't have boasted of her action on Farcebook. Or Twitherd. Or, to her grandmother's sewing circle. Especially not her grandmother's sewing circle.

What about the consequences? Strelastica was fired from her job. Is that consequences enough for you?

"After it was no longer possible to deny her part in this…prank, we had to let June go," said her immediate supervisor, Franklin Pornbang. Polly Amorish, her not quite so urgent supervisor, added, "We were well within our rights to fire Ms. Strelastica. She dirtied the good name of Montreal's Department of Sewage!"

Uhh, okay.

"Can we really blame the women?" said psychologist and part-time computer keyboard Stanathan Blotski. "When the estrogen courses through their bodies, they need to release all that female energy somehow. And, frankly, this is a lot healthier for them than eating a carton of Randy Rocky Rhodes ice cream! Mmm…Randy Rocky Rhodes ice cream…"

"**Yes!**" CBS' Bill Martens, whose live stand-up segment in front of the White House on the US' deteriorating relationship with Russia was interrupted by a woman gleefully shouting ILTFCY, insisted. "**Yes, they should be blamed! Women should totally be blamed!**"

"Blame is such a harsh word," demurred an other psychologist (who dreams of someday being a part-time computer monitor) Monanette Villaneucki. "I prefer to think of it as 'responsibility with extreme prejudice.' In any case, this is a way of demeaning well known men, of putting them in their place, of telling them: 'Bad dog! Bad, bad dog!' And, not in a bedroomily playful way, either."

Okay, as pranks go this one is more silly than bust-a-gut funny, but, ultimately, where is the harm? By deflating the egos of pompous male reporters, don't

A young girl's blond curls appeared on my computer screen, and she shouted, "I'd Love to Fucking Castrate You!" Outraged, I sputtered, "Hey! I thought you only did that to television journalists!"

"What can I tell you?" the girl grinned. "We're branching out." Then, she giggled for a few seconds and vanished.

That was when I realized that ILTFCY was a scourge that must be stopped.

The Old Neighbourhood Goes to Hell

by   CORIANDER   NEUMANEIMANAYMANEEMAMANN, Alternate Reality News Service Urban Issues/Labour Writer

Three years after Fort McMurry was rebuilt, house prices in the city, especially its suburban belt (the part that circles the downtown core and keeps its pants from falling to its knees), have skyrocketed. Why? A highly unusual wave of immigrants have come to Alberta, driving the market ever higher. Who?

"Deeeeeeeeeeeeeeeeeeeeemons!" cried Fort McMurray Pastor Andrew McAndrews. "Demons! Demons! Demons! Demons! De-e-e-e-e-c-c-emons!"

"Christians! Soooooo judgmental," said new Fort McMurray resident Nogar the Odiferous. "We prefer to think of ourselves as 'differently moralled engines of economic growth and prosperity.'"

"Demons!" Pastor McAndrews insisted. "From Hell! They're here to damn all of our souls to eternal perdition!"

Nogar the Odiferous, resplendent in a golf outfit that would make your eyes bleed if you looked at it for too long, tutted. He pointed out that demons were quite capable of mining human souls from Hell, thank you very much. In fact, that was the problem: demons were so good at collecting souls that Hell was heavily oversubscribed. It was like an airplane seat sale that had been tragically overbooked. In short, it was crowded, and getting crowdeder with every cheating spouse and crooked stock dealer.

"We're not here for your souls," Nogar the Odiferous argued. "We're here for your incredibly undervalued real estate!"

Why now? Nogar the Odiferous explained that, until recently, Earth was too cold for his kind to live on comfortably. "The heating bills would have far offset any advantage we would have in buying the land. But, now? Well! I don't want to give credence to crackpot theories of global warming – everybody knows what a hoax **that** is! – I mean, Al Gore? Pfft! We had his soul when he was three years old! He should never have – ahem. Sorry. I can be such a *yenta*. Look: all I'm saying is that the place feels very…homey, now, you know? A place where a differently moralled engine of economic growth and prosperity could lay down roots…so he could uproot them and salt the earth so nothing would ever grow in it again, I mean."

When it comes to figuring out how widespread the immigration of demons to Canada is, hard figures are ha – not easy to come by. When asked about the trend, representatives of the federal Department of Immigration, Refugees and Citizenship, as well as the Alberta Land Registry Office, responded with the chant, "Pri-va-cy. Pri-va-cy. Pri-va-cy. Was there any-thing else?" It was almost as if they had been…I don't know…enchanted somehow.

However, there are other ways of gauging the growth of an immigration population. For example: in the last three months, several "soul food" restaurants catering to demons (and hipsters looking for the next big trend, granted, but mostly demons) have sprung up in Fort McMurray. With such catchy names as The Manna With the Golden Bun, The Sufferin's in the Sauce, and Bruce, they offer such dishes as "braised duck in a white 'virgin' sauce" and "chicken croquettes with your choice of sin on the side."

Newly appointed Mayor of Fort McMurray James McJameson (who took office after former Mayor Melissa Blake had an unfortunate encounter with a Yeti) admitted to having mixed feelings about the development. "On the one hand," he said, "differently moralled engines of economic growth and prosperity don't share our customs, they don't eat the same foods that we eat, and they smell – of sulfur! Don't try to deny it! Ain't enough Axxe in the world to cover that stench! And, then there's their whole business model trading people's souls. Eeeeeewwwww!

"On the other hand, I can't wait to spend the new money that will flow into our enhanced property tax base. Our **greatly** enhanced property tax base. Our **incredibly, stupidly hugely** enhanced property –"

After five minutes of this, I got the distinct impression that the Mayor was not as torn as he would have his constituents believe.

"Oh, we know that the only reason we're being allowed to live here is because of the incredibly, stupidly huge amount of money we bring to the city," Nogar the Odiferous allowed. "We're not fresh off the boat that plies the River Styx, you know. We've been around. For most of human history, if you want the truth of it. Still, we like to think we have a lot to offer Fort McMurray.

"If you just give us a chance, you will be **amazed** at how our presence will transform this community…"

Haters Gotta Hate
Company's Gotta Pro-rate

by GIDEON GINRACHMANJINJa-VITUS, Alternate Reality News Service Economics Writer

Hate is hard work. There's the gnashing of teeth and foaming at the mouth as you scream obscenities at people you don't know but just know you wouldn't get along with. There's the effort required to clench your fist and shake it. When you're really into a good bout of hatred, your whole body can clench up. Hate is like walking through a blizzard being pelted by unhappy raccoons.

Love, by way of contrast, lounges on a comfy couch and grins goofily at anybody who happens to walk by.

The difference between love and hate is obvious. But, can you monetize this psychological insight?

"Boy, can you ever!" enthused Ned Feeblish, MultiNatCorp Vice President, Segregation and Monetization. "You can monetize the shit out of it! Umm…that may come across as too aggressively enthusiastic – could you…could you maybe change the word 'shit' to 'heck?' Much appreciated…"

Leo Strauss, the American economics theorist who is much loved by neoconservatives and playground bullies in high schools across the continent, anticipated this idea in a much-overlooked paper he wrote in 1957 called "Hate is Theft." "The energy that the average worker expends on hating his fellow man is energy that he does not have available to do what is required of him in his workplace," Strauss wrote. "This will cost the economy a skabillion dollars in lost productivity by – let me pick an arbitrary date – one far enough in the future that I won't be alive to be held accountable for my ideas, but I won't be entirely forgotten, either – not by people who matter, in any case – let us say…2023…no – too far – that's not credible…let's say…2015. A skabillion 2015 dollars will be lost to the economy. Ayn Rand villains have faced forbidding fates for far less!"

In his paper, Strauss rejected the possibility of educating people not to hate, arguing that it would cost too much for results that were far from certain. "With sufficient indoctrination, the man who hated all minorities might come to accept redheads, Jews and Armenians," he wrote, "but still hate blacks, lefties and the French. The cost of his indoctrination would far outweigh its benefits. Unless you were Armenian, I suppose, but we cannot allow such emotionalism to affect our thinking on this subject." Penalizing workers depending upon how much hatred they carried in their hearts was much better for the bottom line, he argued.

Unfortunately, it would take decades before Strauss' idea could be implemented. Hatred has always been part of the background noise of American culture, which made it hard to isolate and measure. A combination of the civil rights movement, which pushed organized hate to the margins of society, and technologies that can detect patterns of activity in parts of the brain that govern hatred (and, coincidentally, love of chocolate pudding – make of that what you will, General Foods!), made quantifying levels of animosity in individuals possible.

MultiNatCorp, which pioneered the use of biometric key cards to shunt ambitious underlings into dead-end jobs, was in a perfect position to implement a policy of wage discrimination based on the level of hate shown by an employee. However, not everybody agreed that it was a good idea.

"Whaaaaaat?!" shrieked NAACP spokesperson Lashonda Tendentious. "If you hate a Jew, you lose 43 cents an hour on your base pay, but if you hate a black, you only lose 27 cents? I. DON'T. THINK. SO!"

"Oy," replied Rabbi Horatio Heffernen, putting him in the sweepstakes for the shortest quote ever in an Alternate Reality News Service article.

"Weeeeelllll," Feeblish responded, "in the implementation of any new policy, you will inevitably have to work out some kinks –

oh! That reminds me: I have to look over how to integrate hatred of people who engage in non-traditional sex acts into our compensation penalization matrix. If you will excuse me…"

Other people have…other problems with the policy. "I got hired as a panda extruder at a lower pay level than advertised for the position just because I fly a Confederate flag outside my house," said Atticustard Whitbread. "And have a Confederate flag on my car. And have a Confederate flag tattooed on the back of my neck. And I named my daughter Connie Flagg. But, for me, it's just a symbol of my southern heritage. Nothing else."

When asked about his membership in the KKK, Whitbread spat on the ground, but it was the saliva of chagrin. "Oh. You know about that, hunh? Well, shoot, I guess that may have had something to do with my pay."

"This is just one more excuse to drive down wages for the average working stiff!" roared AFL-CIO-MOUSE President Flaherty McDivot. "Well, my twelve members and I aren't going to stand for it! We aren't going to stand for it, I tell you…although I would happily sit for another pint if you're buying the next round…"

Strauss, who refused to be quoted unless he was given the last word – over 60 years later – the man has power, is what I'm saying – wrote: "The loss of wages will give workers an incentive not to hate their fellow man. Who says markets can't solve every problem in the world?

"I believe that Jesus would have approved."

Innovation? In No…Uhh…Ovation?

by NANCY GONGLIKWANYEOHEEEEEEEH, Alternate Reality News Service Technology Writer

How many patents have Silicon Valley tech companies applied for in the last year? Three. One was for a faster than light propulsion system that looked suspiciously like a bug zapper. Another was for "A New Method of Removing Unwanted Hair" that looks suspiciously like tweezers. Nobody knows what the third application looks suspiciously like: it seems to have been written in English, but the words are strung together in incomprehensible ways that would make both Strunk **and** White blanch.

What happened?

"Well, you know," mused Marc Buzzburker, founder of Farcebook and somebody you wouldn't want to French kiss in a dark alley, "original ideas are like...something that is very similar to them. But, either way, sometimes they dry up – creativity is not an industrial process, much as we have tried to make it one..."

"Not a single real patent application? Just like that?" countermused Tim-Bob McBits, creator of the game *Angry Crustaceans*. "That's not ebb and flow – that's post-apocalyptic nuclear wasteland! I wish I...I could take credit for that metaphor, but I read it in one of Frank L. Baum's books. My point, though, is that it's like...like somehow something that destroys people's creativity got into our water supply!"

Actually, that's exactly what happened.

"It is?" McBits mused. (Sometimes, a random good idea can pop up in conversation and seem like inspiration.)

Two years ago, a janitor, having spent 176 straight hours mopping up the Zachary quinto-triticale containment tanks at the Bubbe Guy factory in southern California, wearily leant on a wall to look with pride on the work that he had done. He accidentally flipped a switch, which opened a circuit which sent a message to a storage tank to open a door that led to a sluice that dumped 1,200 gallons of RUR 312 (proposed commercial name: We Couldn't Think of an Original Thing to Call This Drug: **That** is How Good it is!) into the South Bay Aqueduct, an important source of California's drinking water.

Of course, RUR 312 (proposed commercial name: OUIdi...812) is the drug developed at the Bubba Ghee Foundation that interferes with people's ability to formulate original ideas. Not necessarily "of course," I suppose: it could have been the drug that makes people's ears shrivel up and causes them to pronounce words with the letter "r" in them as though it didn't exist. But, uhh, that would make this a very different article.

"Oh. Well, that might explain –" McBits started to muse, but I wasn't finished.

A couple of days later, a train carrying 600 gallons of the brain disenhancing drug derailed thirty seconds out of the station from the factory. Its contents spilled into the Hetch Hetchey Aqueduct, which also serves California.

"Okay. Well. That might also explain –" McBits started to continue to muse.

This time, he was cut off by Amitabhy Backchanl, representing the Bubbe Guy plant, who mused: "What? You think that just because a drug that makes it hard for people to form original ideas is spilled into a waterway and that everybody who drinks from the waterway starts having trouble forming original ideas that the two events are connected? Do you understand nothing about cause and effect?"

A couple of stunned seconds later, Backchanl turned and mused quite loudly, "Uncle! I think I may not have been cut out for a job in public relations!"

The accidental release of RUR 312 (proposed commercial name: Creativity is for Nerds!) into silicon valley's drinking water hasn't hurt the tech sector's bottom line yet. The release of Panes 27 – Revenge of the Empirical Subroutine, for example, was delayed for six months, but, when it was finally released, users found it generally more friendly and less bug-ridden than typical Microsquish releases. Rovipovich, the production company that produced *Angry Crustaceans*, was bought out by Japanese giant X Corp. and repositioned in the market as a North American games warehouse and distribution centre.

Well, it hasn't hurt Tim-Bob McBits' bottom line, in any case.

Are the effects of the drug permanent? "What good would a drug be that users only had to take once?" Backchanl mused. "Our stock price would plummet, that's what! We've been testing the drug on lab rats for about 15 years, and none of them lived long enough to regain their ability to run mazes that they had never seen before. Still, I imagine it would only be a matter of time before – damn! I really suck at public relations, don't I?"

"Hold on a sec," Buzzburker mused, "I only drink bottled water." Unfortunately, by then the common wisdom about RUR 213 (proposed commercial name: Aww, Do We Have to Come Up With an Original Name? Really? There's Nothing Original Any More, You Know – You Need Something to Call it? Call it Bob. Or, Infidel. Or, Persuasion. Or, a Peruasive Infidel Named Bob. Or Give it Your Own Name – As Long as You Try It Before You Take it

Because…You'll See…) had taken hold, and nothing so insubstantial as facts would move it.

Survival of the Kittenist

by FREDERICA VON McTOAST-HYPHEN, Alternate Reality News Service Pop Culture Writer

Those eyes can melt your heart faster than a wax candle at the purrcise mathematical centre of the sun. Okay, that's a bit of an exaggeration: the purrcise mathematical centre of the sun would vapurrize a candle before those eyes had opened, before the thought of those eyes opening had formed in their owner's brain. Then, the purrressure at the purrcise mathematical centre of the sun would probably fuse the sub-atomic particles that had once been the candle into the gigantic diamond there.

The point is, those eyes are damn cute. And, they belong to kittens. That is, young purrsons. But, what is a cat trying to be cool to do if he is no longer young?

"It's a very simple purrcedure," said Doctor Malenka Visage, Chief Surgeon at the Purrfect You Clinic in Salzpurrg. "We pull back the skin around the eye to give the lens more room. Then, we suture lens material grown in a Petri dish from a sample of your DNA to the existing lens. Of course, your lashes did not develop to be able to lubricate the new, larger area of your eye; fortunately, eyelash extension has been around for centuries. Finally, we must stimulate the visual centres of your brain in order to ensure that they are able to purrocess the larger amount of stimulus coming from your eyes."

That is what you call simple?

"We used to have to enlarge a purrson's eye sockets in their skull to accommodate the changes," Doctor Visage informed me, casually wiping down her hair with a wet paw. "Fortunately, we found a work-around for that!"

The craze for eye enhancement surgery was first embraced by the Japurrnese. Naturally. That country must have an Institute of Weirdonics that comes up with these bizarre ideas. That was over a decade ago. As the fad started to wane in the east, it was eagerly taken up by cosmetic surgeons in the United States.

How do people who have undergone the opurration feel about it?

"The bandages should be off in about six months," forensic furball analyst Chokyar Begonia told me. "At that point, I'll have to bcat the lady cats off with a stick! Not that I ever would – I…I'm a little inexperienced in that area and need all the help I can get!"

"Ever since I recovered from the oppurration, I have had trouble focusing and have suffered from purriodic migraine headaches," answered Russian opera star Olga Purrodina. "But, since I got these eyes, I never lose an argument with a conductor. Never."

"It's been fantastic!" enthused housewife Eloria Flepstein. "You know, I haven't lost a game of bridge since I've had the operation. And, if I don't feel like…you know, with Bobbet, well, my husband and I just don't!"

And, there have been no side effects? "Oh, well, once in a while I do get the urge to lick the insides of my eyeballs. But, I just make myself a campurri and soda – or six – and drink until the feeling goes away!"

What is it about larger eyes that makes them so attractive to older people?

According to Yamaha Aikido, chief historian and grooviness guru of the International Weirdonics Institute of Sappurro, Japan (wait, there is such a thing? Really? I…I was just joking! Honest, I just used the first thing that came to mi – well. Ahem. I called it. Good for me), large eyes are an evolutionary adaptation. "The kitten who

looked the cutest would be the most likely to be fed the most, most often," he explained. (Sorry for splitting the sentence, but the previous paragraph had gotten a bit unwieldy, and I decided to start a fresh one to make it easier to read. Unfortunately, I decided that after I had started the sentence…whiiiiich purrobably made it harder to read. So much for good intentions!)

It's also likely that animals with eyes large enough to elicit an "Aww!" response from purredators would be spared while they went after animals with ordinary eyes. This is borne out by a survey of businesses that suggests that people with large eyes are the last to be fired in a recession.

"I…wouldn't put too much into that," Visage stated. "Other factors may have been in play, like, you know, competence at their jobs and stuff."

Right. So. Do larger eyes really contribute to a purrson's success in life?

That was not a rhetorical question – I would really like to know. Nobody I interviewed for this article was able to give me a definitive answer!

When in Rome, Drone as the Romans Drone

by ALEXANDER BIGGS-TUFTS-MANN, Alternate Reality News Service Sports Writer

It was a strange day in the Coliseum. Kittenus Cuticus' drone had clearly been bested by the drone of top flight gladiator Atticus of Sparta; it was leaking oil and wobbled uncontrollably. Yet, when Emperor Gaullus Maximus gave the thumbs down sign, Atticus lay aside his drone controller and watched as Cuticus proudly flew his drone back to the ground, where he shut it off and returned it to its case.

"I've never seen anything like it," said sportscaster Bob Costus, excited but with an undertone of apprehension. "I mean, when Emperor Maximus gives the order to kill an opponent's drone, you kill the opponent's drone. Gladiators deciding on their own whether to end the existence of another's drone? That would be anarchy! What's next? Female drone gladiators?"

In fact, females have had their own drone competitions in Gaul, but I'd hate to spoil Costus' rhetorical question with an actual fact, so let us set that aside for the time being.

Atticus' drone was heavily favoured by Vegus (that would be Lucius Vegus, oddsmaker to the Emperor): it is a huge black affair with the latest laser and projectile weapons. Cuticus, on the other hand, had a smaller, blue-grey model with previous gen lasers and low-powered energy shields. Moreover, Atticus had won his previous 19 battles in the arena, while Cuticus had yet to be tested in public; it was assumed that Atticus would have been more comfortable wearing the viewing goggles that allowed him to watch the battle from the drone's point of view.

When asked why he spared the other drone, Atticus looked at the floor of his cell and answered, "I dunno. It just kinda felt like, you know, the right thing to do." When pressed, he stated: "Kittenus, he…he made me think. I hate thinking. I wanted to destroy his drone – smash it into a million pieces for that. But, then, he made me laugh. And, I…I just couldn't bring myself to do it. I'm in big trouble, aren't I?"

That's for the praetors to decide.

Angelica Nonsensicus, Emperor Maximus' press secretary, held a meeting in which she explained to journalists that Cuticus' drone would be executed immediately, and that Atticus and his drone would be sent with the Legion to someplace far, far away. Narnius was mentioned. "Gladiators cannot be allowed to make their own decisions about whose drone can live and whose drone can die," Nonsensicus argued. "That would be anarchy. And, what would come next? Female gladiators?"

After a couple of moments of uncomfortable silence, she added, "Outside of Rome, I mean." This broke the tension in the room.

In the undercard, Cingulate Cortexus lost a close drone battle to Michelin Tahyer, while Bassel Faultus easily blew the drone of Perdon-Mai Officur out of the sky. Those bouts will soon be forgotten, however, as both sides in the drone debate used the Atticus/Cuticus battle as an excuse to trot their political positions out in public once again.

"Drone battle in the arena is barbaric!" argued Ellust Causicus, principle secretary for the Popular Front for the Liberation of the Judean People. "Surely, the Roman people no longer need to satisfy our blood lust through such spectacles – we have political primary campaigns!"

"Drone battle in the arena isn't barbaric enough!" countered Violenz Domesticus, spokesman for the Judean People's Popular Liberation Front. "There are no spurts of blood – oil gushing everywhere doesn't have the same dramatic impact! No human limbs getting hacked off – you think watching a drone lose its tail fin gives the same visceral pleasure? Where did you study – in a gymnasium run by Plodicus the Fool? Yes, by all means, stop this nonsense with drone battles, so we can see what civilized people really want: human beings hacking each other to pieces!"

Drone battle was introduced into the Coliseum arena by Emperor Ellactric Cirkus – yes, it was that long ago. Some people just don't know when to move on.

I tried to get into the restricted area of the Coliseum where Cuticus was being held, but the Centurions at the gate refused to let me in. After greasing some palms (cooking oil being in short supply in the capital at the moment), I was given entry, but it didn't help: a large mob of people, most laughing, surrounded the drone star, and I couldn't get near enough to ask him anything.

If he isn't executed within the next 24 hours, this Kittenus Cuticus could bear watching.

Every Breath You Take…A Life!

by HAL MOUNTSAUERKRAUTEN, Alternate Reality News Service Crime Writer

Runfang Zhiang is believed to be the first person in the world to have been killed for his breathing mask. Police report that he was bludgeoned to death by a small statue of Buddha, and that the only unusual thing about the body (aside from the puncture marks in the shape of a head) was the fact that he was found outdoors in Beijing without a mask.

"It wasn't just any breathing mask," pointed out Public Outrage Inspector and amateur time cop Hymie Xuhuan. "It was a Clean Air Jordan!"

Only a limited number of the masks, which feature an image of a stylized human figure stretching one arm with a ball in its hand high above its head while the other arm covers the figure's open mouth, were produced. Even at $175 per mask (in a country where the average worker's wage is 37 cents a week and a promise to be given only two rather than seven daily beatings), the Clean Air Jordan breathing masks almost immediately sold out. They even more immediatelier started popping up on ehBay for over $1,000 each (beatings negotiable).

Many members of China's underclass believe owning a celebrity endorsed breathing mask makes them look like they're members of the country's growing middle class. "They are delusional, of course," Xuhuan, who has no real expertise in this field but was the only person the Chinese government would allow me to speak to (really: I couldn't even speak to the official who told me that the only person I could speak to was Xuhuan – she used a sign language that had been developed for communication with porcupines), said. "Nobody who makes 37 cents a week can enter the middle class, no matter how few beatings they endure! Besides, people who have any real wealth at all are distinguished by their white, logoless masks."

"Aiiieeeee, my little Runfee, he save up money for over 10 years to buy that mask!" moaned amateur outrage aficionado Michelle Zhiang, the victim's mother. "Aiiieeeee, why you say I moan my first sentence?"

You started it with "Aiiieeeee!"

"Aiiieeeee," Mrs. Zhiang told me. "That just a linguistic affectation!"

Celebrity breathing masks have been a hot item in China for many years. There was set of four featuring the likenesses of each member of the band Kiss in full makeup (the concept of the set confused some cultural critics, who pointed out that most people only had one mouth, but that didn't stop it from selling out in under three minutes). Madonna endorsed a breathing mask with such a provocative design that the Communist Party of China debated banning it from the country (the move lost steam when it was revealed that Premier Li Keqiang had bought seven "because she is a role model for the modern Chinese woman"). A mask with a cockroach motif was released as a tribute to Franz Kafka. Unless it was a tribute to the Chinese United Exterminator's Union.

It's very powerful, the Chinese United Exterminator's Union is.

Not all celebrity breathing masks were successfully launched, of course. To take one example, the Gilbert Gottfried mask, which featured an exaggerated version of the brasH (a scrunchuation of the term "abrasive Helot) stand-up comedian's mouth, couldn't be given away to people who were choking on the smog of a normal Beijing rush hour.

Police quickly found Zhiang's murderer: Abelard Quiquig. In retrospect, taking selfies of putting on a dead man's breathing mask **at the crime scene** and posting them to your Weibow (the Chinese equivalent of Farcebook and Twitherd) account isn't how to get away with murder. "Seriously?" Quiquig commented at his trial. "What is the point of going to the trouble of murdering somebody for an article of apparel **if you cannot even share it with your friends?** I'm surprised I have to explain this to you!"

Quiquig was advised by his lawyer to plead guilty. Five minutes after the plea was read into the court, Quiquig was executed. Five minutes after that, his heart, liver, spleen, left eye, right foot and two thirds of his lower intestine were removed for transplant. Ironically, his lungs were not considered strong enough for this purpose; they were believed to have been given to Xuzhou Anying Biologic Technology, a purveyor of fine foods for your cats and dogs.

Despite the harsh sentence meted out to Quiquig, other people have since resorted to violence to get a celebrity breathing mask. A gang in Zigong, for example, beat up a teenage girl for her *Mad Max* mask (which bore the image of Mad Max' mask); they were caught because they got into a flame war on Fiddycent Qzone (a different Chinese equivalent of Farcebook and Twitherd – hey! They've got over a billion people – they need all the social media they can get!) over who should wear it.

Many more people may be killing others for their breathing masks and not getting caught because they do not feel the need to broadcast their act to the world. Some people call them Luddites; others call them prudent.

In the final analysis, is a dubious status symbol really worth killing somebody over? "Are you kidding?" Xuhuan said. "Thirty million people in this country died because of a little red book. This? This doesn't even rate an adjective!"

A Place for Stereotype-A Personalities

by FREDERICA VON McTOAST-HYPHEN, Alternate Reality News Service People Writer

Some come to learn more about their craft. Others come to network and party. Other others come to represent their imagined ethnic identity, fight feuds that reasonable people would have settled aeons ago and otherwise make a terrific nuisance of themselves to the hotel staff.

They are attending the 6278th annual Ethnic Stereotypes Convention, this year held in the Marriott Scrunchie in downtown Moncton, New Brunswick.

"It's always scheduled during Ramadan," complained Swarthy Muslim Terrorist Stereotype as he waited in line for his convention badge. "I tell you, sometimes the disrespect to believers of the one true religion is so blatant, it makes me just want to explode!"

By day, attendees had a choice of a wide array of panels with such titles as "Are Muslims the New Jews? Are Jews the Old Episcopalians?" and "We'll Wait Five Minutes Before Starting to Allow the Blonde Bimbo to Find the Right Room" and "The Ontology of the Racial Epithet, or, How Come They Can Say it But I Can't?" On Saturday night, the convention hosts a masquerade where attendees are invited to dress up as members of other ethnic groups; the Masquerade has not ended in riot police being called in for the last four years, a string of good behaviour that hasn't happened since 217 BCE.

And, there are parties. At a Friday night room party hosted by Southern Redneck Stereotype (you could tell because the walls were adorned with a Confederate flag – to celebrate his heritage, of course, no other reason, and if you insist upon arguing the point you can just give me back my damn alcohol and get the hell out! – and life-size photographs of assault rifles he was not allowed to bring across the border), a young man in a lumberjack shirt wearing a toque was arguing with another young man in a lumberjack shirt wearing a toque over Canada's national food.

"Beer," said the young man with brown hair, Anglophone Hoser Stereotype.

"*Cretin!*" shouted the young man with black hair, Francophone Stereotype. "Beer is not a food! It's the staff of life! Canada's national food is poutine!"

"Aww, take off, bear breath!" Anglophone Hoser Stereotype argued. "Poutine is okay, right? But it's no box of donuts! Mmm…snort! Snort! Donuts…"

"*Tabernac!*" Francophone Stereotype shouted, followed by a string of words, probably in French, that gave our translation software a nervous breakdown, so we're pretty sure they weren't compliments.

Needless to say with so many – why do people start a sentence with the phrase "needless to say" and then go on and say something? Needless to say, if something was truly needless to say, you wouldn't actually need to say it!

Umm, so, it goes without saying in any large group of diverse stereotypes, some will get along better than others. Case en pointe (it did service in a ballet company's programme for the classic *Loon Lake* before it agreed to appear in this article): in a discussion in a room party that spilled out into the hallway (much to the distress of the hotel's janitorial staff), Millennial Stereotype complained, "I have to work seven full time jobs just to be able to not quite make my rent. Whenever I try to talk to my family about it, my grandfather, Self-absorbed Boomer Stereotype, reminisces about how he dropped out of university after three years of attending no classes **and** immediately got a job that allowed him to pay off the mortgage to our house in three months. Am I bitter? Nooooooo. What could I possibly have to be bitter about?"

To which a passing Bohunk Stereotype replied, "Is that a slur against Czechoslovakia? Did you just insult Czechoslovakia?" Before Millennial Stereotype could mentally process the non-sequitur, three people had to be taken to hospital for bruised egos.

No charges were laid in the incident. "'Twas but a mere bit o' spirited hijinks," said the hotel's security head, retired Amiable Irish Beat Cop Stereotype.

As you might expect, a lot of colourful characters could be found at the convention. One example was the elderly Asian woman who wandered around the hallways who didn't appear to contribute anything, mumbling to herself in Mandarin – or possibly Cantonese – for those of us unfamiliar with the language, it may as well have been Klingon – the whole time. I asked Amiable Irish Beat Cop Stereotype what that was about.

"Aww, bless her soul, dat's Just Off Da Boat Asian Stereotype," he told me. "Ye know dey never learn da language. And dey always look like someone just poisoned deir dog – or husband. Still, I'm sure dat in her own way she's enjoyin' de convention as much as anybody!"

This all begs the question: in this – no, it doesn't. To beg the question means to give an answer that acknowledges the question without directly responding to it. The proper phrase to use in this situation would be "This all leads to the question..." Oh, yeah, baby – I'm **on fire** for the English usage tonight!

Still, I'm on a tight deadline, so, in this case, I will bow to common ignorance: this all begs the question: in this more enlightened day and age, should ethnic stereotyping be supported with its own convention?

"Vat? You vant you should take bread out of my children's mouths?" replied the conference organizer, Little Old Jewish Man Stereotype. "*Veismier!* We didn't survive 4,000 years of persecution to have you be so politically correct, already!"

A Hairy Situation

by SASKATCHEWAN KOLONOSCOGRAD, Alternate Reality News Service Fairy Tale Writer

A break in the Tower Kidnapping or Possible Disappearance, We're Not Really Sure case has led to the arrest of a nanotech researcher in Schenectady. Police are certain that it is only a matter of time before the missing woman herself is found.

The country was riveted (literally, bolted to their television sets with hot metal nails) by the story of the disappearance of a beautiful young woman known only as Rapunzel (which, in Lithuanian, means "yak enlightener"). For years, she lived in the Penthouse Suite of Drumpf Great Wall of China Casino Tower, named after its creator, billionaire (in his own mind) Tonalt Drumpf, although currently owned by billionaire (on paper, but he would never sell off his stocks for fear of flooding the market and getting far less than what they are currently listed for on stock exchanges) Carl Ikon.

Rapunzel, who had been a top fashion model from the age of seven, was believed to be a prisoner; the only elevator leading to the Penthouse had been disabled. Carrot sticks and water were provided for her by a witch in Drumpf's employ named Dame Goathell.

Six months ago, Dame Goathell noticed that the carrot sticks and water were not being consumed. At first, she thought Rapunzel was on a diet. After a couple of weeks, she investigated, finding the young woman gone. Dame Goathell immediately called the police on her Scryphone 3000; Drumpf showed how happy he was to cooperate with the investigation by getting an injunction to keep them out of the building that had his name on it.

As it happened, they didn't need his cooperation. You know how when detectives on TV cop shows send evidence "to the lab," the subsequent analysis helps them solve the crime? That never happens in real life.

Until now.

Ten storey long strands of hair discovered outside the casino were found to contain nanotech. Police now believe that the nanotech made Rapunzel's hair grow at an accelerated rate, strengthening it until it could hold hundreds of kilos of weight. Then, she used it to make a slipknot which she climbed down and, with one tug, she was gone.

"Ain't technology grand?" asked Dylan "To Rome, Do Lead All" Rhodes, the FBI agent assigned to the case.

The hair-strengthening nanobots were created by VisiCompTech, a start-up that was believed to have been end-downed two years ago. The company's founder, Jack McJackman, disappeared, and he wouldn't have been found except that he tweeped the fashion model: "Rapunzel, Rapunzel, let down your hair, so that you may climb your golden stair." (A video of the song based on the tweep has already become popular on YahooTube, and a house mix is rumoured to be in the works.)

"We traced the tweet from a phone Rapunzel threw into a garbage can back to McJackman's home on the Scottish/Australian border," Rhodes explained. "When he was arrested by Interpol, he told us everything. How he had fallen in love with – what did he call her? Rap Pretzel? Rap Denzel? Raw Pun Sells? – when she did a spread for *Peanut Butter on a Bagel* magazine. How he discovered that she had been held captive by Tonalt Drumpf. How he watched security feeds of her brushing her long, blonde hair for hours on end while listening to Duran Duran. Up and down. Up and down. Over and over again. Always with the brushing. When I say he told us everything, I mean he told us way too much. My partner was in an information coma for twelve hours. Eeeeeeverything. He told us everything."

Except where Rapunzel is now.

She was so grateful to McJackman for helping her get free that she stayed with him a whole three minutes before disappearing into the Circuits Circuits Casino next door. You might think that somebody with ten storey long hair would stand out in a crowd, but this is Vegas. And, in any case, most of the hair was found in a dumpster on the outskirts of town. That's the last trace of the woman.

"I like to think that she's run off to a tropical island with a hunk named Bruno or Pierre or Monkeyman or something else foreign-sounding," said McJackman's sworn affidavit. "That she's lounging on a deck chair, her brown skin shining in the sun, sipping a pina colada while Bruno or Pierre or Monkeyman or something else foreign-sounding slathers sunscreen or whipped cream or something I'm too love-struck to even dream all over her slender, sensuous..."

Eeeeeeverything.

The idea of a woman being held captive in a tall tower seems medieval. On the other hand, the idea of nanobots helping that woman escape seems futuristic. Despite this clash of literary tropes, the detective on the case insisted that it really happened.

"Any sufficiently advanced narrative looks like science fiction," Rhodes stated. "Now, if you'll excuse me, I have to look into a report of some kind of fast-growing stalk destroying a downtown neighbourhood..."

The Dirtbucket Stops Here

by BRENDA BRUNDTLAND-GOVANNI, Alternate Reality News Service Editrix-in-Chief

Okay, Internet trolls, you win.

As of this morning (yesterday morning in France), the Alternate Reality News Service has terminated the comments sections on our Web portal (not ^{TM} because we're not giving [EXPLETIVE DELETED] Bill Gates a penny!) with extreme prejudice. Personally, I'm not surprised: when upper management started spewing phrases like "reader engagement," "starting a conversation with the community" and "wage cuts for those wastrel scallywags in editorial" (this last one may have been left over from the last union negotiations), I warned Mikhail Lo-fi that it was a bad, bad, bad, bad, bad idea. Except for the last rationalization. Still.

All the best publications were doing it, Lo-fi argued; I had never taken him for such a Joyner, but we all have high school track moments, I suppose. The move took some of the sting out of the fact that newspapers were cutting back on actual journalists; in his perfect world, newspapers would consist entirely of reader-contributed comments without any original reporting. I will admit that it was a seductive argument, but my doubts were tenacious (they had clearly learned the wrong lessons from the Opiepic *In the Heart of the Sea*).

As the comments started coming in, I quickly devised a five slap system for rating them:

one slap: responding to an article with a comment that makes no logical, grammatical or hygienic sense; gratuitous bad language, under five usages; EXAMPLES: 1. Obviously, FDR is responsible for kids' lack of respect for their elders these days! 2. What a [EXPLETIVE DELETED] moron! The [EXPLETIVE DELETED] Crusades wouldn't have happened if [EXPLETIVE DELETED] hadn't blown up the moon!

two slaps: completely ignoring the article you're supposed to be commenting on and spewing random nonsense; gratuitous bad language, five usages and over; EXAMPLES: 1. Anything responding to an article on Barack Obama, the 2008 market meltdown or #squigglelivesmatter. 2. You suck, you [EXPLETIVE DELETED] [EXPLETIVE DELETED] piece of [EXPLETIVE DELETED] [EXPLETIVE DELETED] squidmashing [EXPLETIVE DELETED]! And, your [EXPLETIVE DELETED] dog is [EXPLETIVE DELETED] ugly, too!

three slaps: gratuitous Nazi references (the only exception being comments on articles about Earth Prime 7-9-2-2-5-3 dash omega, where a Dalek invasion was fended off by – you guessed it – Nazis); EXAMPLE: Passing a law that claims that sunshine is a good thing in moderation is **exactly** what Hitler did in 1943!

four slaps: ist postings (racist, sexist, ageist, speciesist, Squigglist – not that those bastard Squiggles don't deserve close, harsh, in-your-face scrutiny, but…uhh, that's not relevant here); EXAMPLE: Any post that starts, I'm not [racist, sexist, ageist, agronomist, Klipponist, ADD YOUR OWN PERSONAL PET PREJUDICE HERE], but…"

five slaps: anything the least bit negative about me; EXAMPLE: I'm not going to give you any [EXPLETIVE DELETED] examples of this! If you want to know what it was like, take the worst thing anybody has ever said about you and substitute my name for yours!

I must admit that, at first, rating the comments was fun; the thought of slapping all of those barely coherent, semi-literate, semi-evolved readers had me giddy with anticipation. People in the office wondered why so much gleeful tittering was coming from my office, a sound that was much more frightening than the moans and growling that they had come to expect.

Over time, however, the pleasure began to pall. As the average number of slaps per posted comment started to asymptotically (literally: the symptom of being an ass) approach five, the joy I took in rating the comments went down, to the point where I actually dreaded reading them.

My personal physician, Doctor Emulio Schlossberg, told me that I had a condition known as "slapping fatigue." Slapping fatigue, an occupational hazard of editors, cellists and Bingo number callers, occurs when the centre of the brain that gets pleasure out of thoughts of physical violence is overused, temporarily burning it out. I had to admit that Doctor Schlossberg had a point when I realized that the thought of slapping him for making this diagnosis gave me no pleasure at all.

The cure was two weeks rest in a dark room while listening to a constant stream of Enya. I decided to close down the comments section of the Web site instead – if I can't enjoy myself, why should anybody else be able to? Besides, Celtic music makes me break out in Pan flutes.

As for people who complain that this is censorship, **You're damn right it's censorship! I don't have any responsibility to publish comments by angry, ignorant, bigoted, barely literate people whose only goal in life is to become the Chinese smog of public discourse! Not those we don't have a columnist's contract with, in any case!** Besides, isn't the rest of the Internet big enough for you monsters?

Allowing reader comments on our Web site was a noble experiment (by which I mean: gaseous and inert), but I'm happy it's over: those were the longest 12 minutes of my life!

8. ALTERNATE INDEX

9. ALTERNATE BIOGRAPHY

Ira Nayman is profilic. Proficlic. Proclif - he writes a lot.

If you enjoyed *Futures in the Mirror are Closer Than They Appear*, you will probably love the six previously published Alternate Reality News Service books. *Alternate Reality Ain't What It Used To Be*, *What Were Once Miracles Are Now Children's Toys*, *Luna for the Lunies!* and *The Street Finds its Own Uses for Mutant Technologies* are general collections of news, reviews, interviews and anything else you might find in your local newspaper. *The Alternate Reality News Service's Guide to Love, Sex and Robots* and *What the Hell Were You Thinking? Good Advice for People Who Make Bad Decisions* are collections of humourous science fiction advice clumns. Print versions of all of the books are available online at Amazon, Barnes and Noble, Chapters/Indigo and other fine bookstores.

New Alternate Reality News Service stories appear weekly on Ira's Web site: *Les Pages aux Folles* (http://www.lespagesauxfolles.ca). These include two advice columns: Ask Amritsar (about love and romance and technology) and Ask the Tech Answer Guy (about anything to do with technology except love and romance). Readers are encouraged to submit their own questions for the advice columns. *Les Pages aux Folles* also contains topical political and social satire and surreal cartoons.

The Weight of Information, the pilot for a radio series based on Alternate Reality News Service articles, can be heard on YouTube.

Ira has written a series of short stories set in a universe where all matter is conscious featuring object psychologist Antonio Van der Whall. As of this writing, eight of the stories are in print, including: "A Really Useful Engine," which appeared in the anthology *Even Birds Are Chained To The Sky and Other Tales: The Fine Line Short Story Collection*; "Thinking is the **Worst** Way to Travel," which can be read in *Explorers: Beyond the Horizon*, and; "If the Mountain Won't Come to Mohammed," which appeared in *Here Be Monsters*.

Ira has also written four novels set in the multiverse that follow the adventures of investigators for the Transdimensional Authority, the organization that monitors and polices travel between dimensions, or the Time Agency, which monitors and polices travel in time. If you are somewhere you don't belong, doing something you shouldn't be doing, they find you, stop you and try and figure out what to do with you. The four novels in the series are: *Welcome to the Multiverse**, *You Can't Kill the Multiverse***, *Random Dingoes* and *It's Just the Chronosphere Unfolding as it Should*. These books can be purchased from all of the usual suspects online, or from the home page of the publisher, Elsewhen Press.

Fans of Ira Nayman's science fiction writing are encouraged to check *Les Pages aux Folles* periodically for news about the availability of these and future stories.

* *Sorry for the Inconvenience*
** *But You Can Mess With its Head*

Connect with Ira online:

Twitter: https://twitter.com/#!/ARNSProprietor
Facebook: http://www.facebook.com/ira.nayman

www.ingramcontent.com/pod-product-compliance
Lightning Source LLC
Chambersburg PA
CBHW070817120626
46556CB00002B/551